D1297061

CARTOON NETWORK

STEVEN UNIVERSE

CHERISHED MEMORIES

Published by

kaboom!

WWW.**BOOM-STUDIOS**.COM

STEVEN UNIVERSE ONGOING Volume Nine, December 2020.
Published by KaBOOM!, a division of Boom Entertainment, Inc.
Copyright © 2020 Cartoon Network. STEVEN UNIVERSE and all
related characters and elements © & ™ Cartoon Network. WB
SHIELD © & ™ WBEI (s20). KaBOOM!™ and the KaBOOM! logo are
trademarks of Boom Entertainment, Inc., registered in various
countries and categories. All characters, events, and institutions
depicted herein are fictional. Any similarity between any of the
names, characters, persons, events, and/or institutions in this
publication to actual names, characters, and persons, whether
living or dead, events, and/or institutions is unintended and
purely coincidental. KaBOOM! does not read or accept unsolicited
submissions of ideas, stories, or artwork.

BOOM! Studios, 5670 Wilshire Boulevard, Suite 400, Los Angeles,
CA 90036-5679. Printed in China. First Printing.

ISBN: 978-1-68415-627-6, eISBN: 978-1-64668-039-9

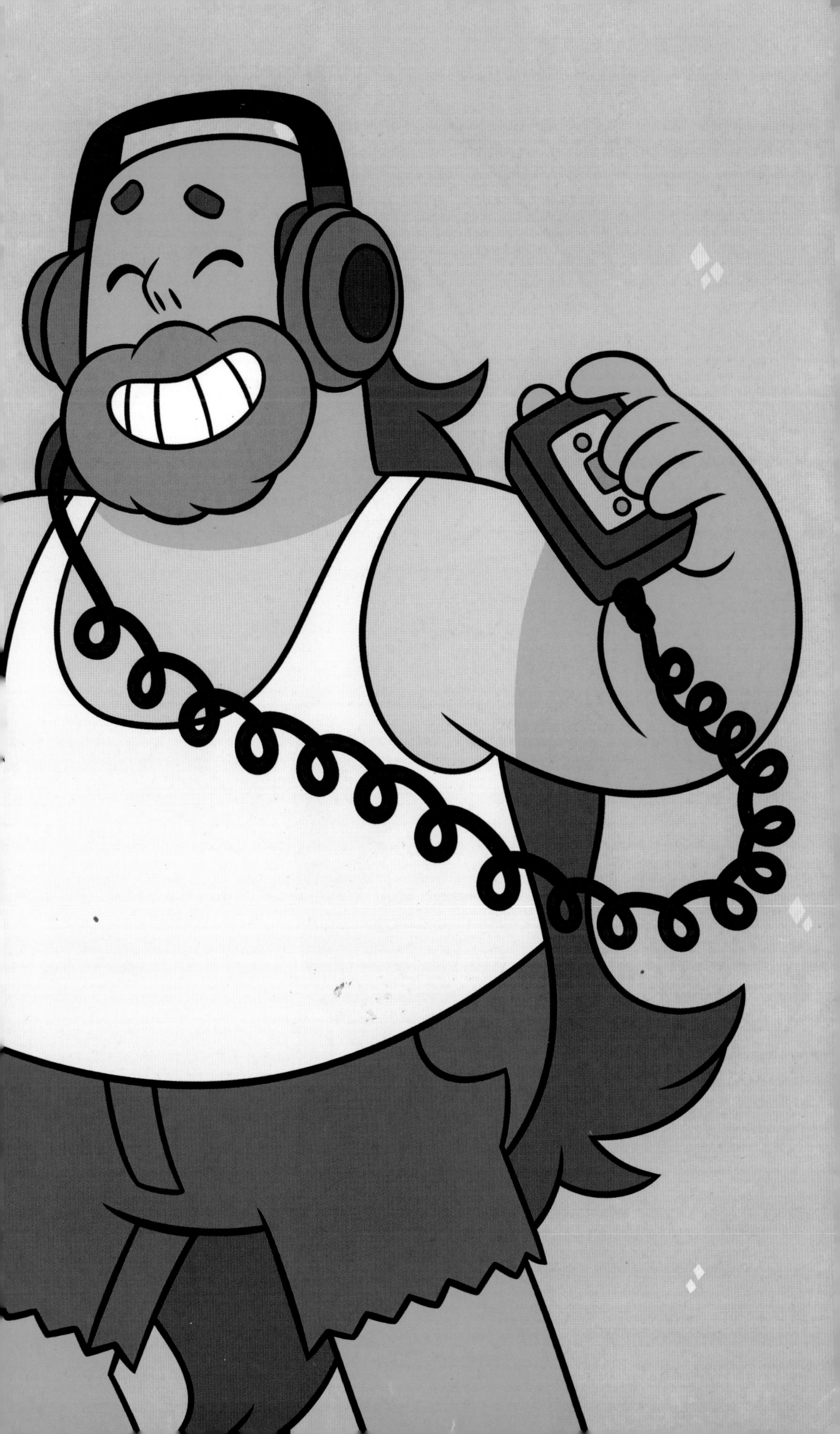

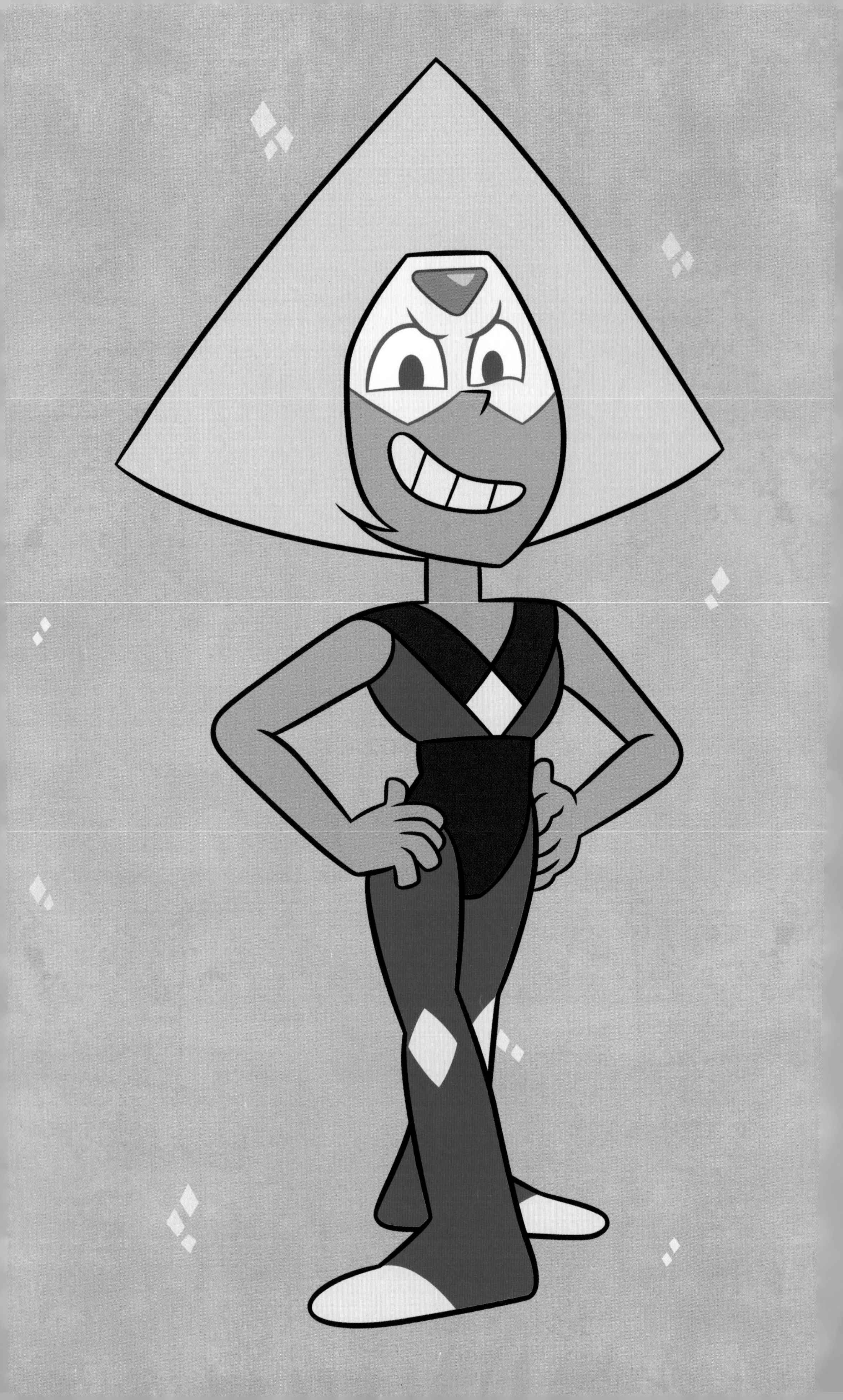

STEVEN UNIVERSE
CHERISHED MEMORIES

created by
REBECCA SUGAR

written by
TAYLOR ROBIN

illustrated by
S.M. MARA

colors by
ZIYED Y. AYOUB
chapters 33 & 34
WHITNEY COGAR
chapters 35 & 36

letters by
MIKE FIORENTINO

cover by
MISSY PEÑA

series designer
GRACE PARK

collection designer
MARIE KRUPINA

editor
MATTHEW LEVINE

Special thanks to
Marisa Marionakis, Janet No, Austin Page,
Conrad Montgomery, Jackie Buscarino and the
wonderful folks at Cartoon Network.

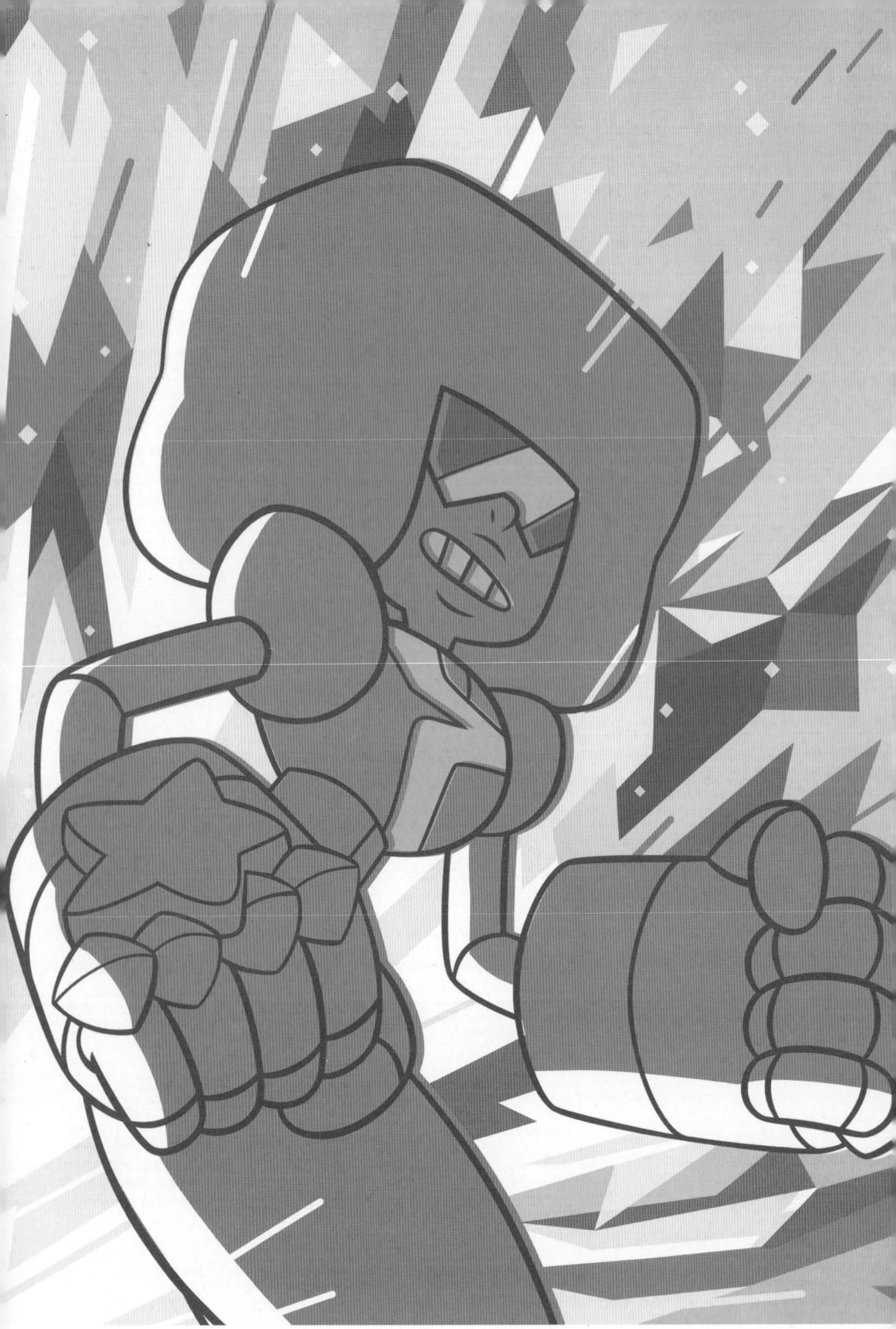

CHAPTER THIRTY-THREE

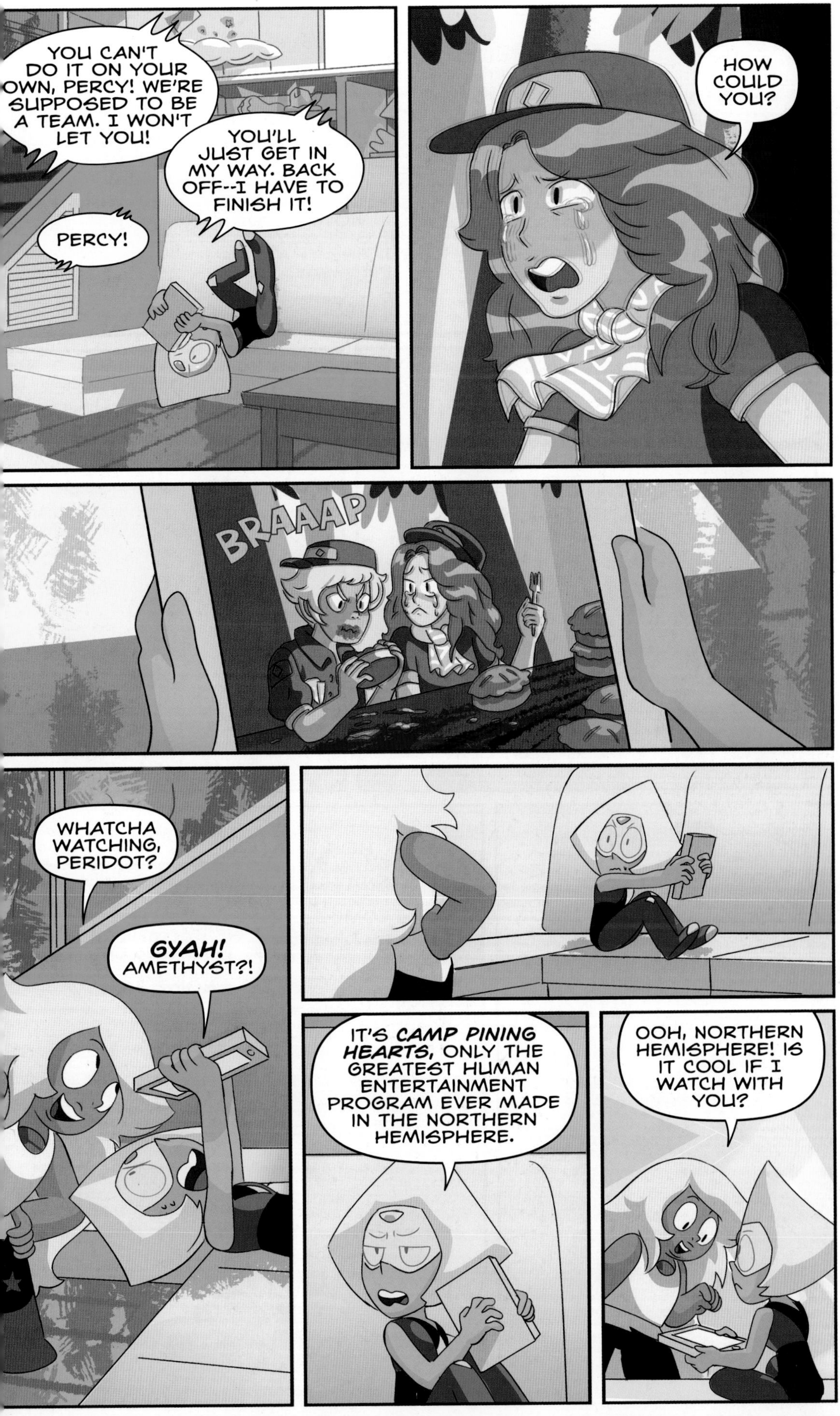
YOU CAN'T DO IT ON YOUR OWN, PERCY! WE'RE SUPPOSED TO BE A TEAM. I WON'T LET YOU!
YOU'LL JUST GET IN MY WAY. BACK OFF--I HAVE TO FINISH IT!
PERCY!
HOW COULD YOU?
BRAAAP
WHATCHA WATCHING, PERIDOT?
GYAH! AMETHYST?!
IT'S CAMP PINING HEARTS, ONLY THE GREATEST HUMAN ENTERTAINMENT PROGRAM EVER MADE IN THE NORTHERN HEMISPHERE.
OOH, NORTHERN HEMISPHERE! IS IT COOL IF I WATCH WITH YOU?

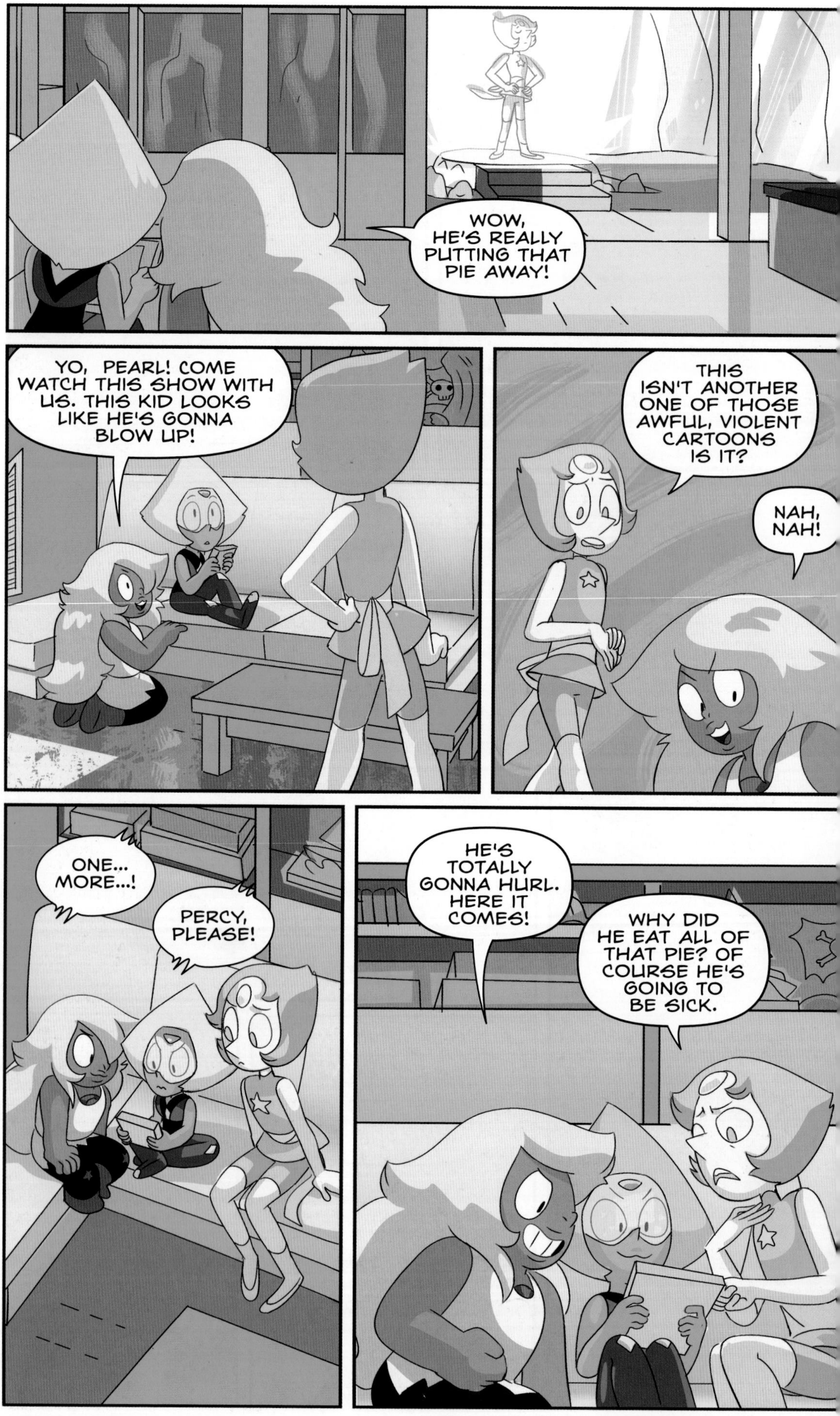
WOW, HE'S REALLY PUTTING THAT PIE AWAY!
YO, PEARL! COME WATCH THIS SHOW WITH US. THIS KID LOOKS LIKE HE'S GONNA BLOW UP!
THIS ISN'T ANOTHER ONE OF THOSE AWFUL, VIOLENT CARTOONS IS IT?
NAH, NAH!
ONE... MORE...!
PERCY, PLEASE!
HE'S TOTALLY GONNA HURL. HERE IT COMES!
WHY DID HE EAT ALL OF THAT PIE? OF COURSE HE'S GOING TO BE SICK.

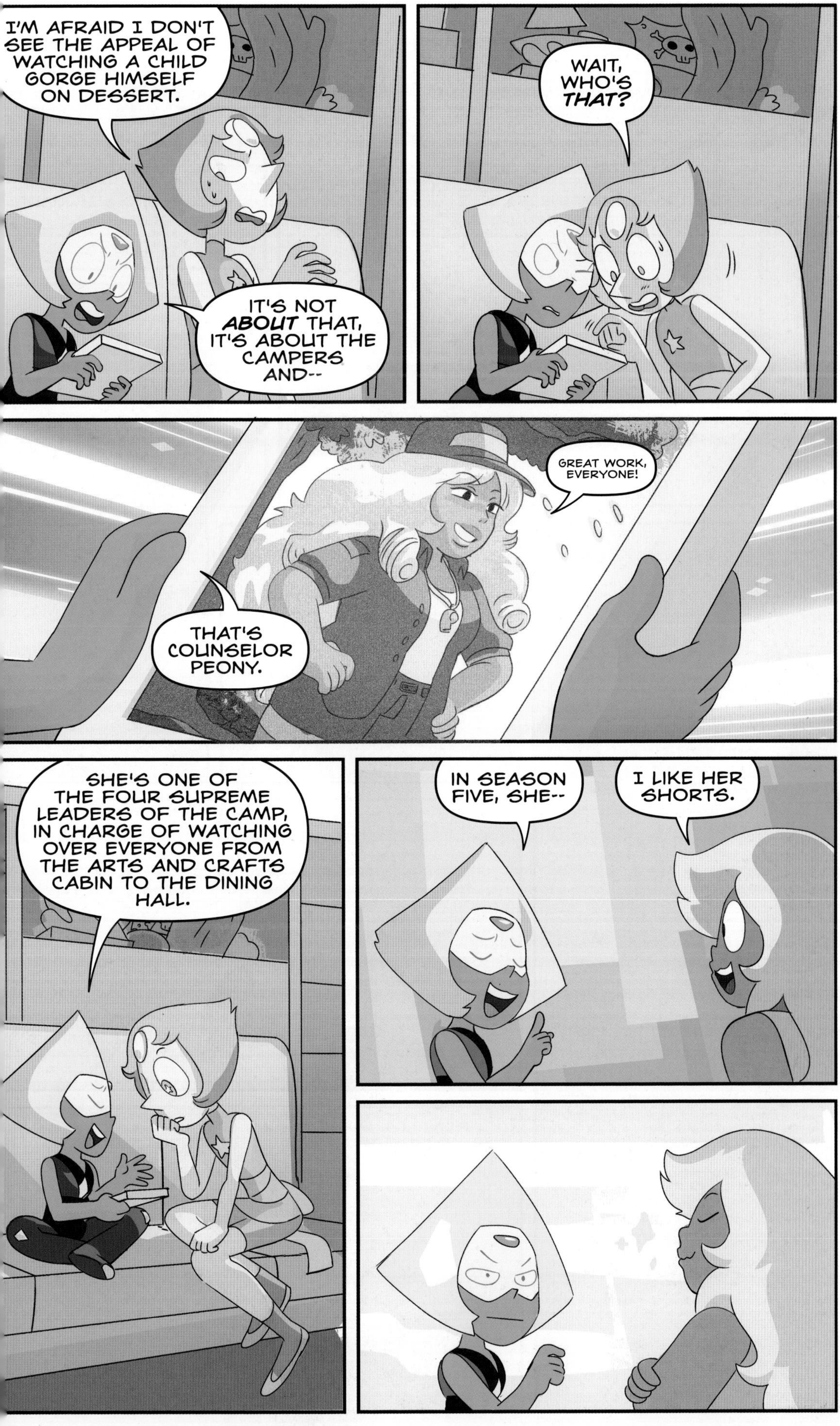
I'M AFRAID I DON'T SEE THE APPEAL OF WATCHING A CHILD GORGE HIMSELF ON DESSERT.
IT'S NOT ABOUT THAT, IT'S ABOUT THE CAMPERS AND--
WAIT, WHO'S THAT?
GREAT WORK, EVERYONE!
THAT'S COUNSELOR PEONY.
SHE'S ONE OF THE FOUR SUPREME LEADERS OF THE CAMP, IN CHARGE OF WATCHING OVER EVERYONE FROM THE ARTS AND CRAFTS CABIN TO THE DINING HALL.
IN SEASON FIVE, SHE--
I LIKE HER SHORTS.

...ANYWAY. CAMP PINING HEARTS IS A *CLASSIC* EARTH ENTERTAINMENT PROGRAM ABOUT THE RELATIONSHIPS BETWEEN CAMPERS AND THE MYSTERIES THAT UNFOLD AROUND THEIR CAMP.

NOPE.

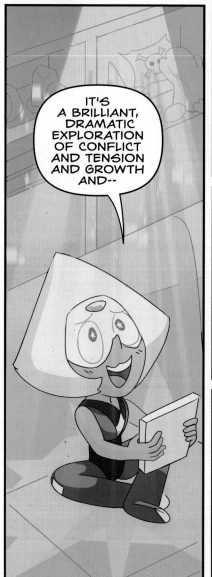

IT'S A BRILLIANT, DRAMATIC EXPLORATION OF CONFLICT AND TENSION AND GROWTH AND--

BLEUUGGH!

PERCY!

WE SHOULD START FROM THE FIRST EPISODE.

I'M NOT SURE I HAVE TIME TO--

NUH-UH, P-- TV TIME!

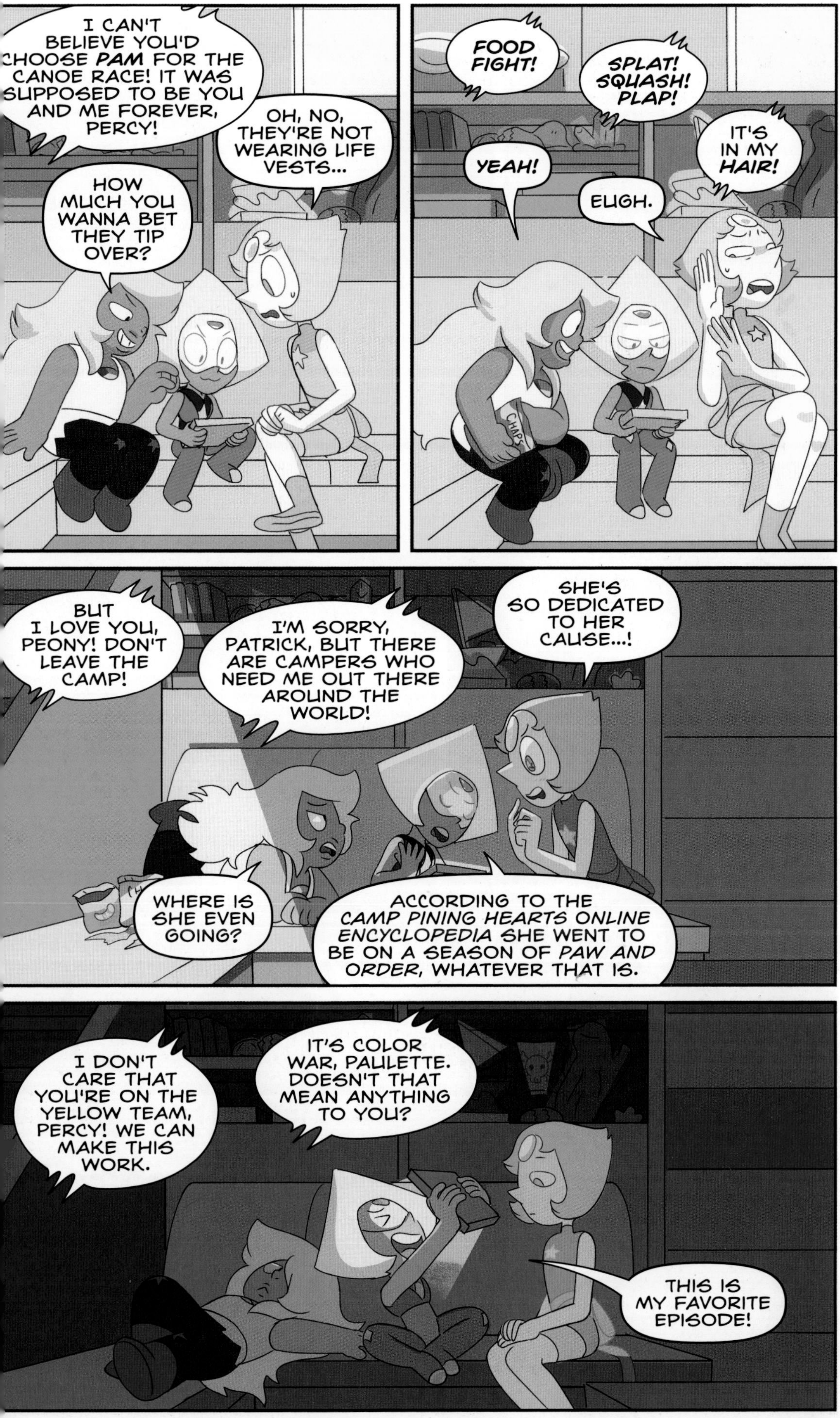
I CAN'T BELIEVE YOU'D CHOOSE PAM FOR THE CANOE RACE! IT WAS SUPPOSED TO BE YOU AND ME FOREVER, PERCY!
OH, NO, THEY'RE NOT WEARING LIFE VESTS...
HOW MUCH YOU WANNA BET THEY TIP OVER?
FOOD FIGHT!
SPLAT! SQUASH! PLAP!
YEAH!
EUGH.
IT'S IN MY HAIR!
CHAPS
BUT I LOVE YOU, PEONY! DON'T LEAVE THE CAMP!
I'M SORRY, PATRICK, BUT THERE ARE CAMPERS WHO NEED ME OUT THERE AROUND THE WORLD!
SHE'S SO DEDICATED TO HER CAUSE...!
WHERE IS SHE EVEN GOING?
ACCORDING TO THE CAMP PINING HEARTS ONLINE ENCYCLOPEDIA SHE WENT TO BE ON A SEASON OF PAW AND ORDER, WHATEVER THAT IS.
I DON'T CARE THAT YOU'RE ON THE YELLOW TEAM, PERCY! WE CAN MAKE THIS WORK.
IT'S COLOR WAR, PAULETTE. DOESN'T THAT MEAN ANYTHING TO YOU?
THIS IS MY FAVORITE EPISODE!

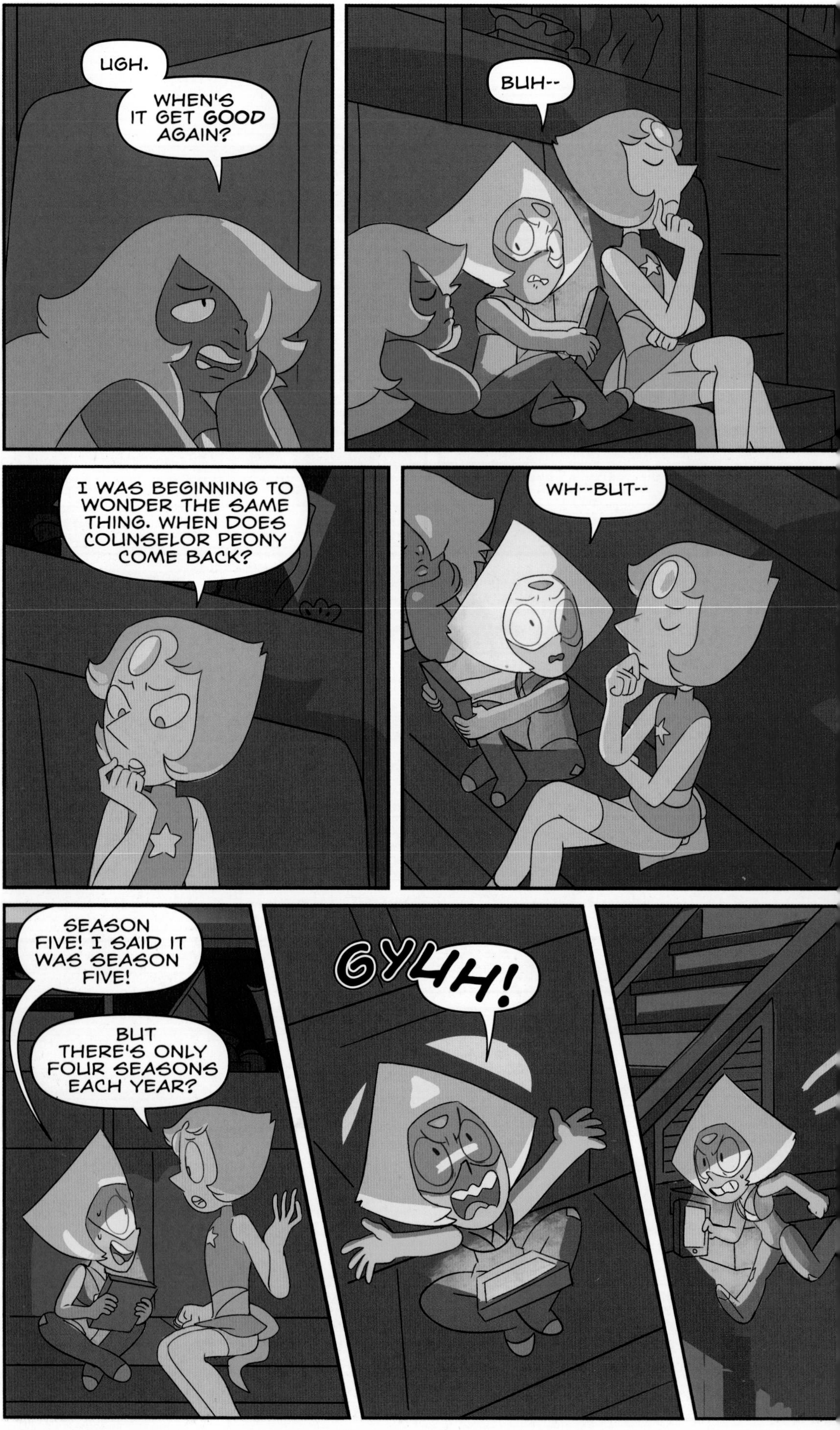
UGH.
WHEN'S IT GET GOOD AGAIN?
BUH--
I WAS BEGINNING TO WONDER THE SAME THING. WHEN DOES COUNSELOR PEONY COME BACK?
WH--BUT--
SEASON FIVE! I SAID IT WAS SEASON FIVE!
BUT THERE'S ONLY FOUR SEASONS EACH YEAR?
GYUH!

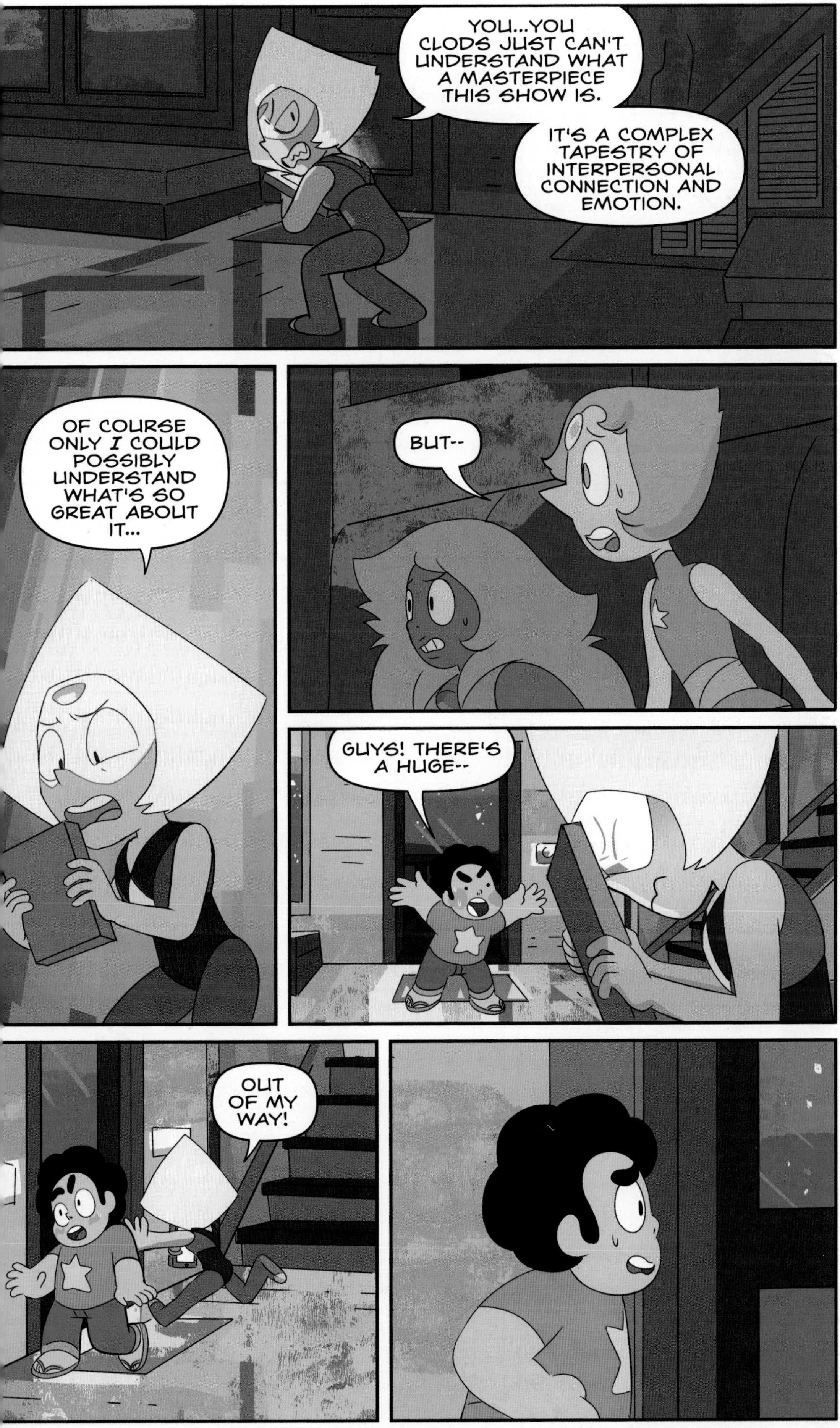
YOU...YOU CLODS JUST CAN'T UNDERSTAND WHAT A MASTERPIECE THIS SHOW IS.
IT'S A COMPLEX TAPESTRY OF INTERPERSONAL CONNECTION AND EMOTION.
OF COURSE ONLY *I* COULD POSSIBLY UNDERSTAND WHAT'S SO GREAT ABOUT IT...
BUT--
GUYS! THERE'S A HUGE--
OUT OF MY WAY!

WHAT WAS THAT ABOUT?

WE WERE WATCHING CAMP PINING HEARTS BUT SHE GOT MAD ALL OF A SUDDEN AND LEFT!

I WANTED TO KNOW WHO WAS GOING TO WIN THE COLOR WAR...

YOU'VE BEEN WATCHING IT ALL DAY?

WELL, YES! WE LIKED IT.

SHE'S JUST MAD WE DIDN'T LIKE HER FAVORITE EPISODE.

IT WAS JUST A BUNCH OF THREE-LEGGED RACE AND KISSING. I WANTE TO GET BACK TO THE COOL STUFF!

BUT I GUESS THAT'S WH SHE THINK IS THE COO STUFF...

SHE TAKES THAT SHOW REALLY SERIOUSLY.

IT'S JUST A SHOW...

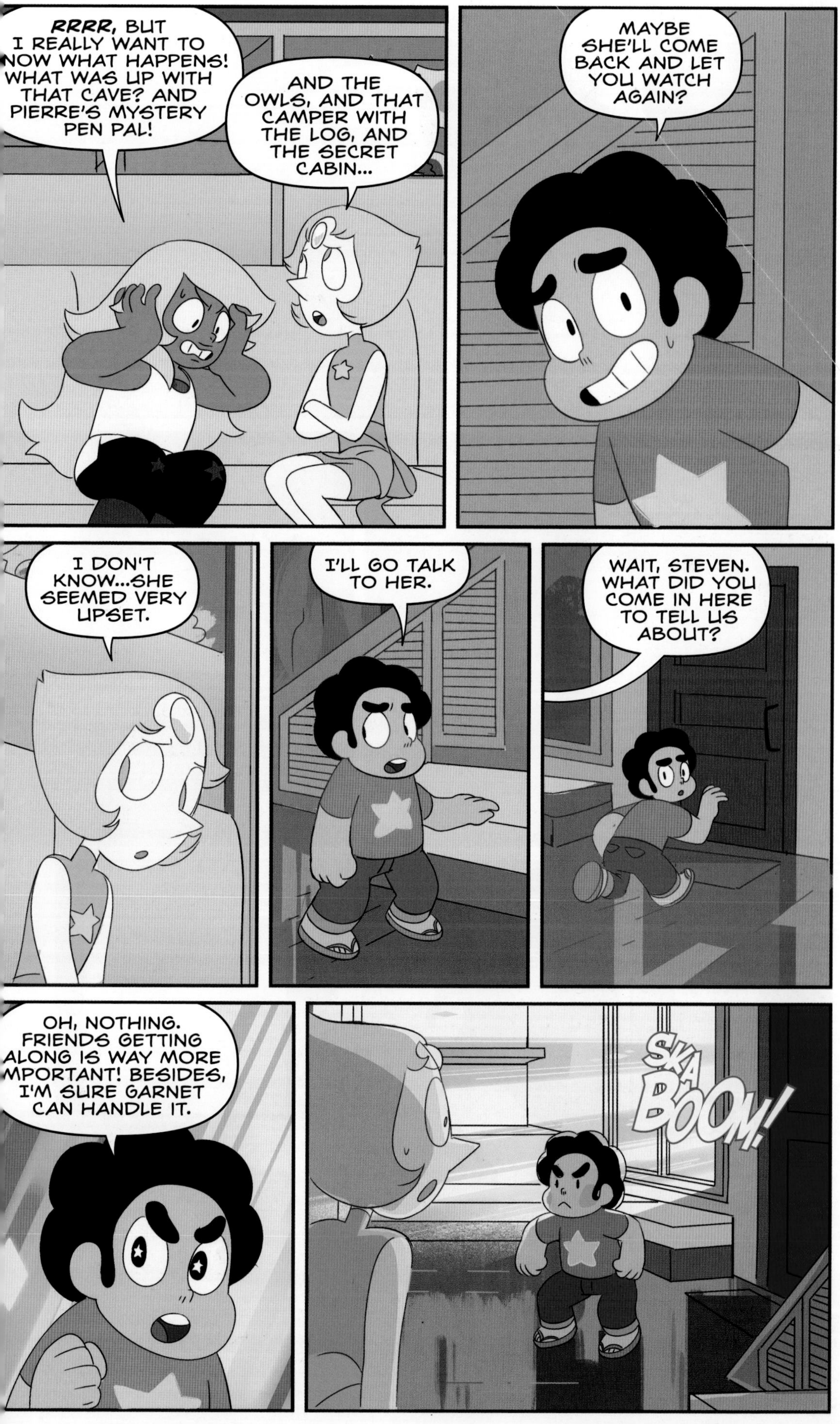
RRRR, BUT I REALLY WANT TO NOW WHAT HAPPENS! WHAT WAS UP WITH THAT CAVE? AND PIERRE'S MYSTERY PEN PAL!
AND THE OWLS, AND THAT CAMPER WITH THE LOG, AND THE SECRET CABIN...
MAYBE SHE'LL COME BACK AND LET YOU WATCH AGAIN?
I DON'T KNOW...SHE SEEMED VERY UPSET.
I'LL GO TALK TO HER.
WAIT, STEVEN. WHAT DID YOU COME IN HERE TO TELL US ABOUT?
OH, NOTHING. FRIENDS GETTING ALONG IS WAY MORE MPORTANT! BESIDES, I'M SURE GARNET CAN HANDLE IT.
SKA BOOM!

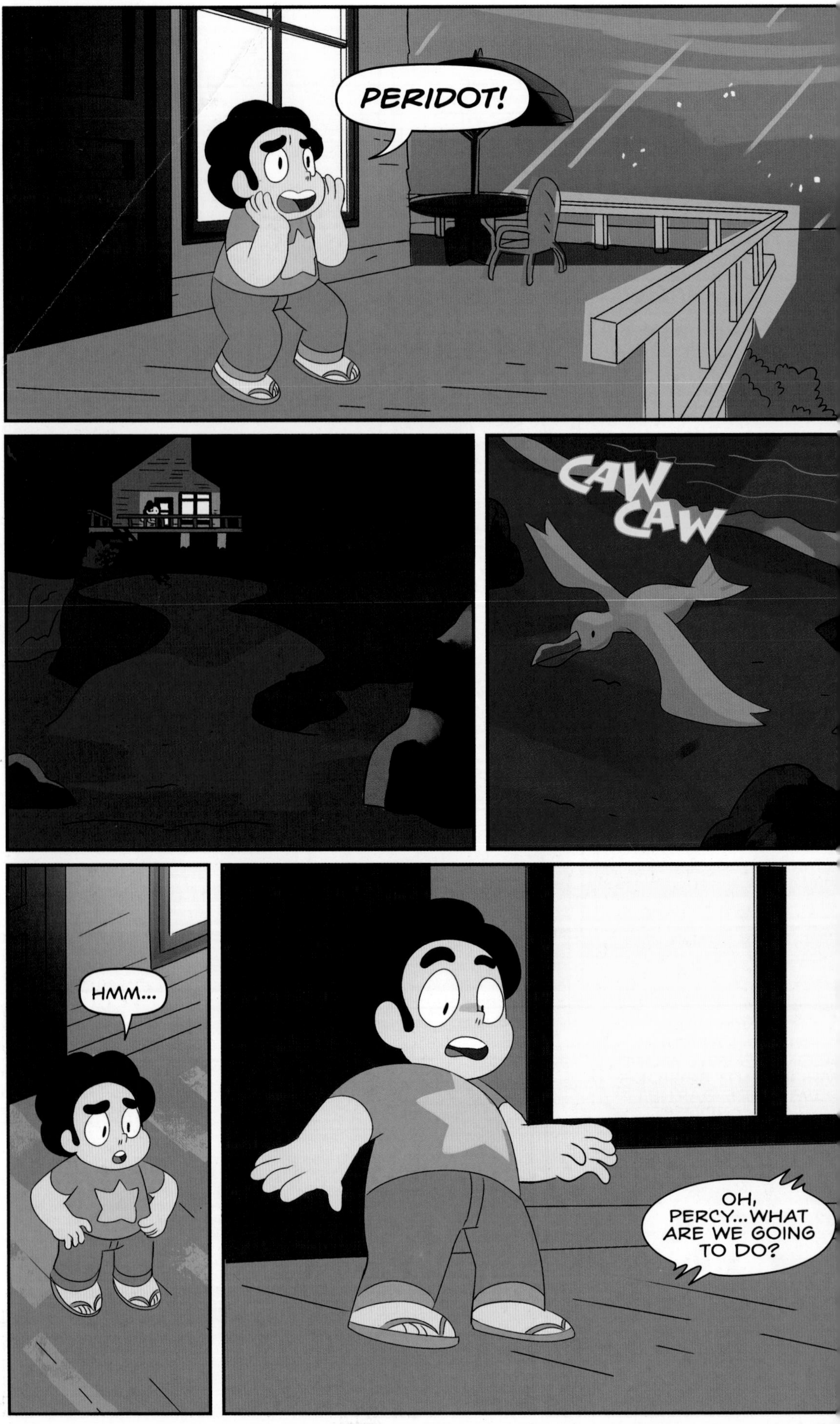
PERIDOT!
CAW
CAW
HMM...
OH, PERCY...WHAT ARE WE GOING TO DO?

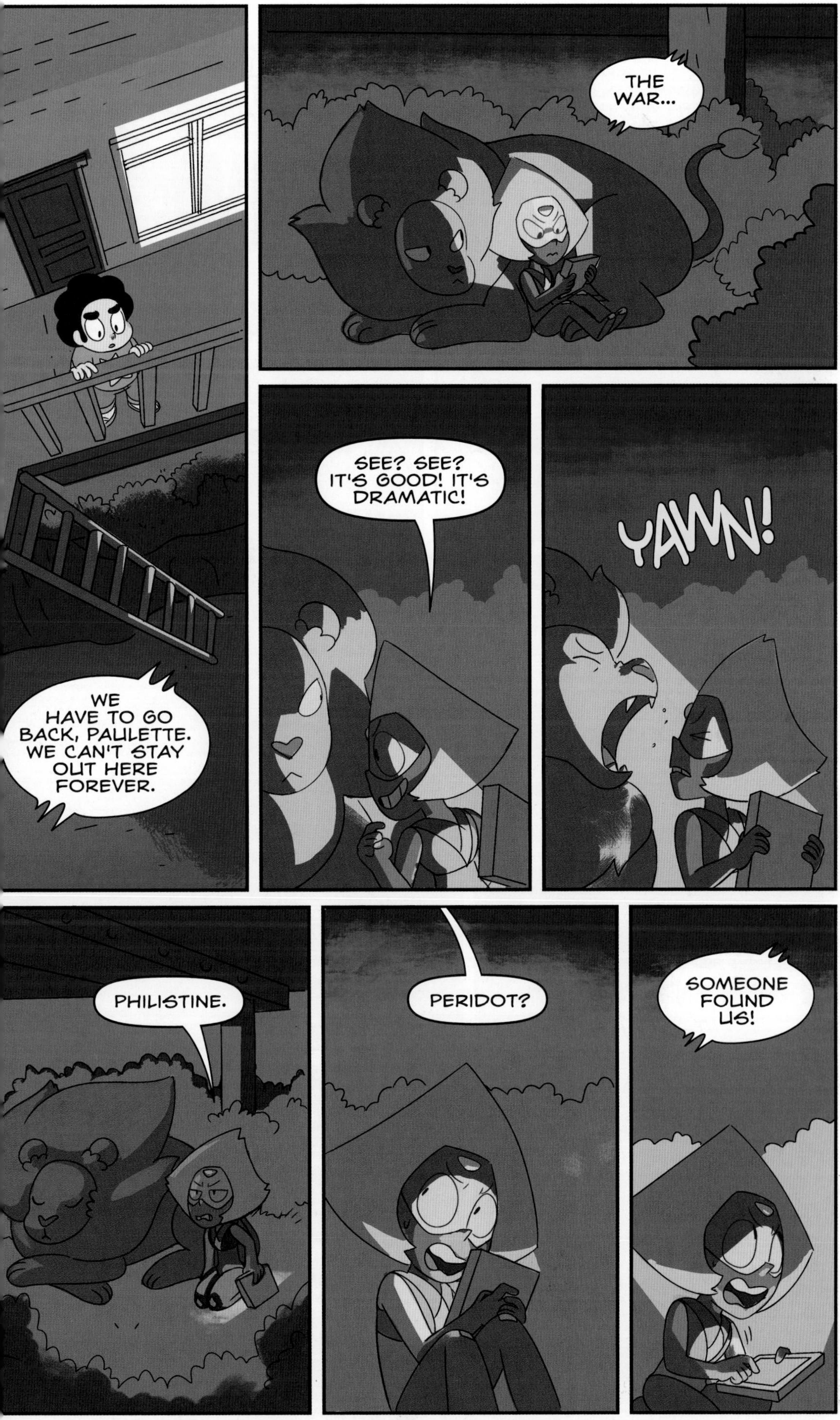
THE WAR...
WE HAVE TO GO BACK, PAULETTE. WE CAN'T STAY OUT HERE FOREVER.
SEE? SEE? IT'S GOOD! IT'S DRAMATIC!
YAWN!
PHILISTINE.
PERIDOT?
SOMEONE FOUND US!

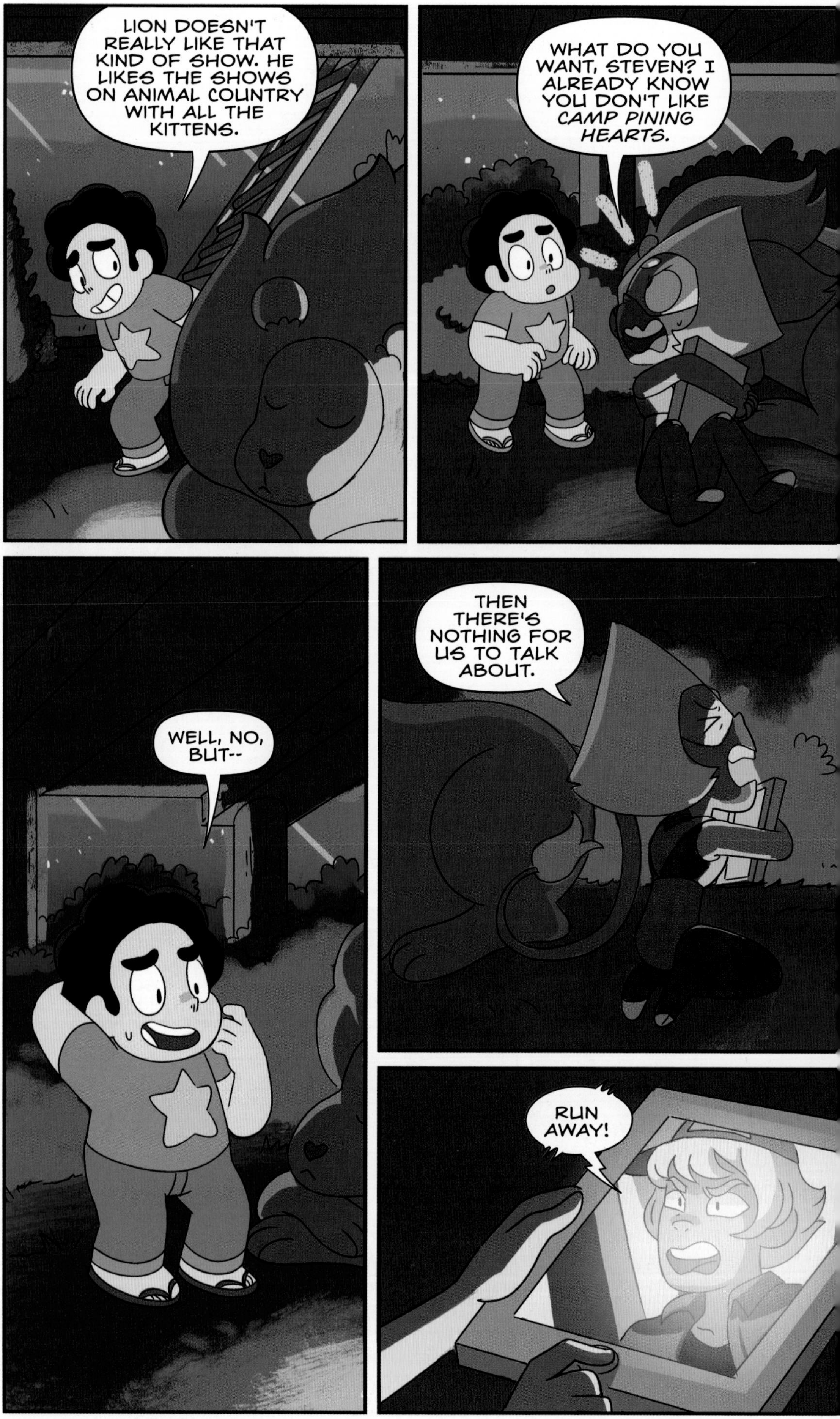
LION DOESN'T REALLY LIKE THAT KIND OF SHOW. HE LIKES THE SHOWS ON ANIMAL COUNTRY WITH ALL THE KITTENS.
WHAT DO YOU WANT, STEVEN? I ALREADY KNOW YOU DON'T LIKE *CAMP PINING HEARTS.*
WELL, NO, BUT--
THEN THERE'S NOTHING FOR US TO TALK ABOUT.
RUN AWAY!

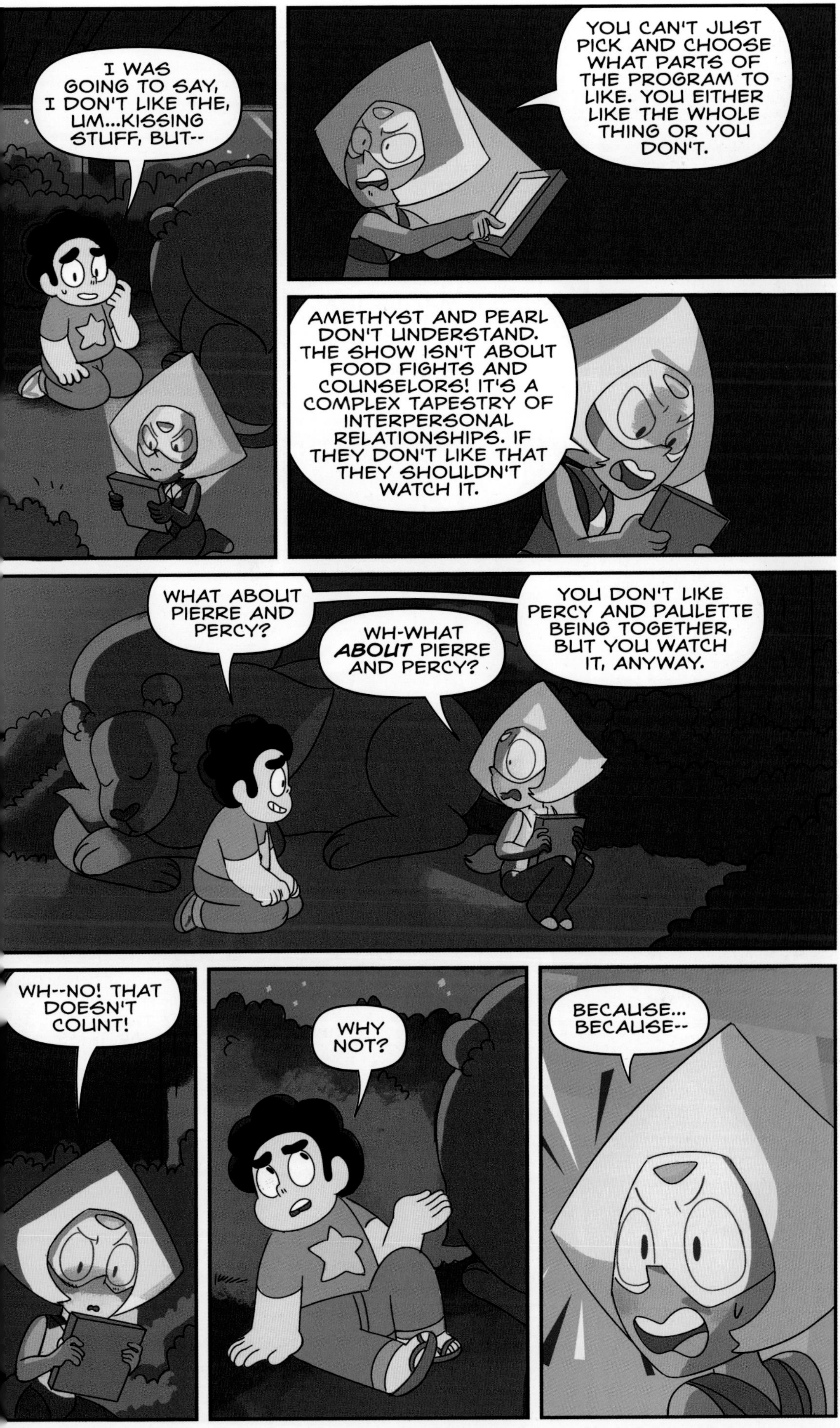
I WAS GOING TO SAY, I DON'T LIKE THE, UM...KISSING STUFF, BUT--
YOU CAN'T JUST PICK AND CHOOSE WHAT PARTS OF THE PROGRAM TO LIKE. YOU EITHER LIKE THE WHOLE THING OR YOU DON'T.
AMETHYST AND PEARL DON'T UNDERSTAND. THE SHOW ISN'T ABOUT FOOD FIGHTS AND COUNSELORS! IT'S A COMPLEX TAPESTRY OF INTERPERSONAL RELATIONSHIPS. IF THEY DON'T LIKE THAT THEY SHOULDN'T WATCH IT.
YOU DON'T LIKE PERCY AND PAULETTE BEING TOGETHER, BUT YOU WATCH IT, ANYWAY.
WHAT ABOUT PIERRE AND PERCY?
WH-WHAT *ABOUT* PIERRE AND PERCY?
WH--NO! THAT DOESN'T COUNT!
WHY NOT?
BECAUSE... BECAUSE--

A CRITICAL EXAMINATION OF THE INFORMATION PRESENTED IN THE PROGRAM!

IT'S DIFFERENT! I STILL LIKE IT MORE THAN THEY DO!

--BECAUSE THAT'S ANALYSIS!

WHY'S IT MATTER THAT YOU LIKE IT *MORE*? EVEN IF THEY DIDN'T LIKE EVERY PART OF IT, THEY STILL LIKED IT ENOUGH TO WATCH IT WITH YOU.

ISN'T THAT MORE IMPORTANT? SPENDING TIME WITH YOUR FRIENDS...?

NO!

PERIDOT...

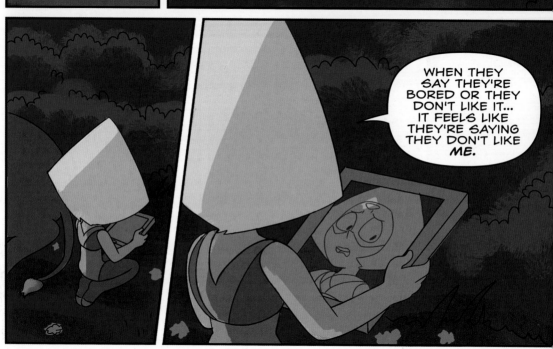

WHEN THEY SAY THEY'RE BORED OR THEY DON'T LIKE IT... IT FEELS LIKE THEY'RE SAYING THEY DON'T LIKE *ME*.

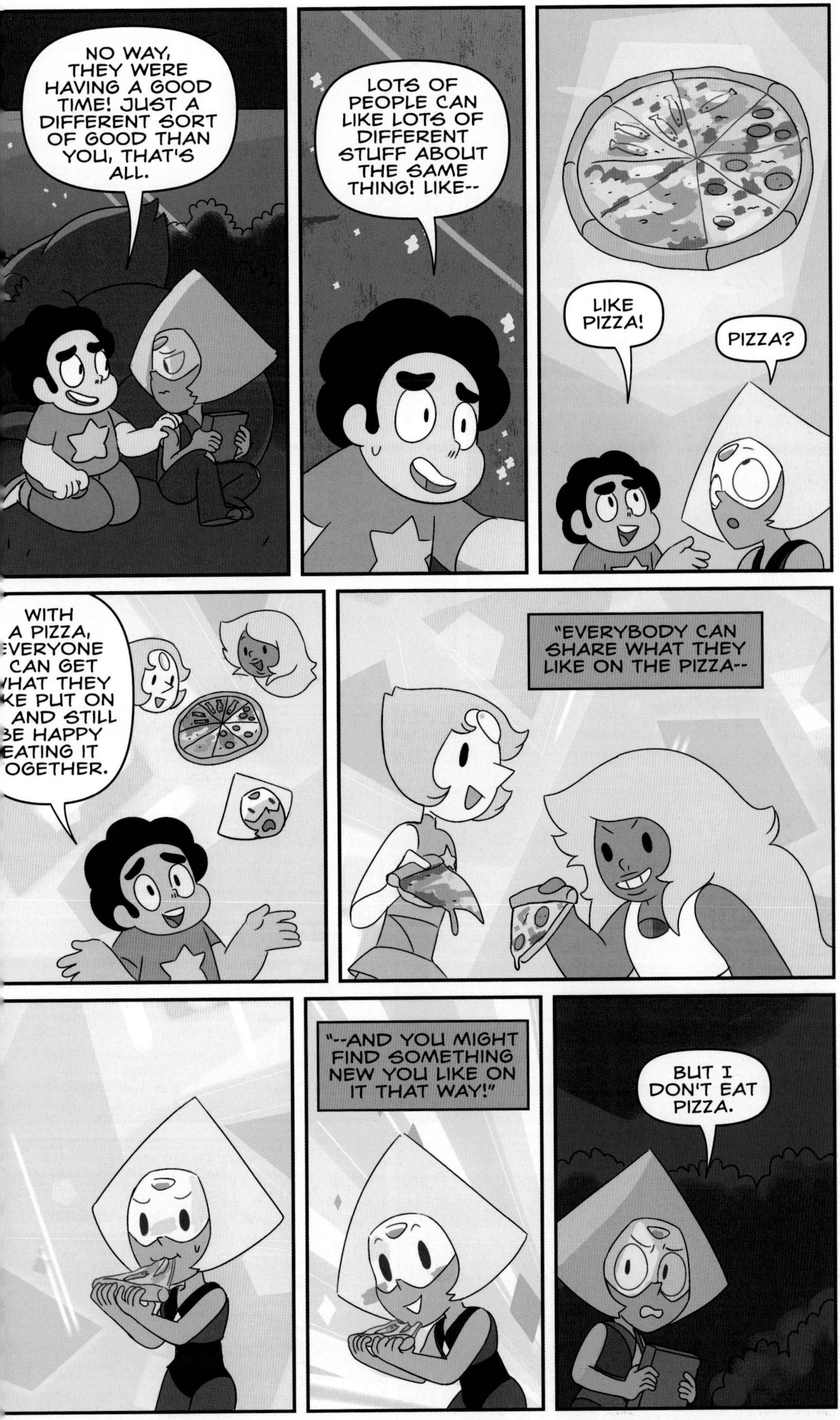
NO WAY, THEY WERE HAVING A GOOD TIME! JUST A DIFFERENT SORT OF GOOD THAN YOU, THAT'S ALL.
LOTS OF PEOPLE CAN LIKE LOTS OF DIFFERENT STUFF ABOUT THE SAME THING! LIKE--
LIKE PIZZA!
PIZZA?
WITH A PIZZA, EVERYONE CAN GET WHAT THEY LIKE PUT ON AND STILL BE HAPPY EATING IT TOGETHER.
"EVERYBODY CAN SHARE WHAT THEY LIKE ON THE PIZZA--
"--AND YOU MIGHT FIND SOMETHING NEW YOU LIKE ON IT THAT WAY!"
BUT I DON'T EAT PIZZA.

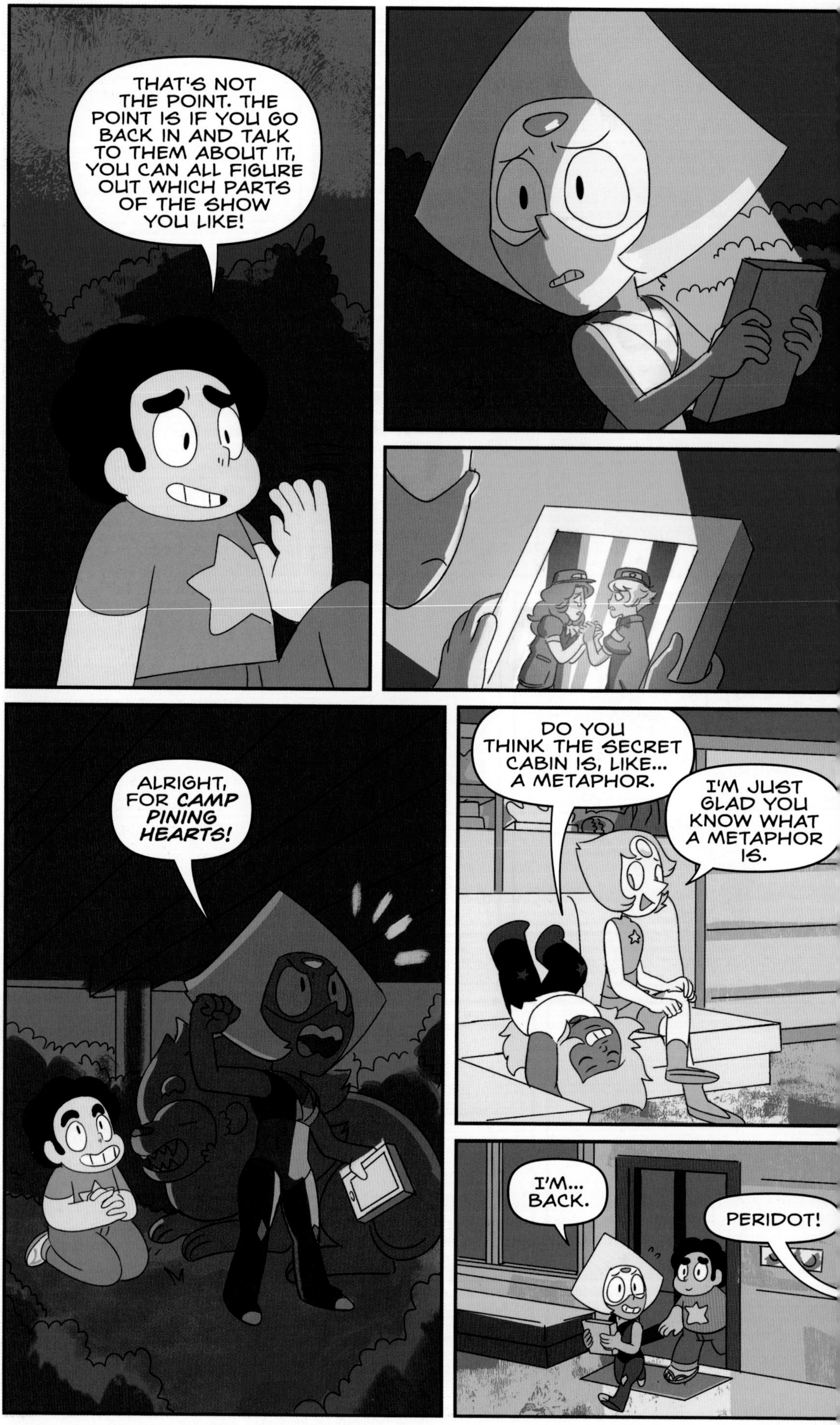
THAT'S NOT THE POINT. THE POINT IS IF YOU GO BACK IN AND TALK TO THEM ABOUT IT, YOU CAN ALL FIGURE OUT WHICH PARTS OF THE SHOW YOU LIKE!
ALRIGHT, FOR *CAMP PINING HEARTS*!
DO YOU THINK THE SECRET CABIN IS, LIKE... A METAPHOR.
I'M JUST GLAD YOU KNOW WHAT A METAPHOR IS.
I'M... BACK.
PERIDOT!

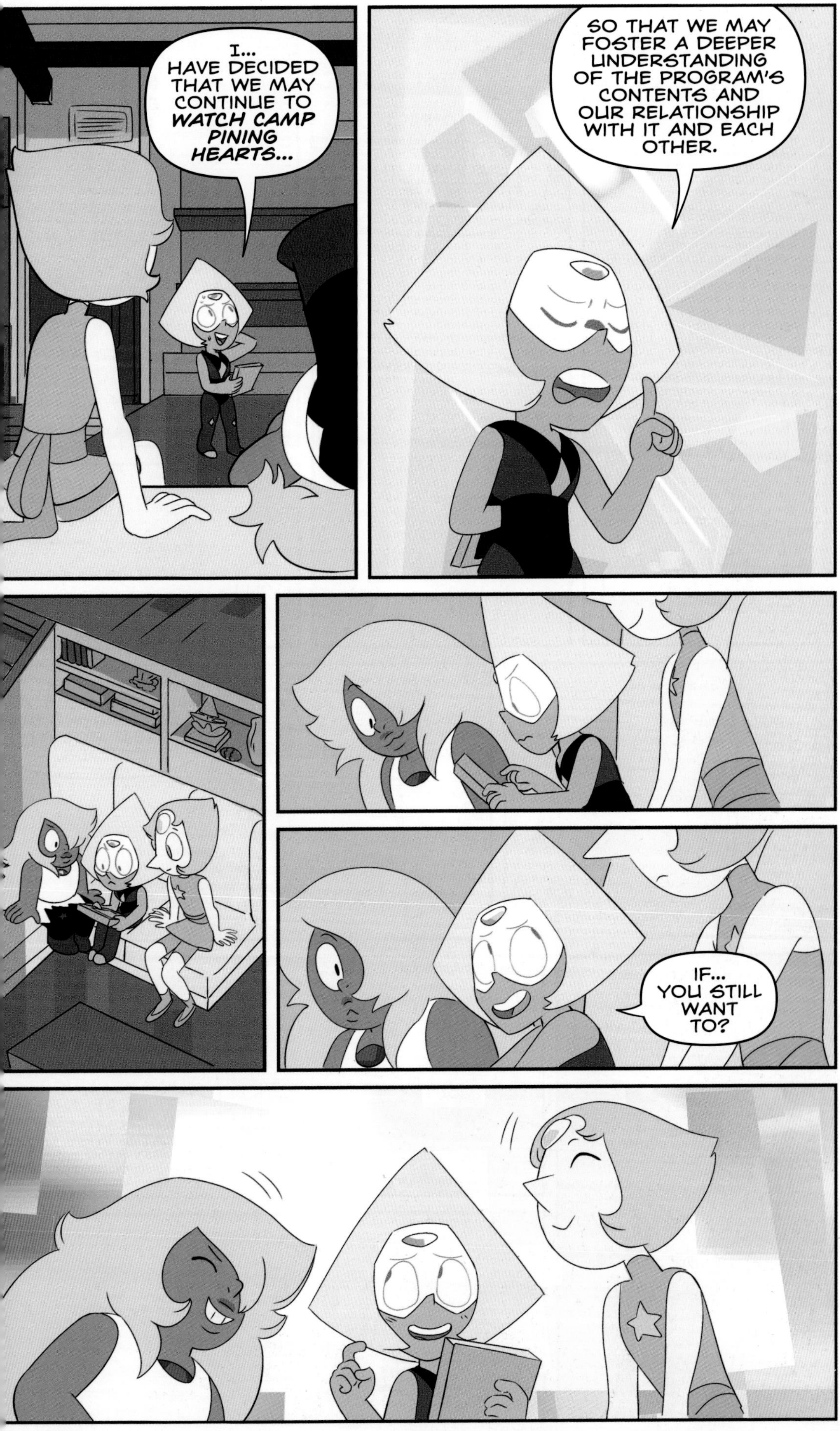
I... HAVE DECIDED THAT WE MAY CONTINUE TO *WATCH CAMP PINING HEARTS...*
SO THAT WE MAY FOSTER A DEEPER UNDERSTANDING OF THE PROGRAM'S CONTENTS AND OUR RELATIONSHIP WITH IT AND EACH OTHER.
IF... YOU STILL WANT TO?

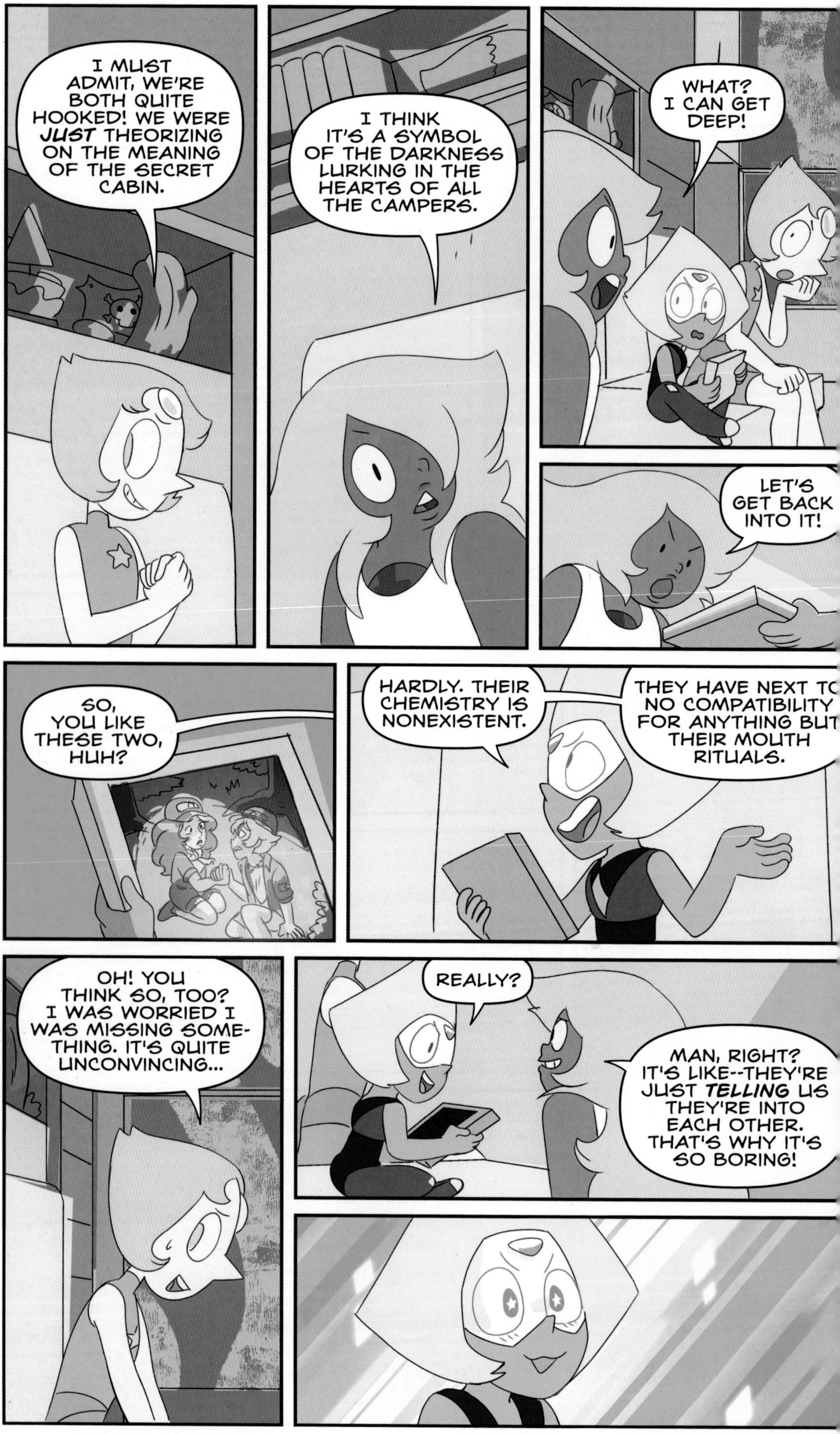
I MUST ADMIT, WE'RE BOTH QUITE HOOKED! WE WERE JUST THEORIZING ON THE MEANING OF THE SECRET CABIN.
I THINK IT'S A SYMBOL OF THE DARKNESS LURKING IN THE HEARTS OF ALL THE CAMPERS.
WHAT? I CAN GET DEEP!
LET'S GET BACK INTO IT!
SO, YOU LIKE THESE TWO, HUH?
HARDLY. THEIR CHEMISTRY IS NONEXISTENT.
THEY HAVE NEXT TO NO COMPATIBILITY FOR ANYTHING BUT THEIR MOUTH RITUALS.
OH! YOU THINK SO, TOO? I WAS WORRIED I WAS MISSING SOME-THING. IT'S QUITE UNCONVINCING...
REALLY?
MAN, RIGHT? IT'S LIKE--THEY'RE JUST TELLING US THEY'RE INTO EACH OTHER. THAT'S WHY IT'S SO BORING!

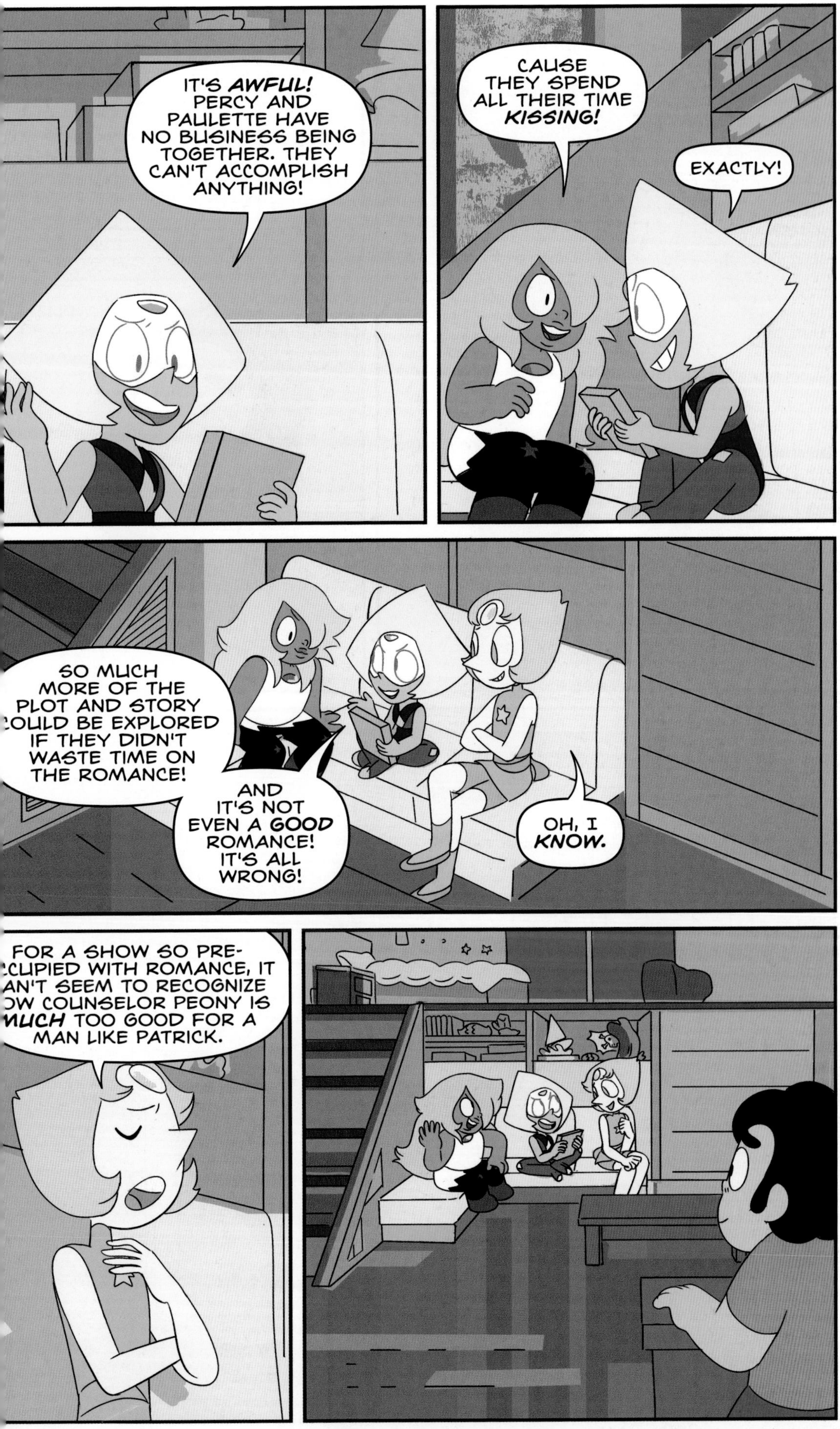

IT'S AWFUL! PERCY AND PAULETTE HAVE NO BUSINESS BEING TOGETHER. THEY CAN'T ACCOMPLISH ANYTHING!
CAUSE THEY SPEND ALL THEIR TIME KISSING!
EXACTLY!
SO MUCH MORE OF THE PLOT AND STORY COULD BE EXPLORED IF THEY DIDN'T WASTE TIME ON THE ROMANCE!
AND IT'S NOT EVEN A GOOD ROMANCE! IT'S ALL WRONG!
OH, I KNOW.
FOR A SHOW SO PRE-CCUPIED WITH ROMANCE, IT AN'T SEEM TO RECOGNIZE OW COUNSELOR PEONY IS MUCH TOO GOOD FOR A MAN LIKE PATRICK.

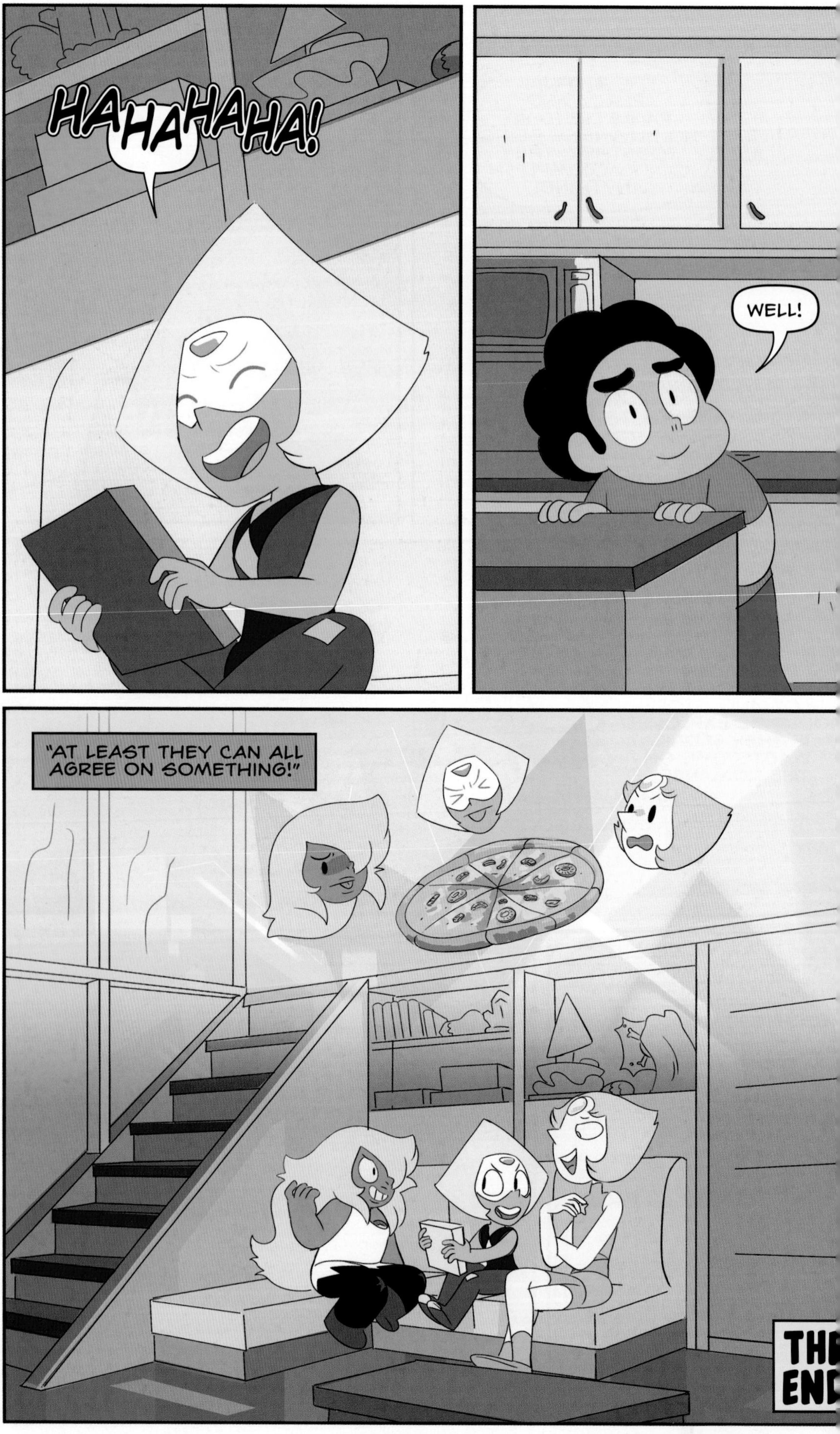
HAHAHAHAHA!
WELL!
"AT LEAST THEY CAN ALL AGREE ON SOMETHING!"

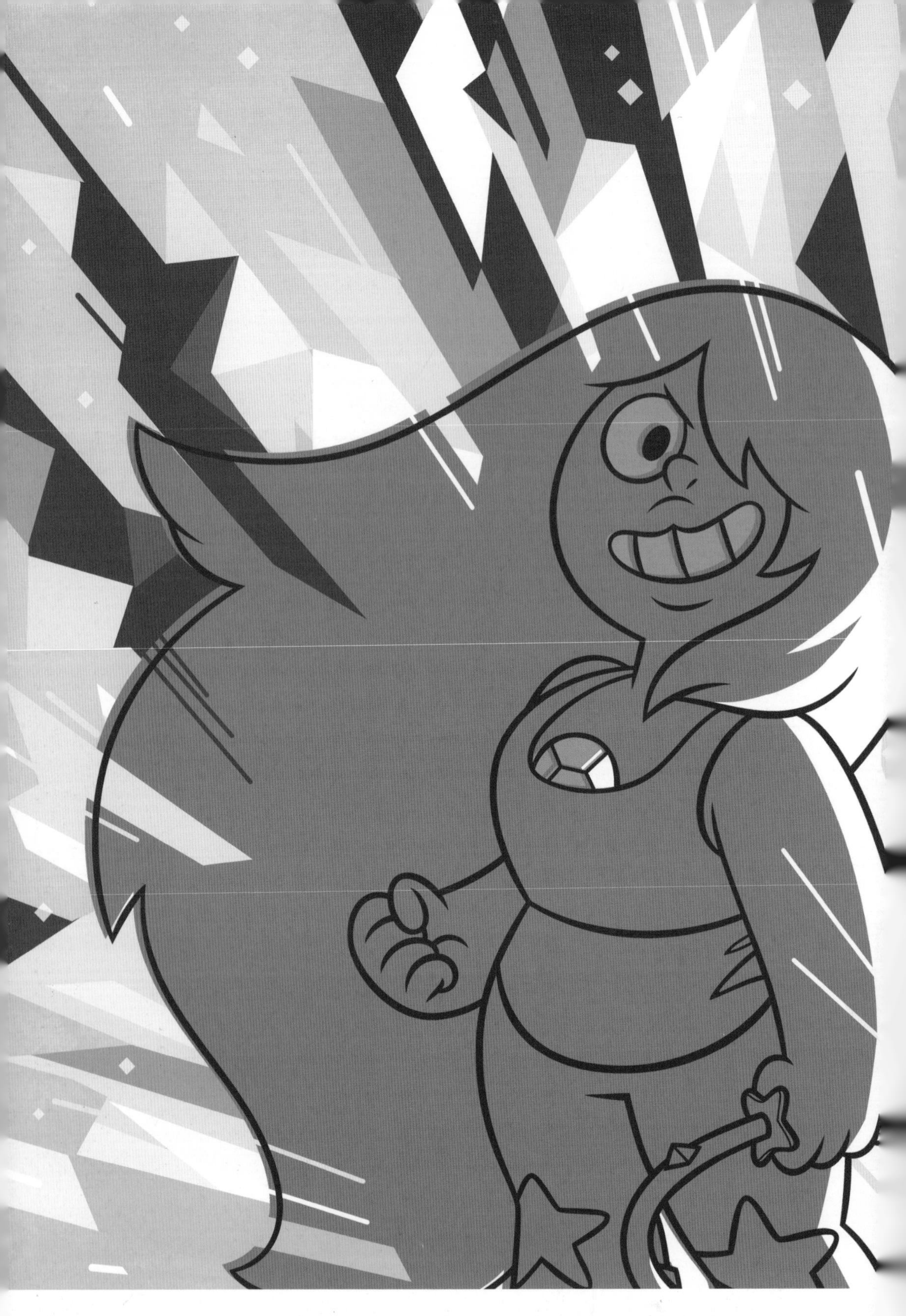

CHAPTER THIRTY-FOUR

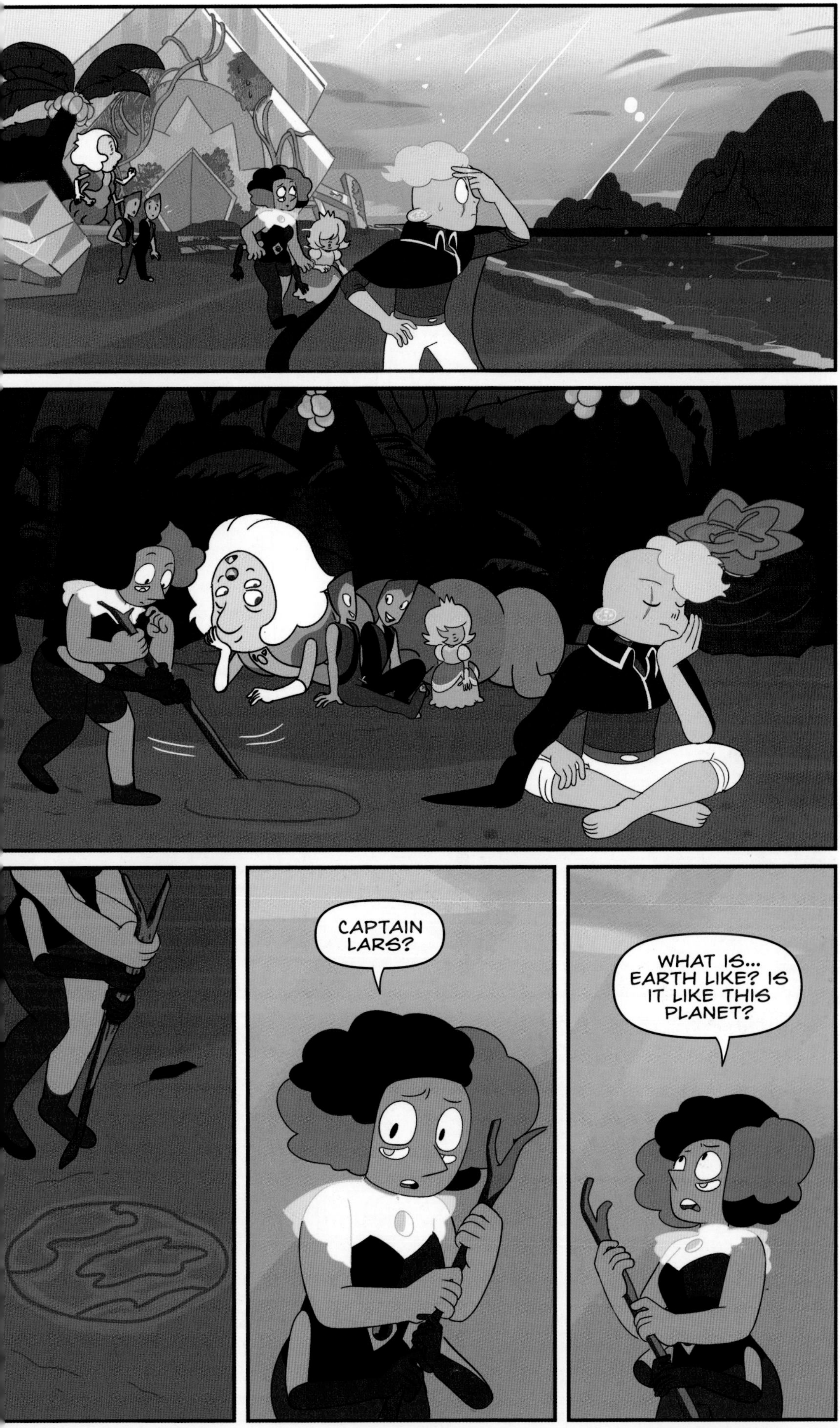
CAPTAIN LARS?
WHAT IS... EARTH LIKE? IS IT LIKE THIS PLANET?

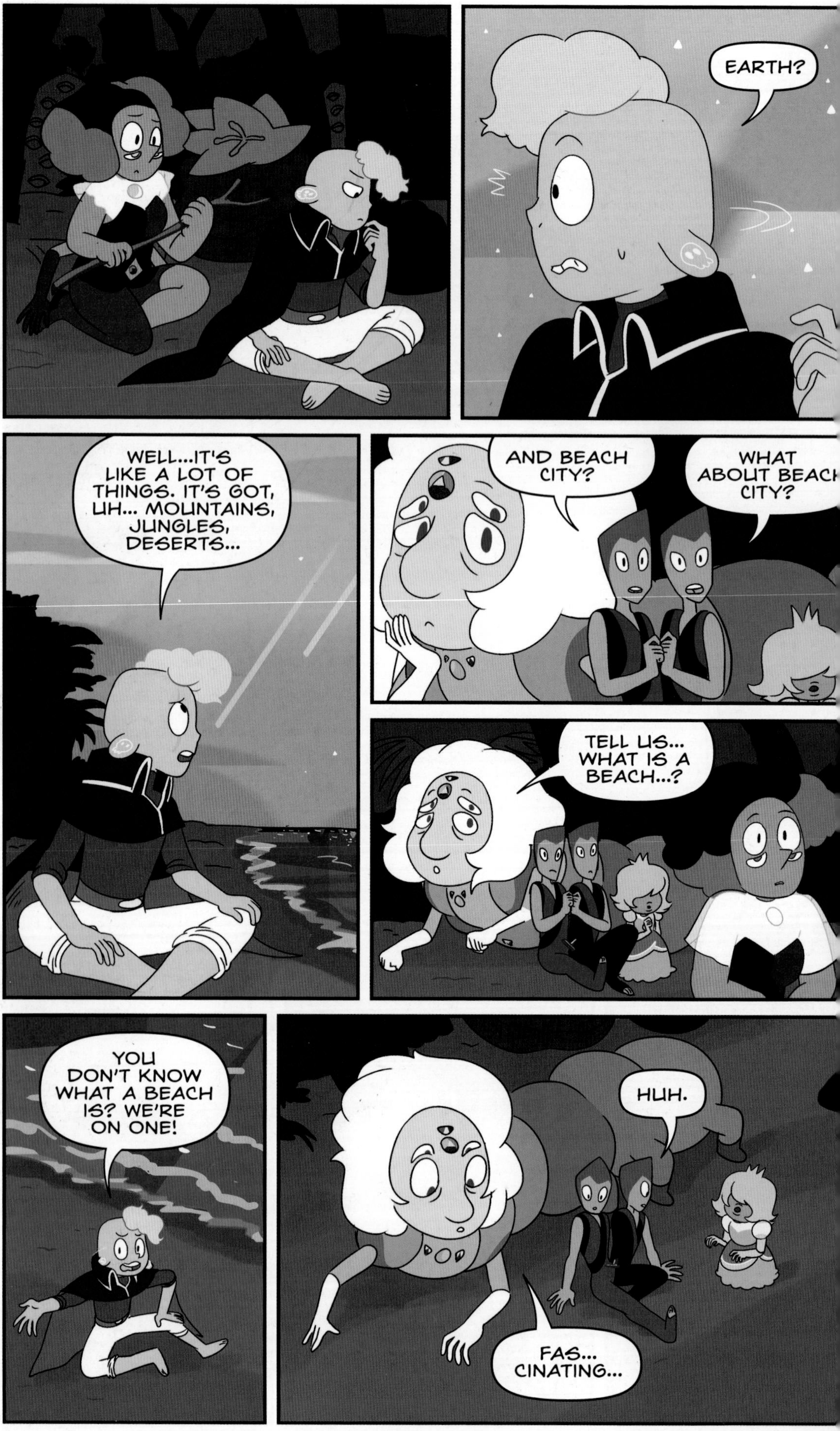
EARTH?
WELL...IT'S LIKE A LOT OF THINGS. IT'S GOT, UH... MOUNTAINS, JUNGLES, DESERTS...
AND BEACH CITY?
WHAT ABOUT BEACH CITY?
TELL US... WHAT IS A BEACH...?
YOU DON'T KNOW WHAT A BEACH IS? WE'RE ON ONE!
HUH.
FAS... CINATING...

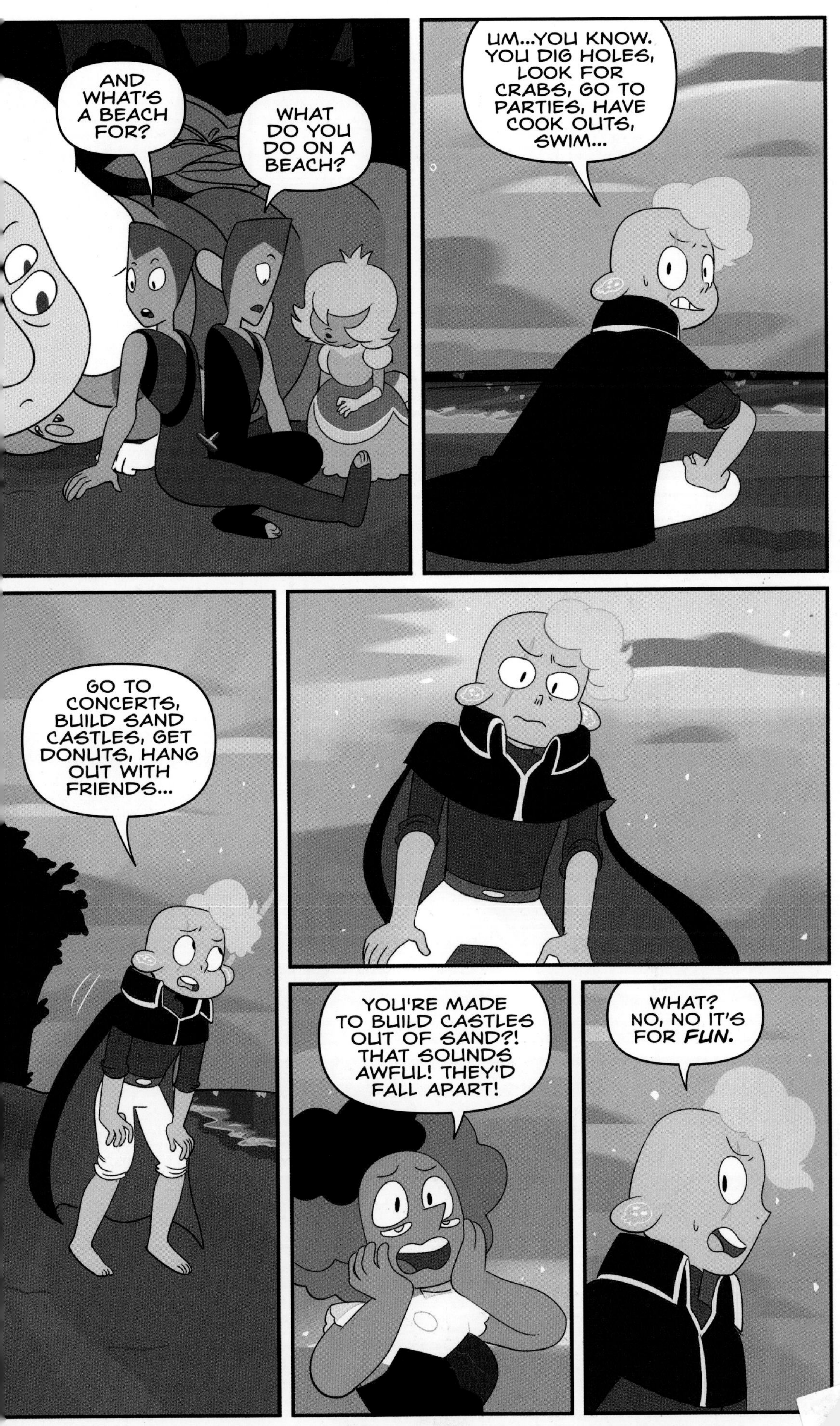
AND WHAT'S A BEACH FOR?
WHAT DO YOU DO ON A BEACH?
UM...YOU KNOW. YOU DIG HOLES, LOOK FOR CRABS, GO TO PARTIES, HAVE COOK OUTS, SWIM...
GO TO CONCERTS, BUILD SAND CASTLES, GET DONUTS, HANG OUT WITH FRIENDS...
YOU'RE MADE TO BUILD CASTLES OUT OF SAND?! THAT SOUNDS AWFUL! THEY'D FALL APART!
WHAT? NO, NO IT'S FOR *FUN.*

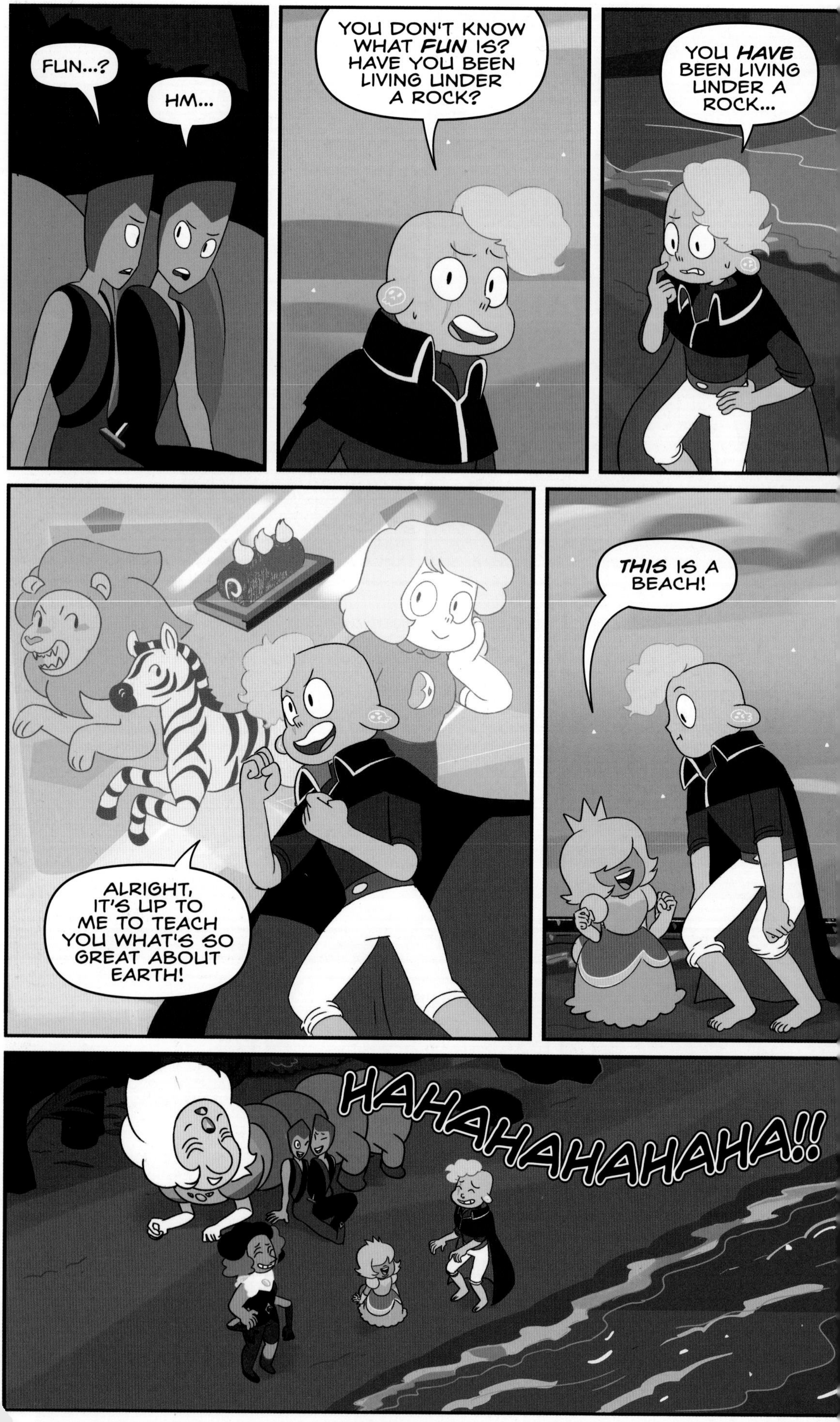
FUN...?
HM...
YOU DON'T KNOW WHAT *FUN* IS? HAVE YOU BEEN LIVING UNDER A ROCK?
YOU *HAVE* BEEN LIVING UNDER A ROCK...
ALRIGHT, IT'S UP TO ME TO TEACH YOU WHAT'S SO GREAT ABOUT EARTH!
THIS IS A BEACH!
HAHAHAHAHAHAHA!!

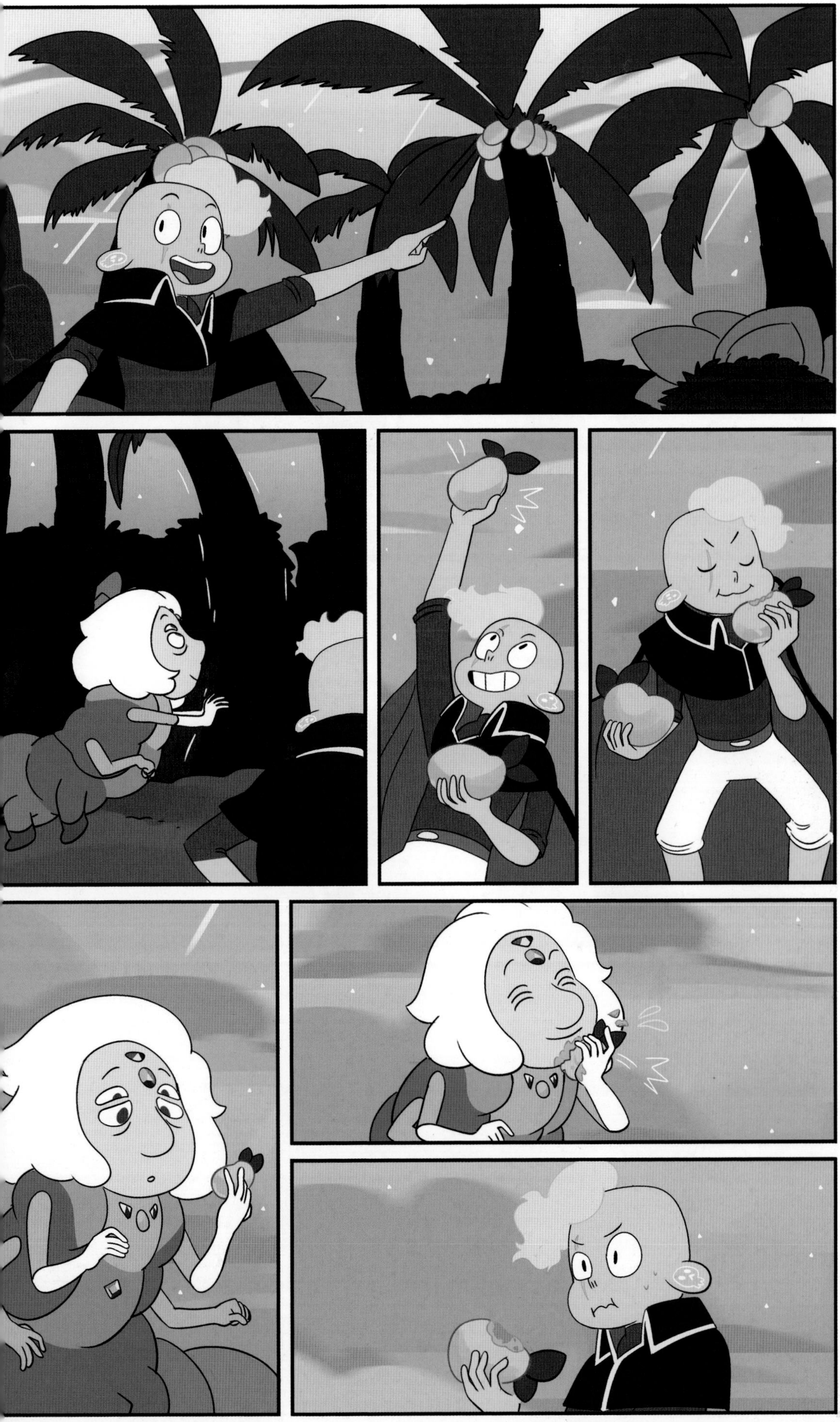

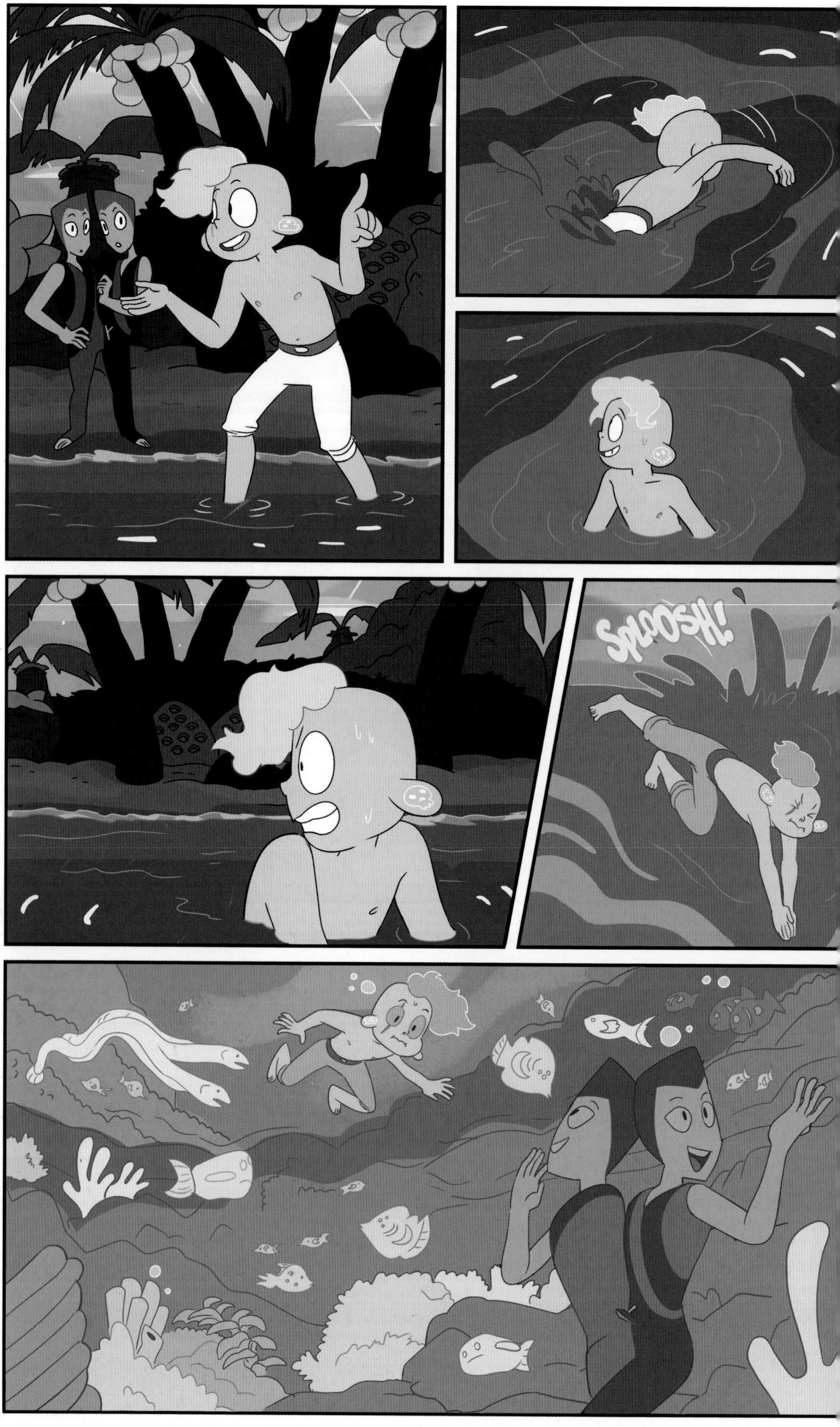
SPLOOSH!

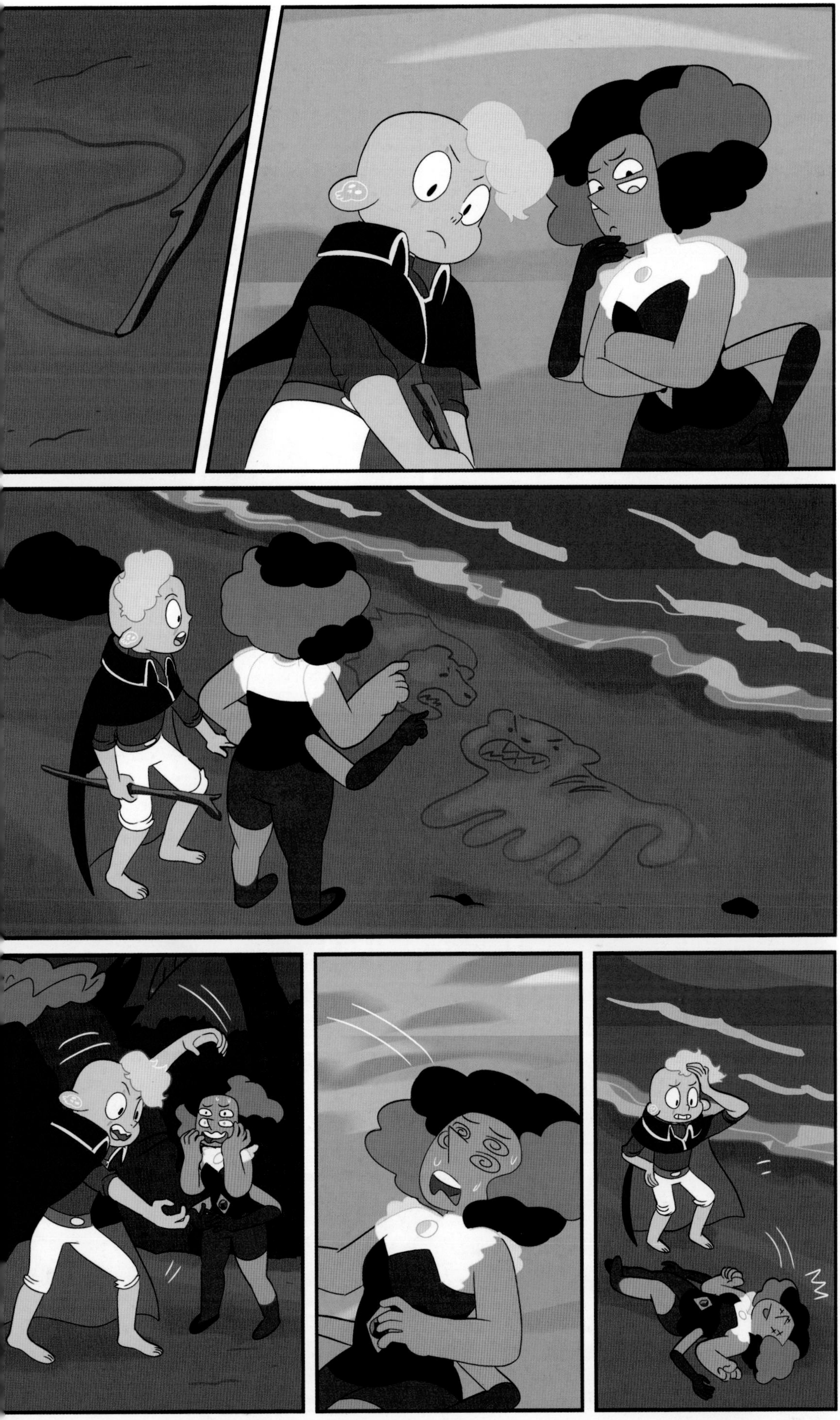

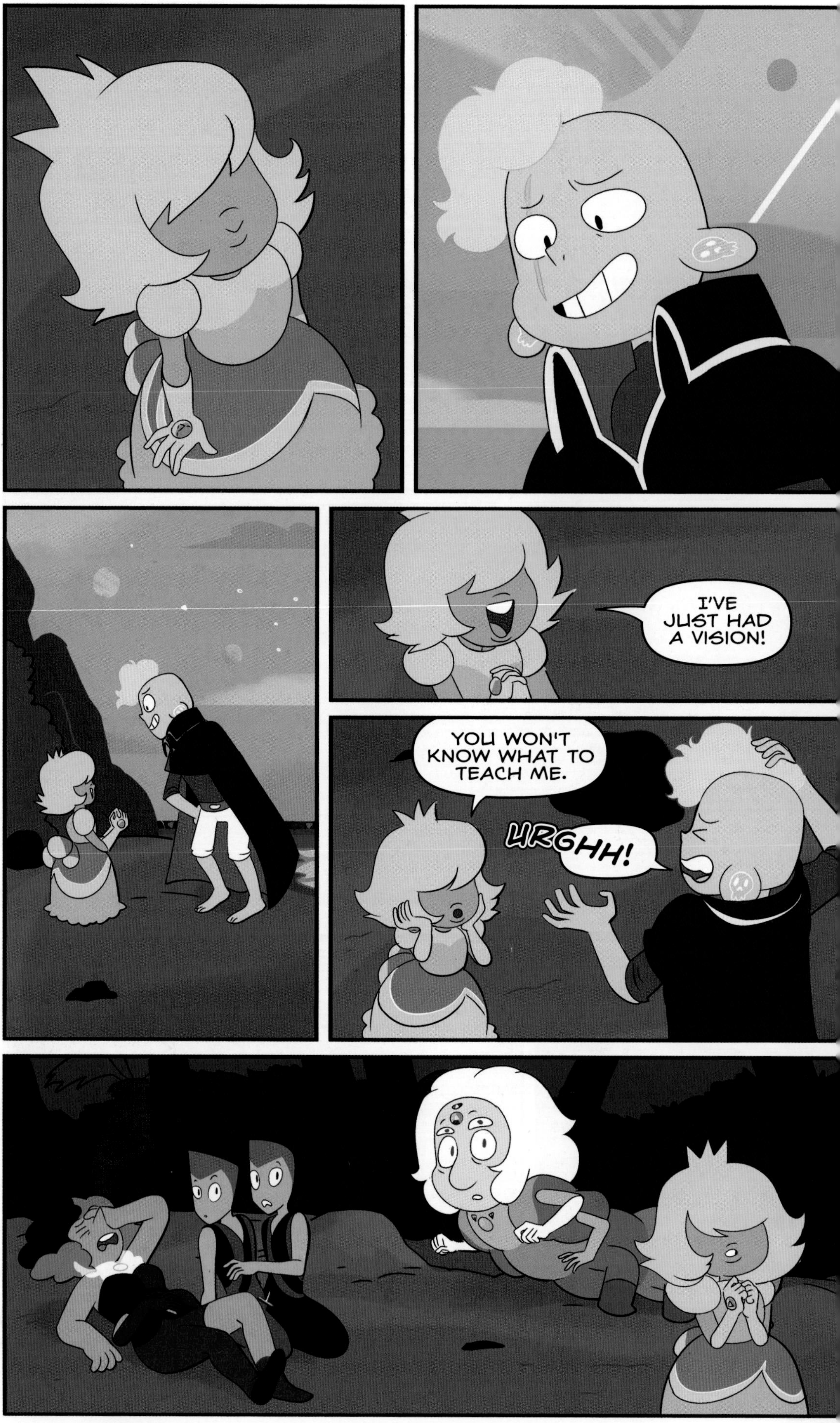
I'VE JUST HAD A VISION!
YOU WON'T KNOW WHAT TO TEACH ME.
URGHH!

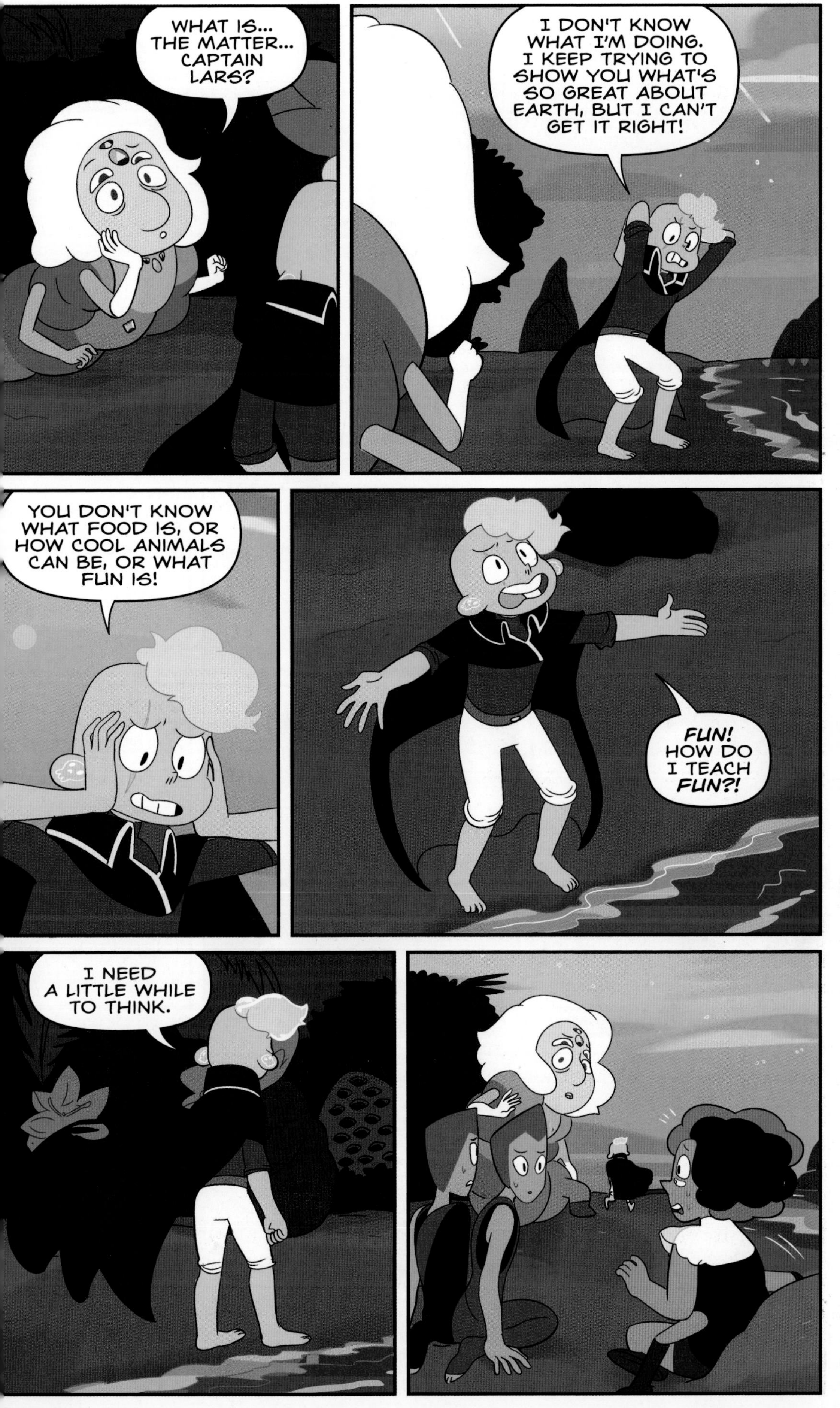
WHAT IS... THE MATTER... CAPTAIN LARS?
I DON'T KNOW WHAT I'M DOING. I KEEP TRYING TO SHOW YOU WHAT'S SO GREAT ABOUT EARTH, BUT I CAN'T GET IT RIGHT!
YOU DON'T KNOW WHAT FOOD IS, OR HOW COOL ANIMALS CAN BE, OR WHAT FUN IS!
FUN! HOW DO I TEACH FUN?!
I NEED A LITTLE WHILE TO THINK.

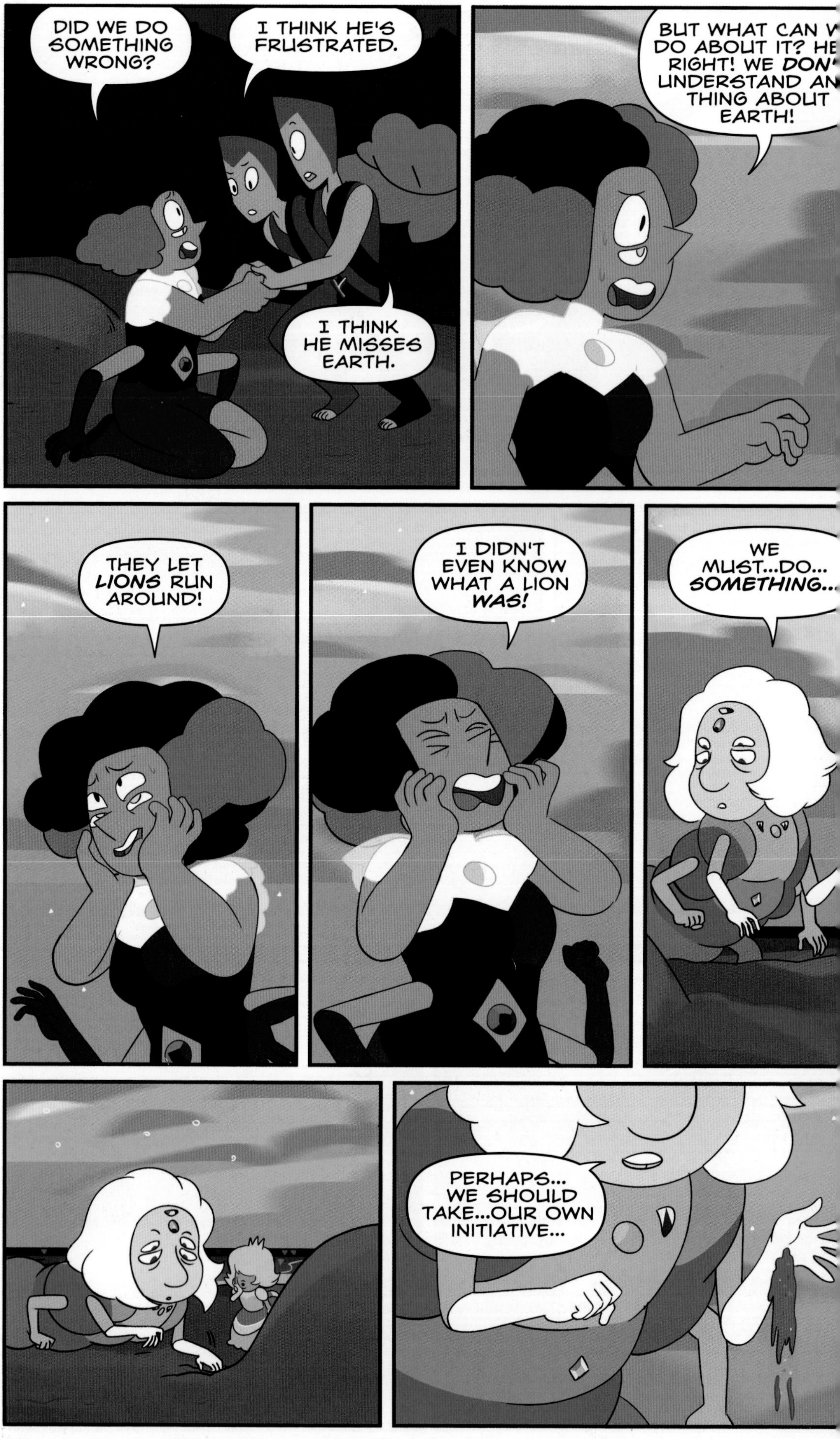
DID WE DO SOMETHING WRONG?
I THINK HE'S FRUSTRATED.
I THINK HE MISSES EARTH.
BUT WHAT CAN W
DO ABOUT IT? HE
RIGHT! WE *DON'*
UNDERSTAND AN
THING ABOUT
EARTH!
THEY LET *LIONS* RUN AROUND!
I DIDN'T EVEN KNOW WHAT A LION *WAS!*
WE MUST...DO... *SOMETHING...*
PERHAPS... WE SHOULD TAKE...OUR OWN INITIATIVE...

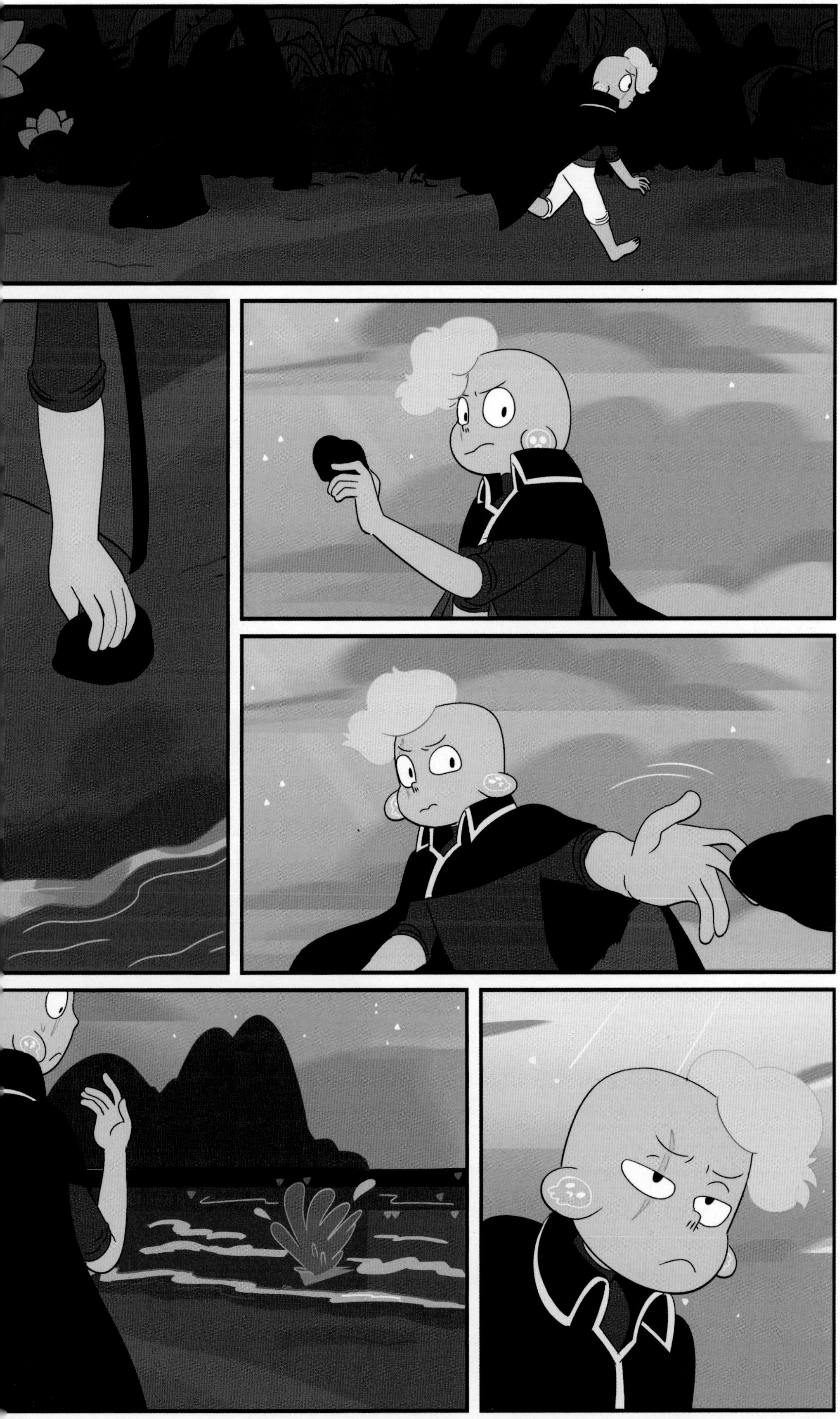

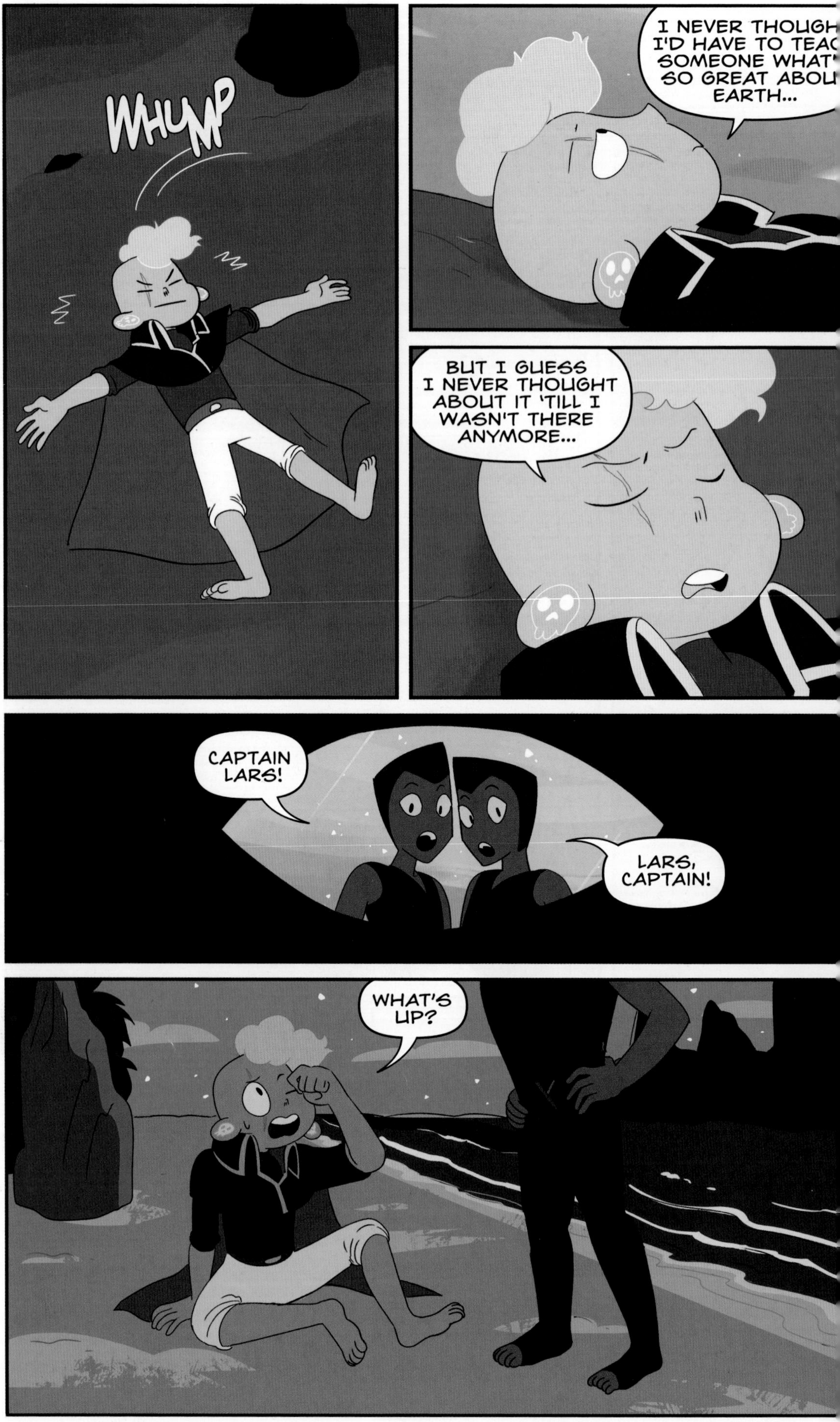
WHUMP
I NEVER THOUGH
I'D HAVE TO TEAC
SOMEONE WHAT'
SO GREAT ABOU
EARTH...
BUT I GUESS I NEVER THOUGHT ABOUT IT 'TILL I WASN'T THERE ANYMORE...
CAPTAIN LARS!
LARS, CAPTAIN!
WHAT'S UP?

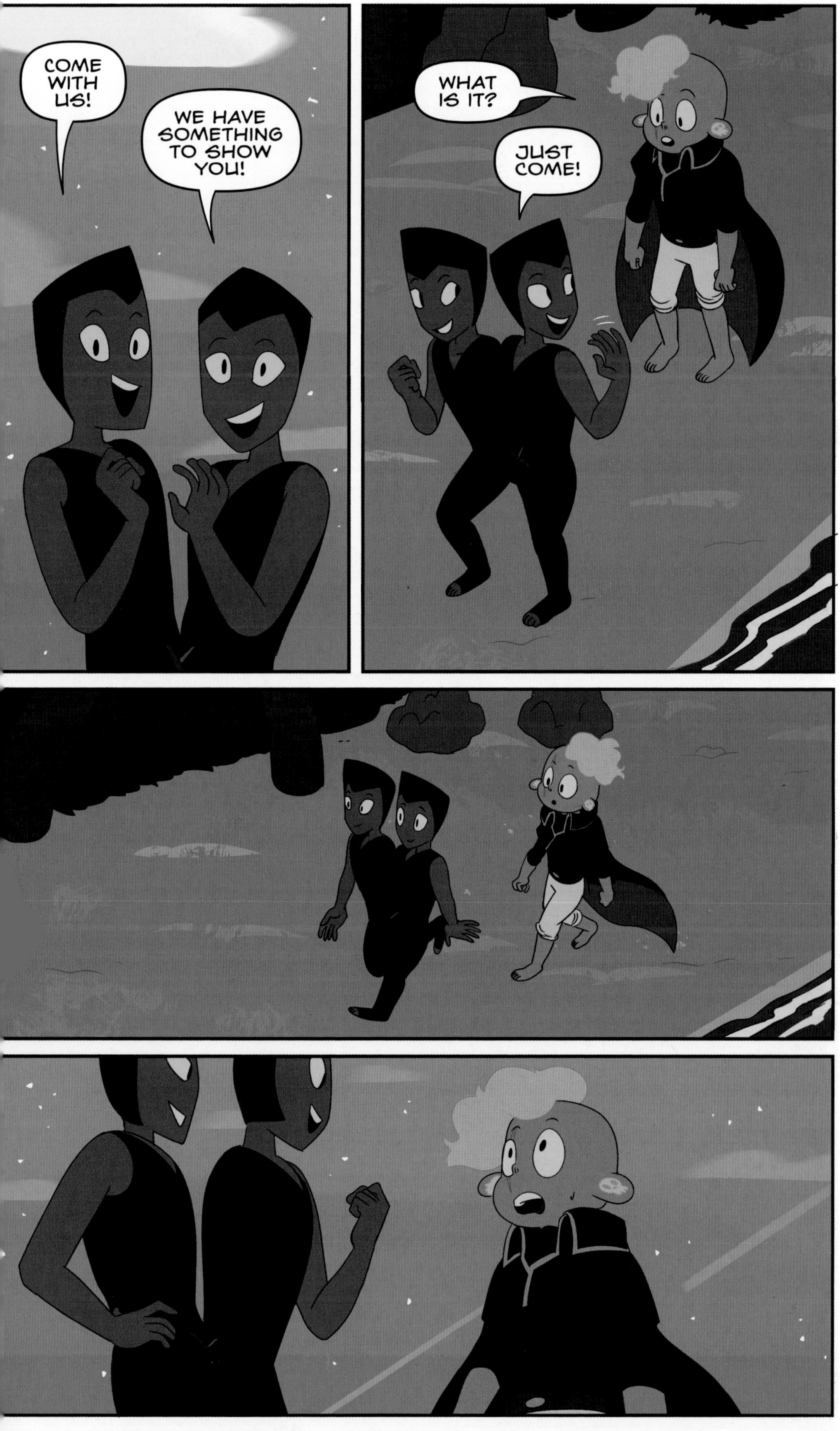
COME WITH US!
WE HAVE SOMETHING TO SHOW YOU!
WHAT IS IT?
JUST COME!

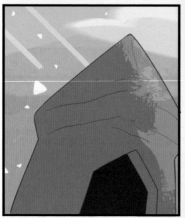

YOU GUYS DID ALL THIS?

ACK!

LARS IS ABOUT TO ARRIVE!

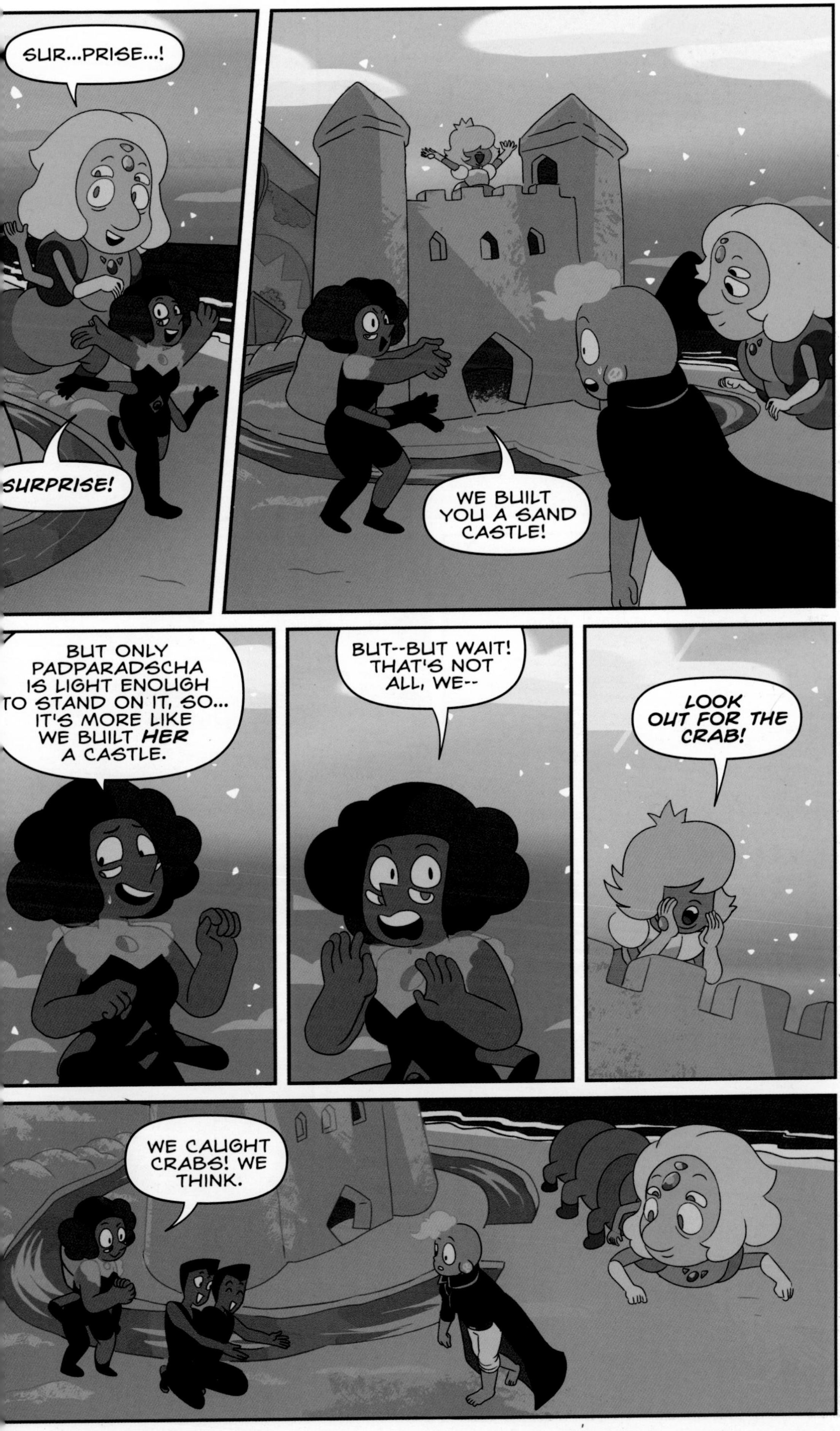
SUR...PRISE...!
SURPRISE!
WE BUILT YOU A SAND CASTLE!
BUT ONLY PADPARADSCHA IS LIGHT ENOUGH TO STAND ON IT, SO... IT'S MORE LIKE WE BUILT *HER* A CASTLE.
BUT--BUT WAIT! THAT'S NOT ALL, WE--
LOOK OUT FOR THE CRAB!
WE CAUGHT CRABS! WE THINK.

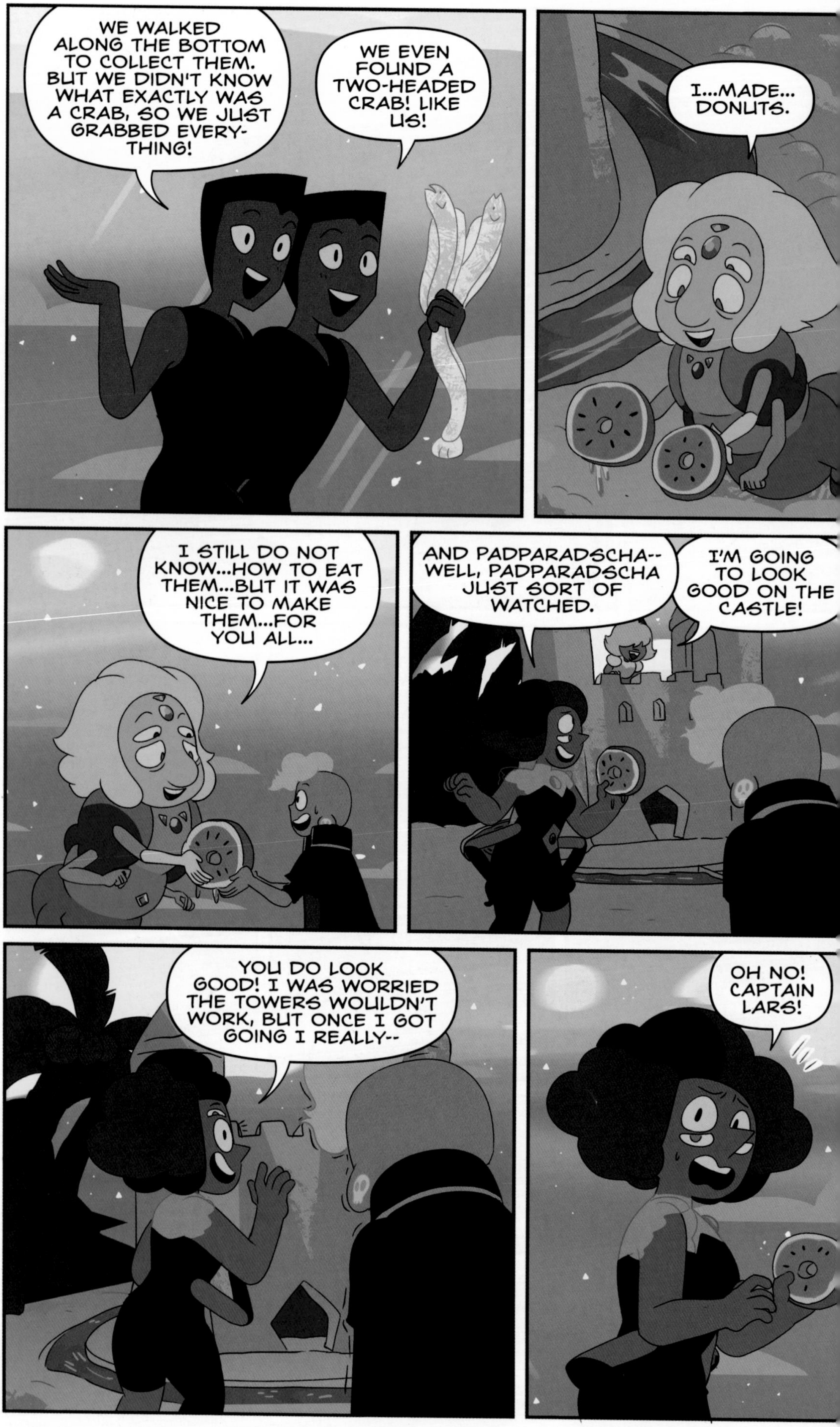
WE WALKED ALONG THE BOTTOM TO COLLECT THEM. BUT WE DIDN'T KNOW WHAT EXACTLY WAS A CRAB, SO WE JUST GRABBED EVERY-THING!
WE EVEN FOUND A TWO-HEADED CRAB! LIKE US!
I...MADE... DONUTS.
I STILL DO NOT KNOW...HOW TO EAT THEM...BUT IT WAS NICE TO MAKE THEM...FOR YOU ALL...
AND PADPARADSCHA-- WELL, PADPARADSCHA JUST SORT OF WATCHED.
I'M GOING TO LOOK GOOD ON THE CASTLE!
YOU DO LOOK GOOD! I WAS WORRIED THE TOWERS WOULDN'T WORK, BUT ONCE I GOT GOING I REALLY--
OH NO! CAPTAIN LARS!

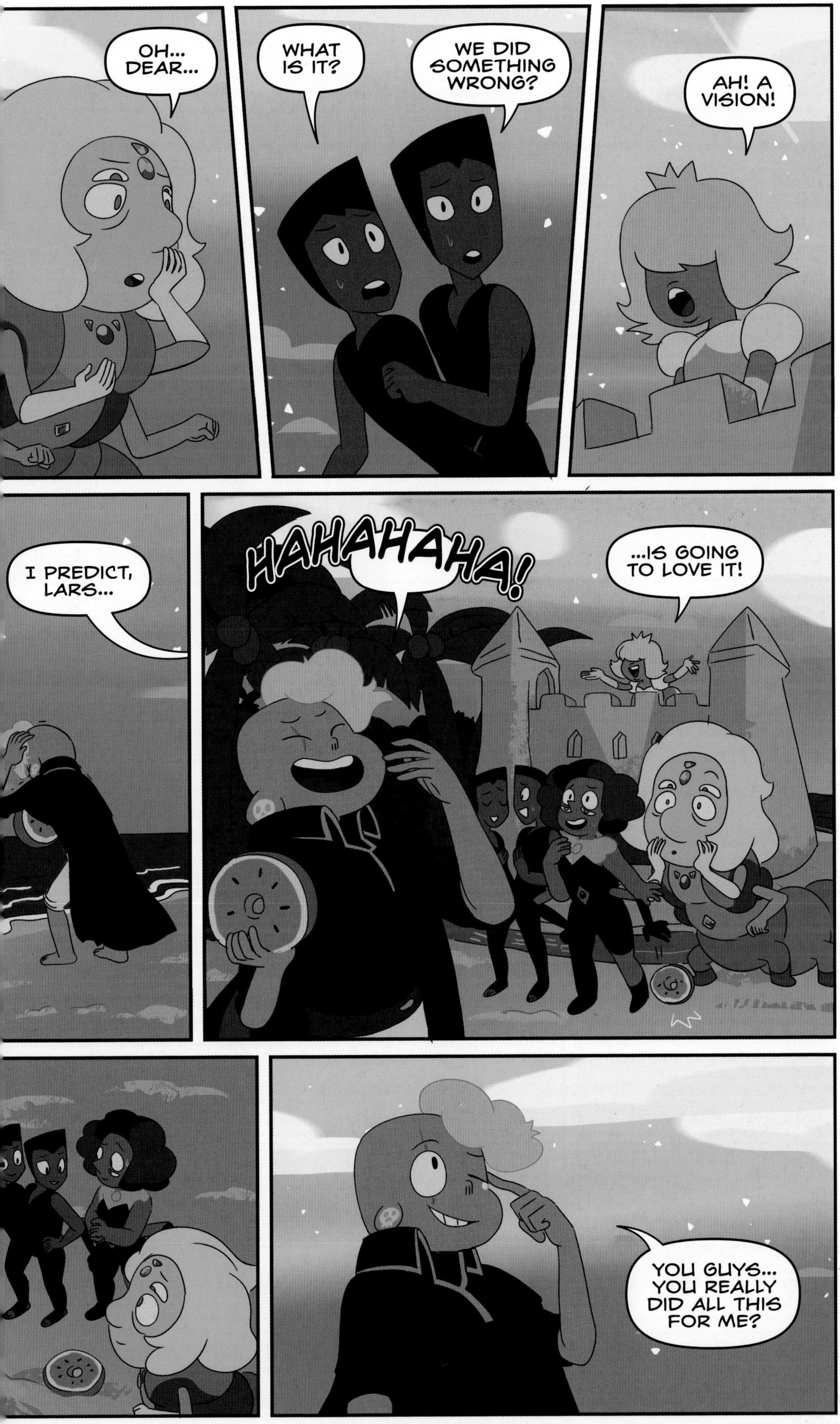

OH... DEAR...
WHAT IS IT?
WE DID SOMETHING WRONG?
AH! A VISION!
I PREDICT, LARS...
HAHAHAHA!
...IS GOING TO LOVE IT!
YOU GUYS... YOU REALLY DID ALL THIS FOR ME?

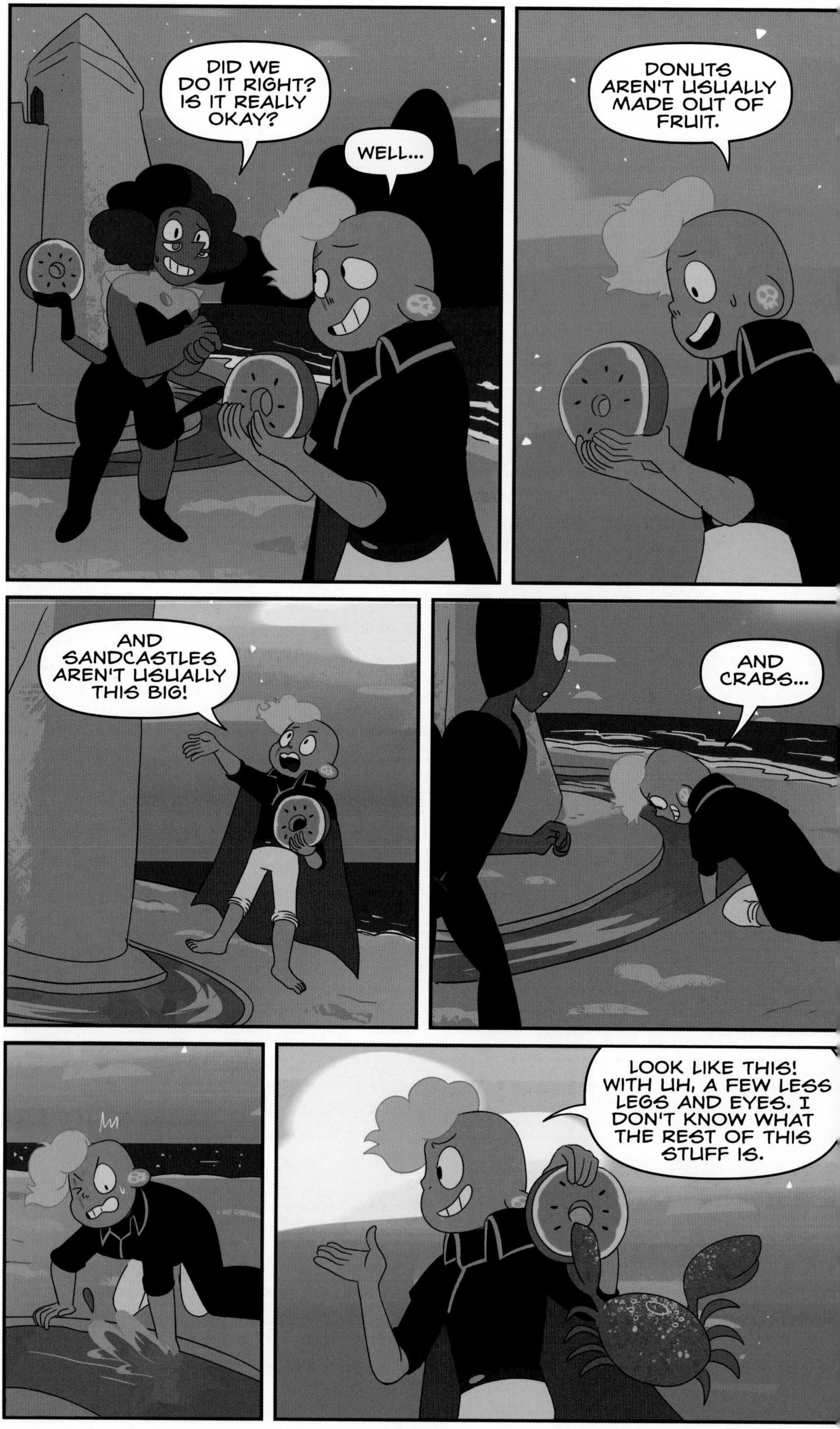
DID WE DO IT RIGHT? IS IT REALLY OKAY?
WELL...
DONUTS AREN'T USUALLY MADE OUT OF FRUIT.
AND SANDCASTLES AREN'T USUALLY THIS BIG!
AND CRABS...
LOOK LIKE THIS! WITH UH, A FEW LESS LEGS AND EYES. I DON'T KNOW WHAT THE REST OF THIS STUFF IS.

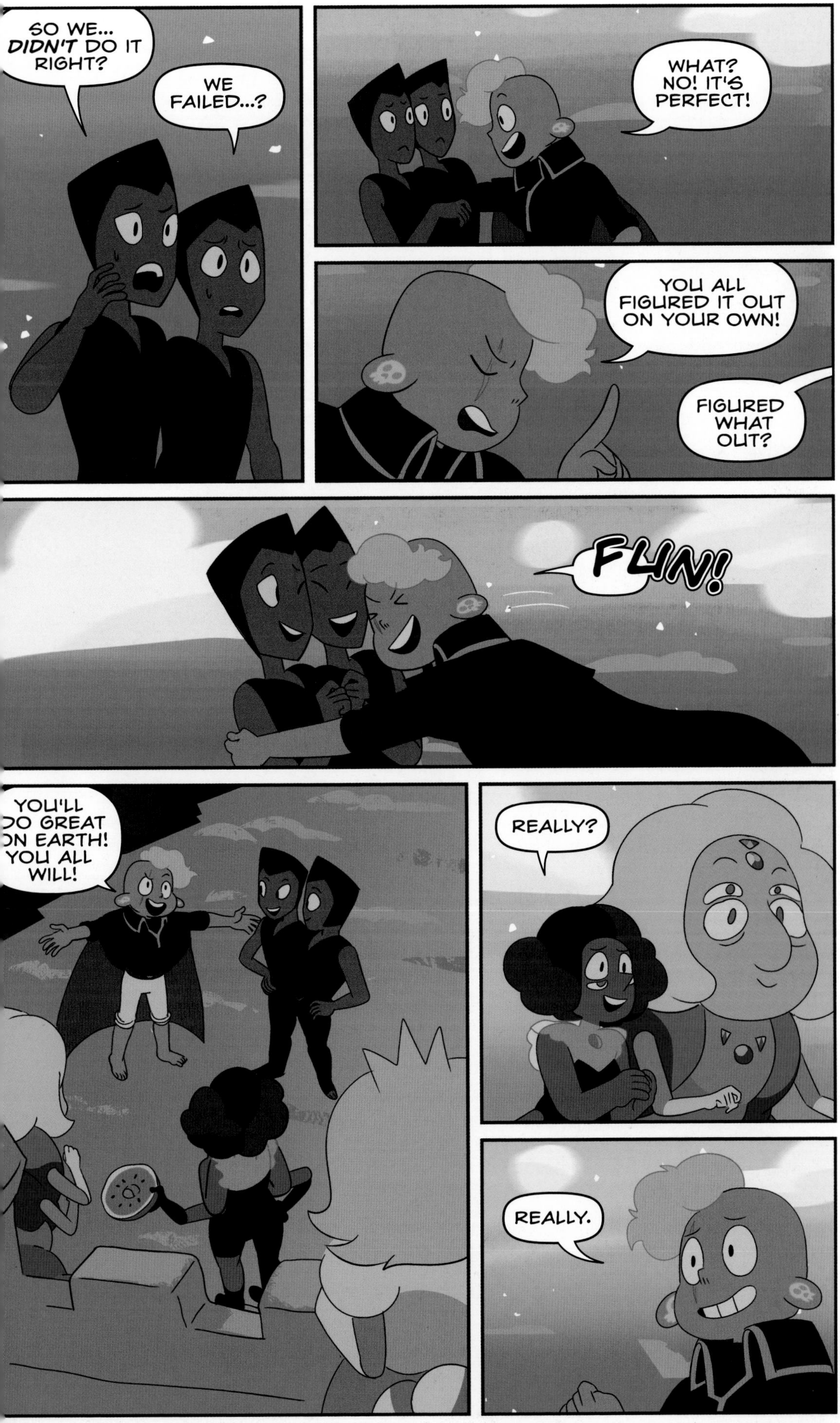
SO WE... *DIDN'T* DO IT RIGHT?
WE FAILED...?
WHAT? NO! IT'S PERFECT!
YOU ALL FIGURED IT OUT ON YOUR OWN!
FIGURED WHAT OUT?
FUN!
YOU'LL DO GREAT ON EARTH! YOU ALL WILL!
REALLY?
REALLY.

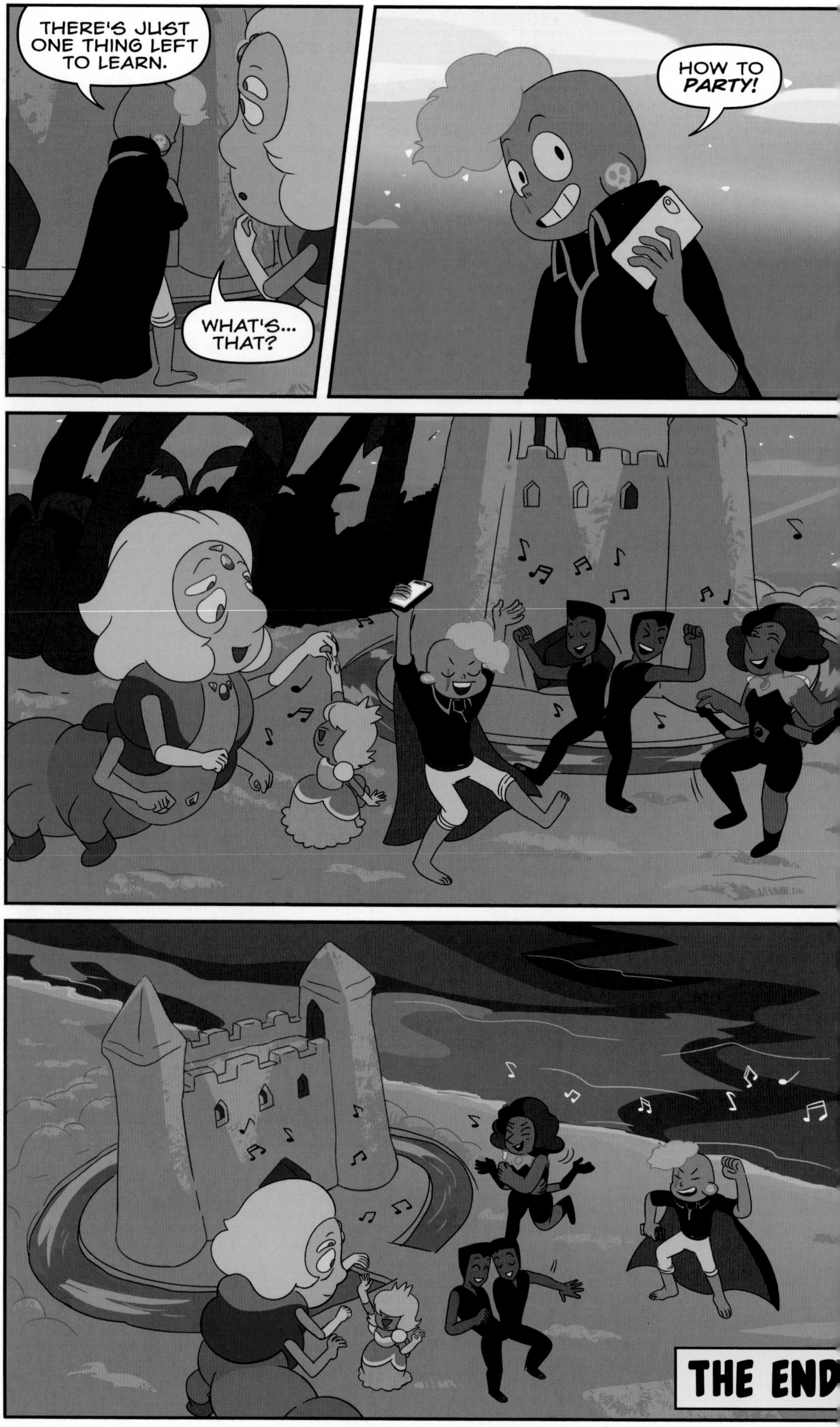
THERE'S JUST ONE THING LEFT TO LEARN.
WHAT'S... THAT?
HOW TO *PARTY!*
THE END

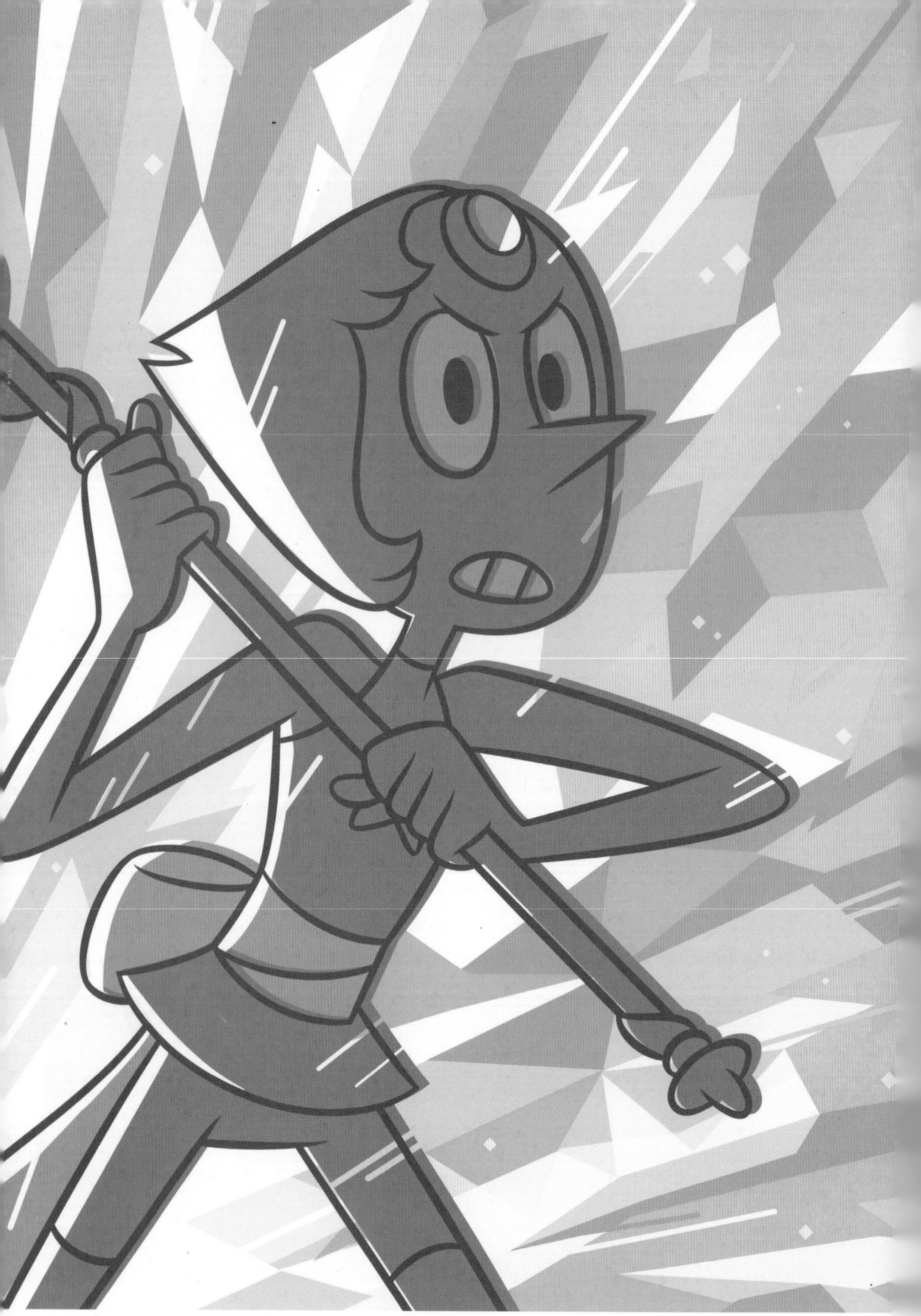

CHAPTER THIRTY-FIVE

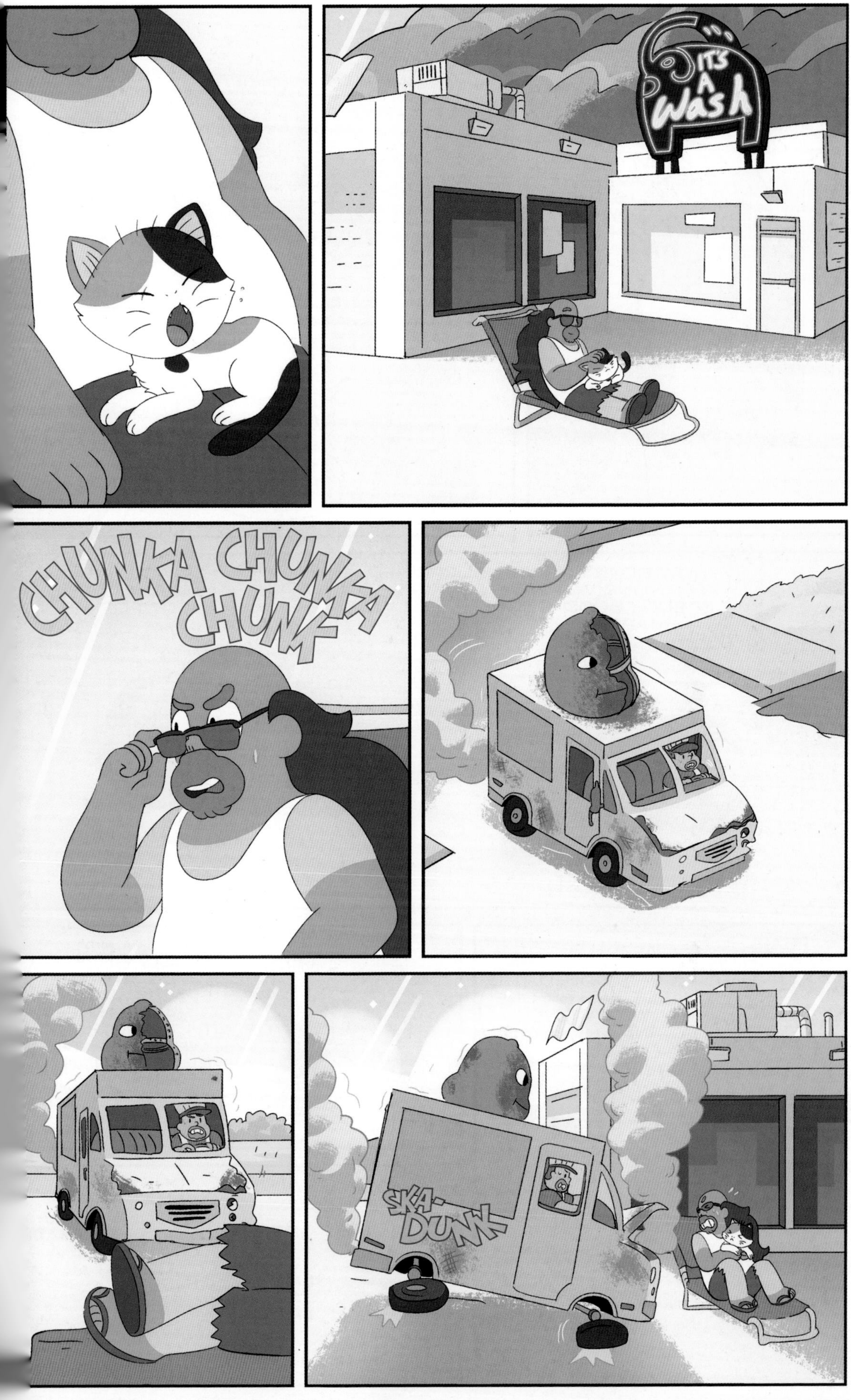
IT'S A Wash
CHUNKA CHUNKA CHUNK
SKA-DUNK

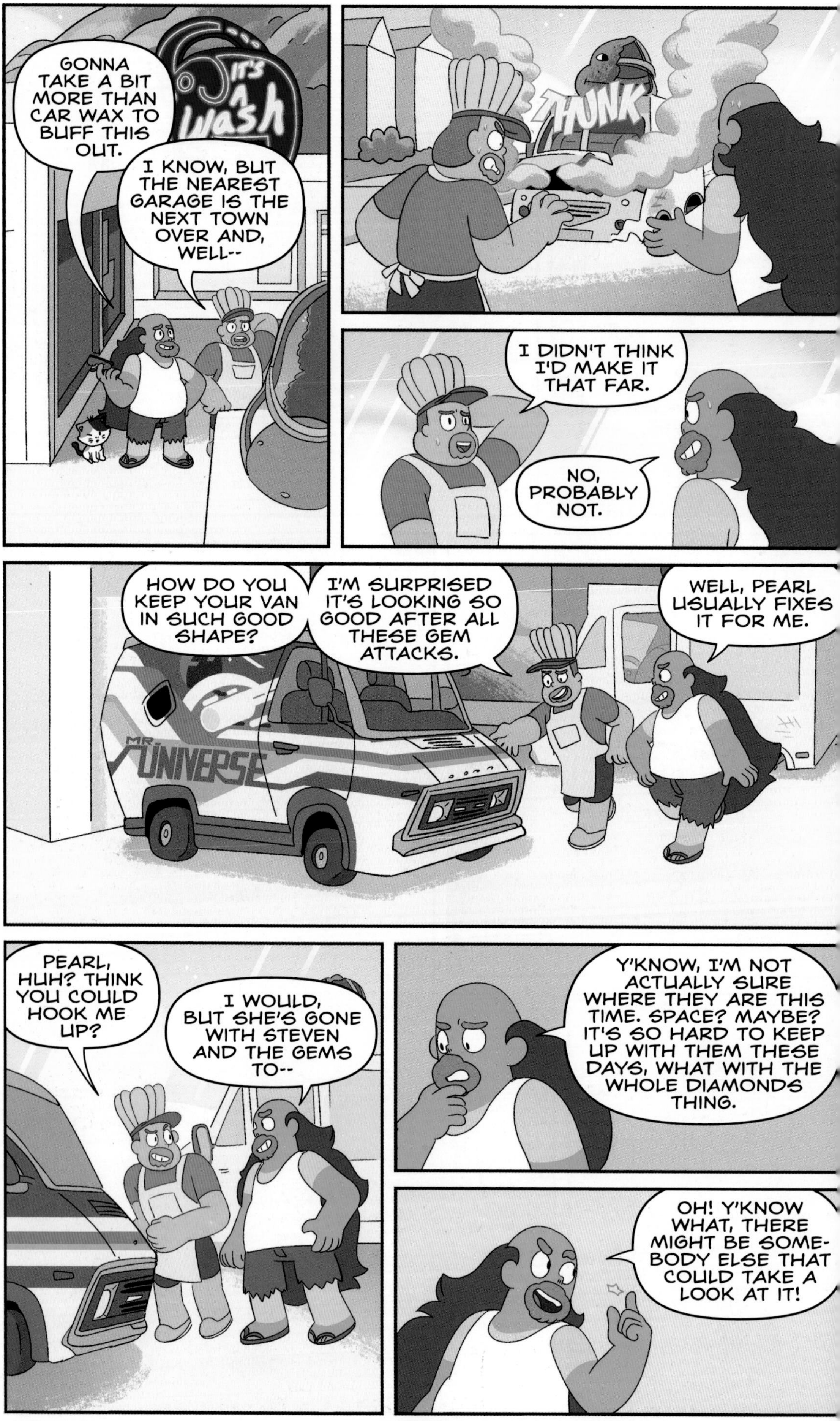

GONNA TAKE A BIT MORE THAN CAR WAX TO BUFF THIS OUT.
IT'S A WASH
I KNOW, BUT THE NEAREST GARAGE IS THE NEXT TOWN OVER AND, WELL--
THUNK
I DIDN'T THINK I'D MAKE IT THAT FAR.
NO, PROBABLY NOT.
HOW DO YOU KEEP YOUR VAN IN SUCH GOOD SHAPE?
I'M SURPRISED IT'S LOOKING SO GOOD AFTER ALL THESE GEM ATTACKS.
WELL, PEARL USUALLY FIXES IT FOR ME.
MR. UNIVERSE
PEARL, HUH? THINK YOU COULD HOOK ME UP?
I WOULD, BUT SHE'S GONE WITH STEVEN AND THE GEMS TO--
Y'KNOW, I'M NOT ACTUALLY SURE WHERE THEY ARE THIS TIME. SPACE? MAYBE? IT'S SO HARD TO KEEP UP WITH THEM THESE DAYS, WHAT WITH THE WHOLE DIAMONDS THING.
OH! Y'KNOW WHAT, THERE MIGHT BE SOME-BODY ELSE THAT COULD TAKE A LOOK AT IT!

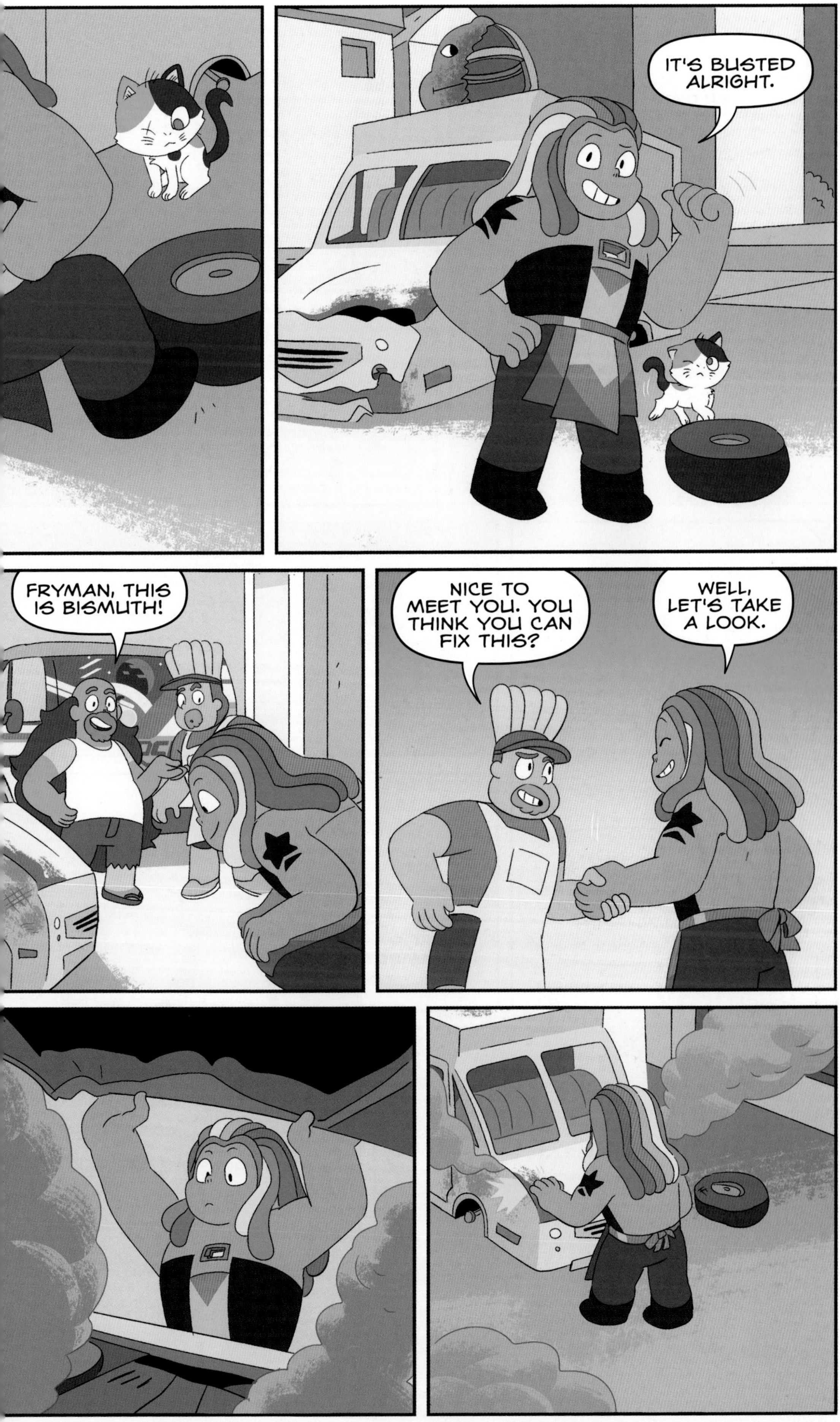
IT'S BUSTED ALRIGHT.
FRYMAN, THIS IS BISMUTH!
NICE TO MEET YOU. YOU THINK YOU CAN FIX THIS?
WELL, LET'S TAKE A LOOK.

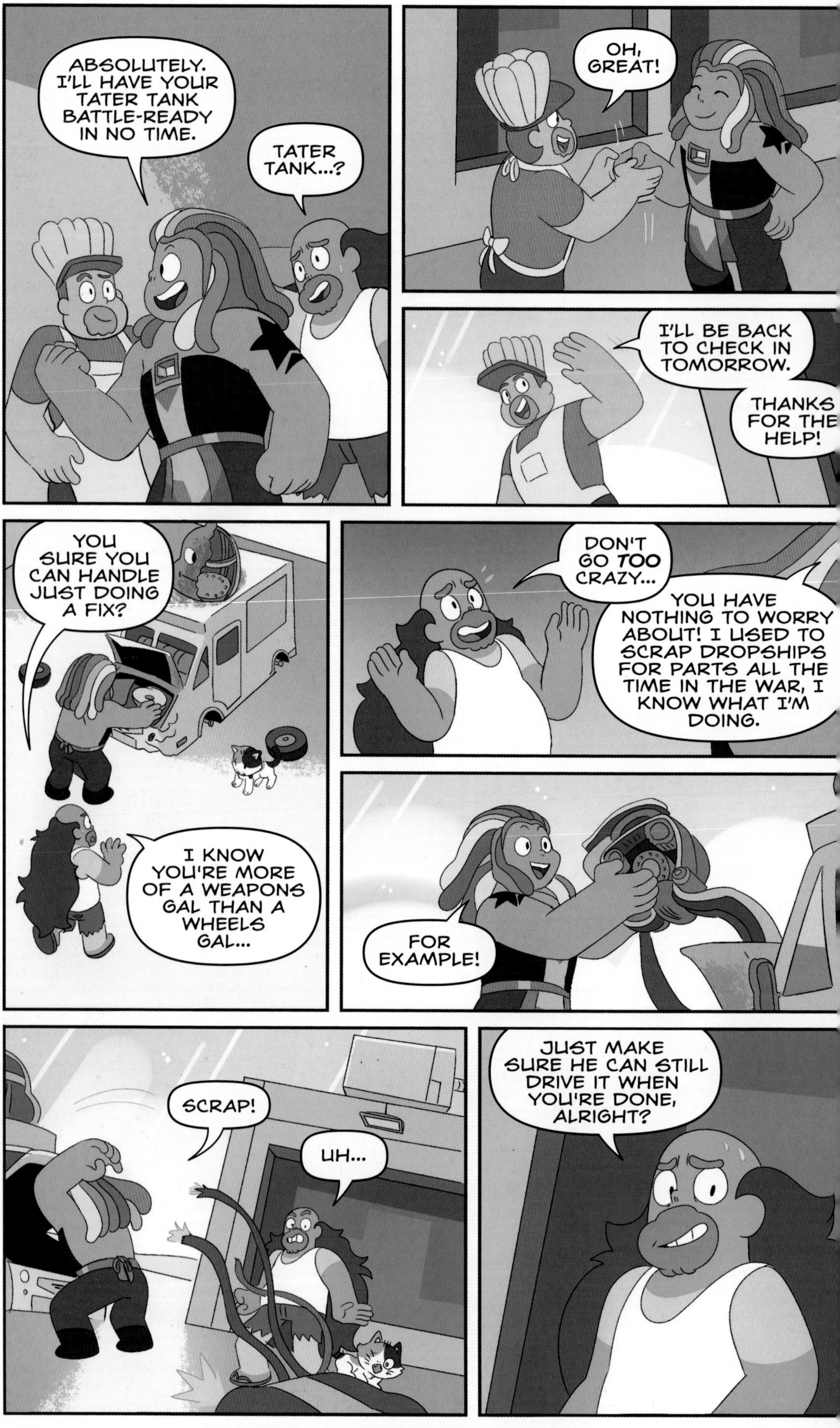
ABSOLUTELY. I'LL HAVE YOUR TATER TANK BATTLE-READY IN NO TIME.
TATER TANK...?
OH, GREAT!
I'LL BE BACK TO CHECK IN TOMORROW.
THANKS FOR THE HELP!
YOU SURE YOU CAN HANDLE JUST DOING A FIX?
I KNOW YOU'RE MORE OF A WEAPONS GAL THAN A WHEELS GAL...
DON'T GO *TOO* CRAZY...
YOU HAVE NOTHING TO WORRY ABOUT! I USED TO SCRAP DROPSHIPS FOR PARTS ALL THE TIME IN THE WAR, I KNOW WHAT I'M DOING.
FOR EXAMPLE!
SCRAP!
UH...
JUST MAKE SURE HE CAN STILL DRIVE IT WHEN YOU'RE DONE, ALRIGHT?

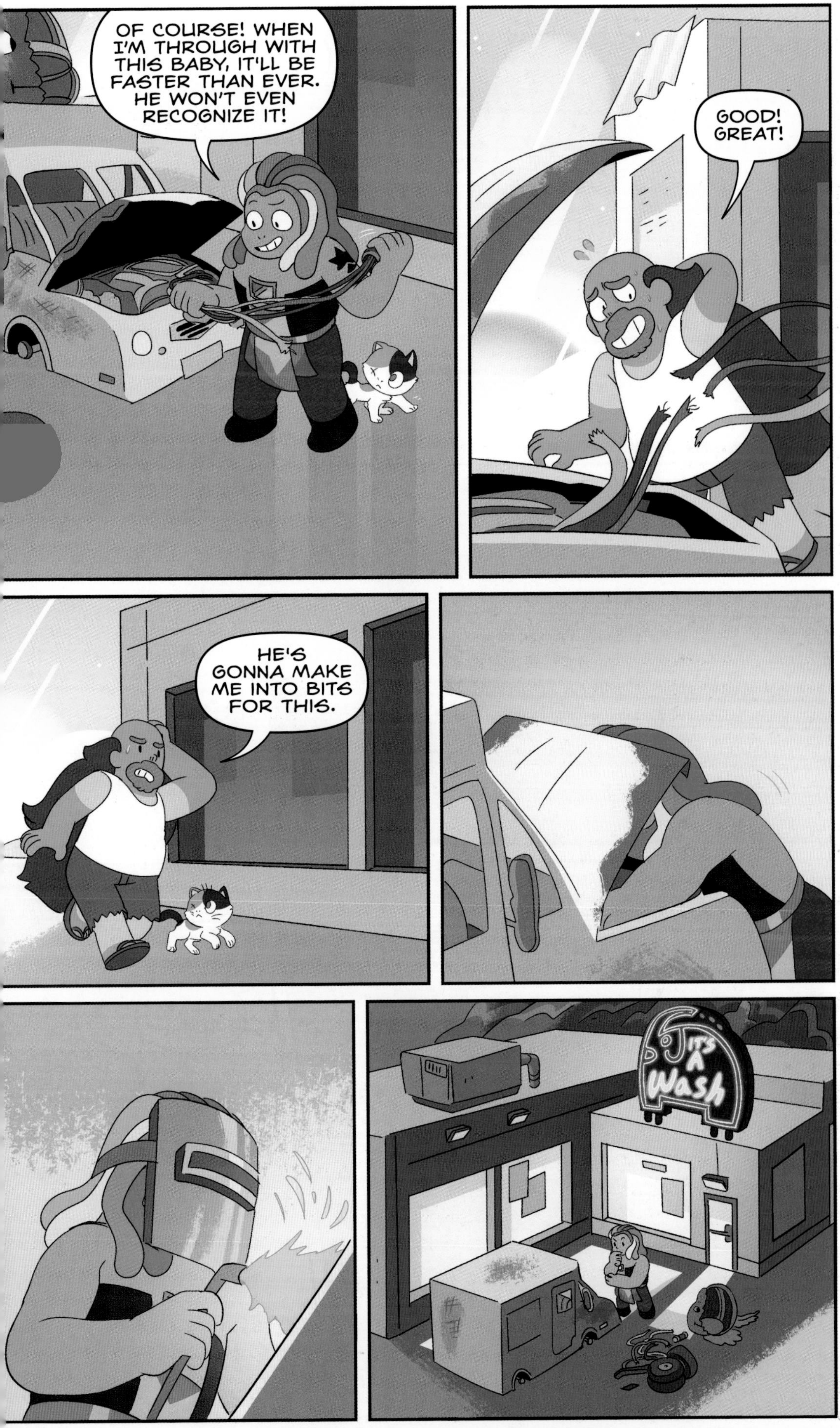
OF COURSE! WHEN I'M THROUGH WITH THIS BABY, IT'LL BE FASTER THAN EVER. HE WON'T EVEN RECOGNIZE IT!
GOOD! GREAT!
HE'S GONNA MAKE ME INTO BITS FOR THIS.
IT'S A Wash

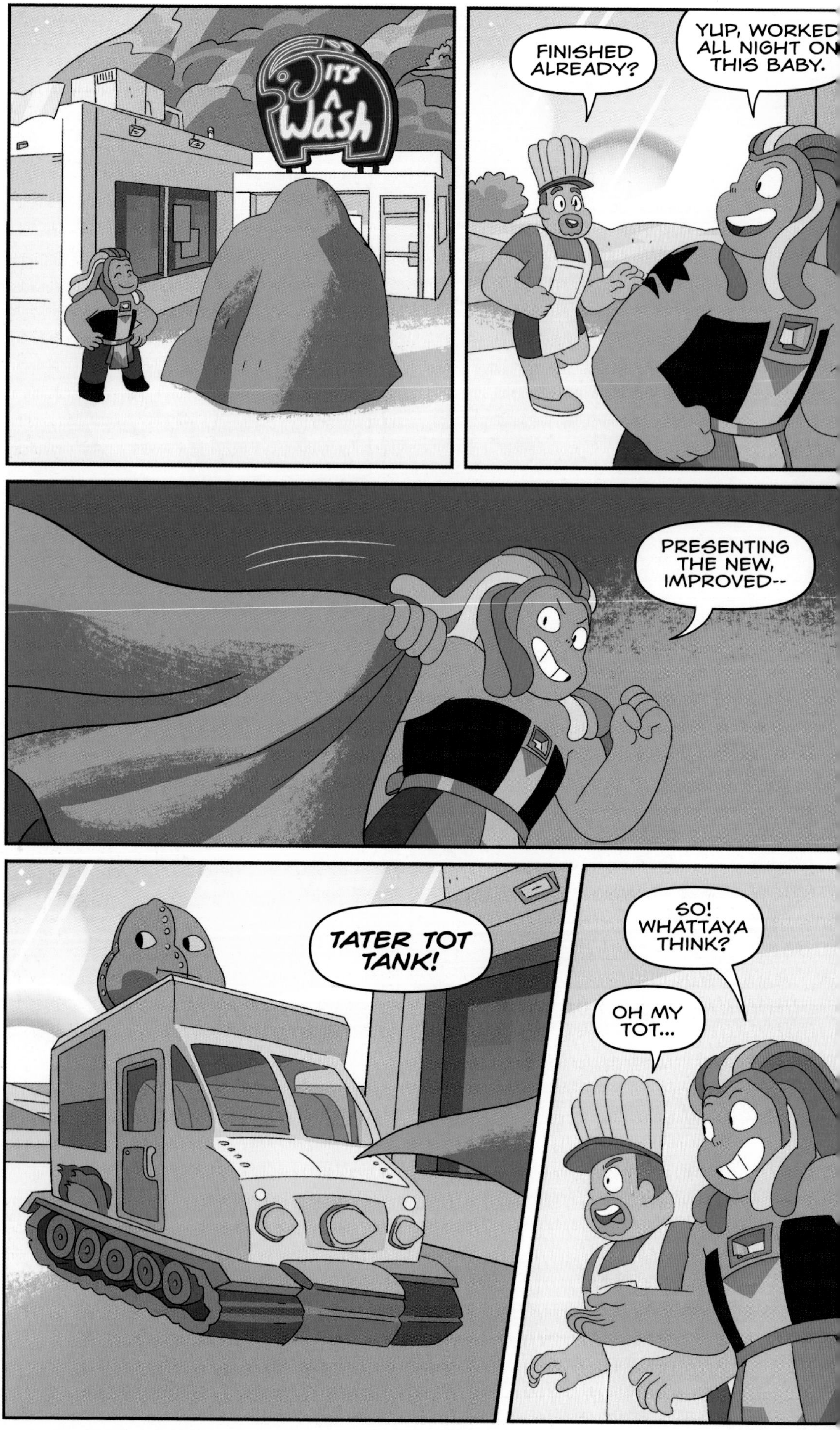
IT'S A WASH
FINISHED ALREADY?
YUP, WORKED ALL NIGHT ON THIS BABY.
PRESENTING THE NEW, IMPROVED--
TATER TOT TANK!
SO! WHATTAYA THINK?
OH MY TOT...

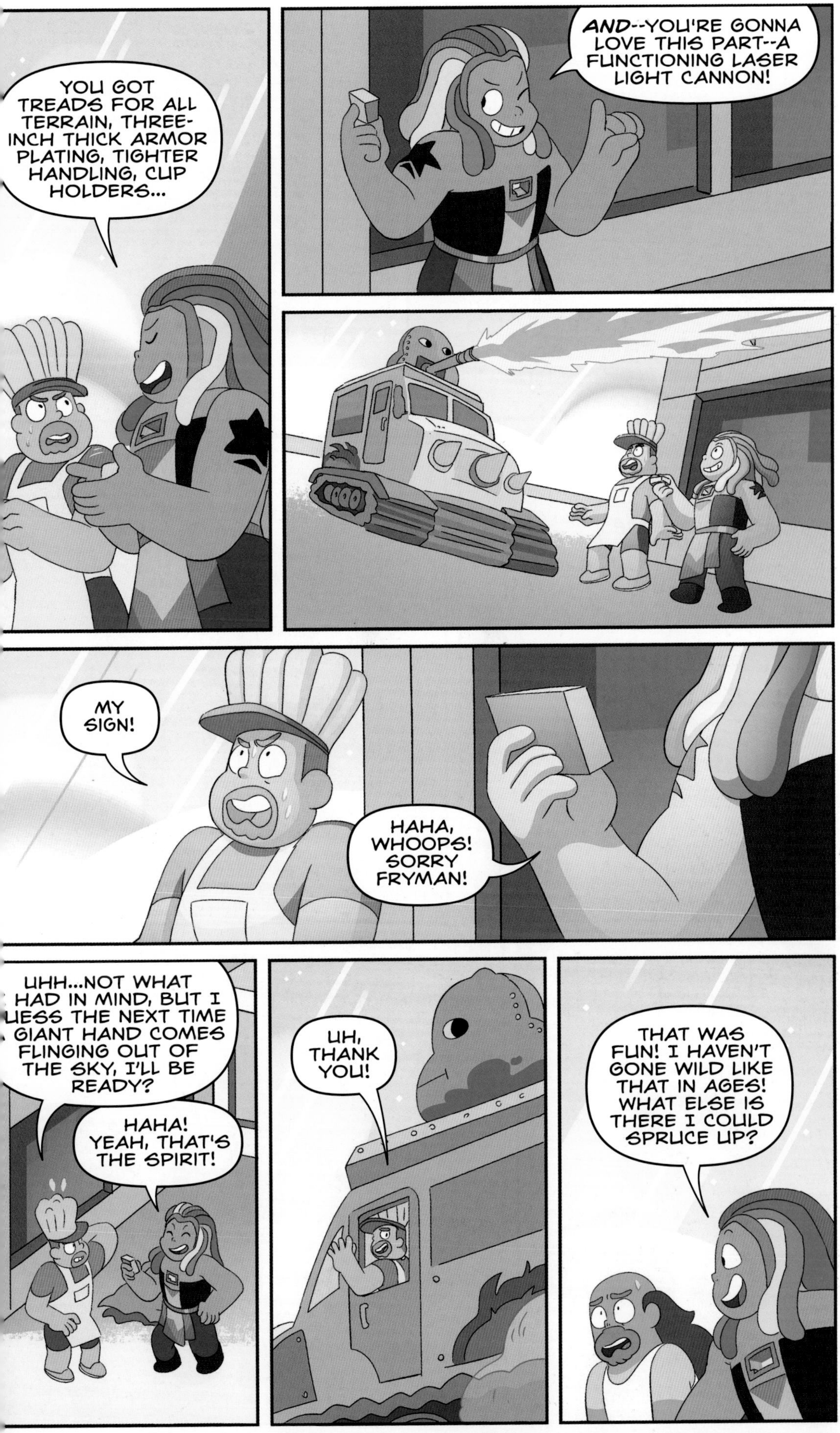
YOU GOT TREADS FOR ALL TERRAIN, THREE-INCH THICK ARMOR PLATING, TIGHTER HANDLING, CUP HOLDERS...
AND--YOU'RE GONNA LOVE THIS PART--A FUNCTIONING LASER LIGHT CANNON!
MY SIGN!
HAHA, WHOOPS! SORRY FRYMAN!
UHH...NOT WHAT HAD IN MIND, BUT I UESS THE NEXT TIME GIANT HAND COMES FLINGING OUT OF THE SKY, I'LL BE READY?
HAHA! YEAH, THAT'S THE SPIRIT!
UH, THANK YOU!
THAT WAS FUN! I HAVEN'T GONE WILD LIKE THAT IN AGES! WHAT ELSE IS THERE I COULD SPRUCE UP?

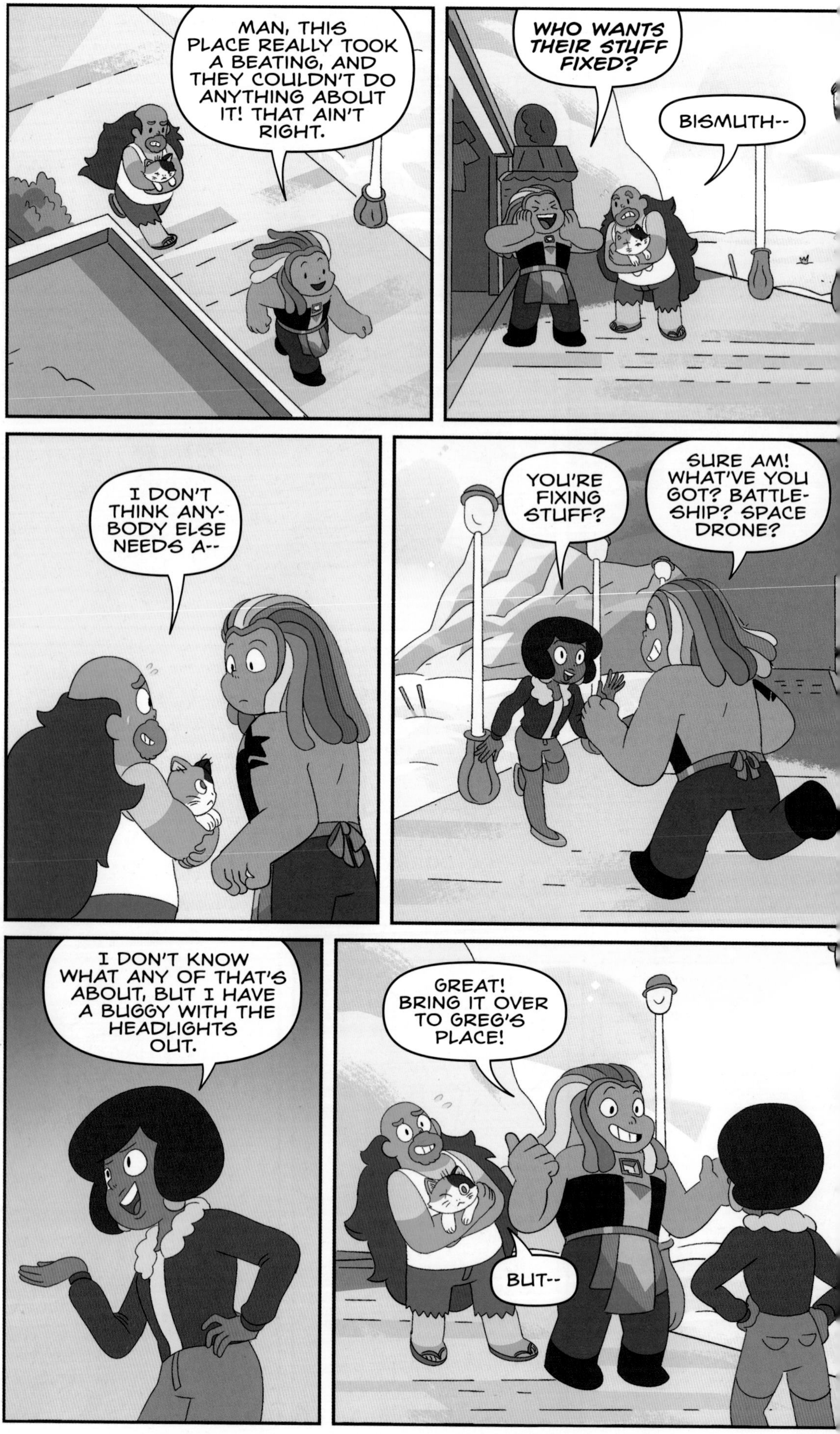
MAN, THIS PLACE REALLY TOOK A BEATING, AND THEY COULDN'T DO ANYTHING ABOUT IT! THAT AIN'T RIGHT.
WHO WANTS THEIR STUFF FIXED?
BISMUTH--
I DON'T THINK ANYBODY ELSE NEEDS A--
YOU'RE FIXING STUFF?
SURE AM! WHAT'VE YOU GOT? BATTLESHIP? SPACE DRONE?
I DON'T KNOW WHAT ANY OF THAT'S ABOUT, BUT I HAVE A BUGGY WITH THE HEADLIGHTS OUT.
GREAT! BRING IT OVER TO GREG'S PLACE!
BUT--

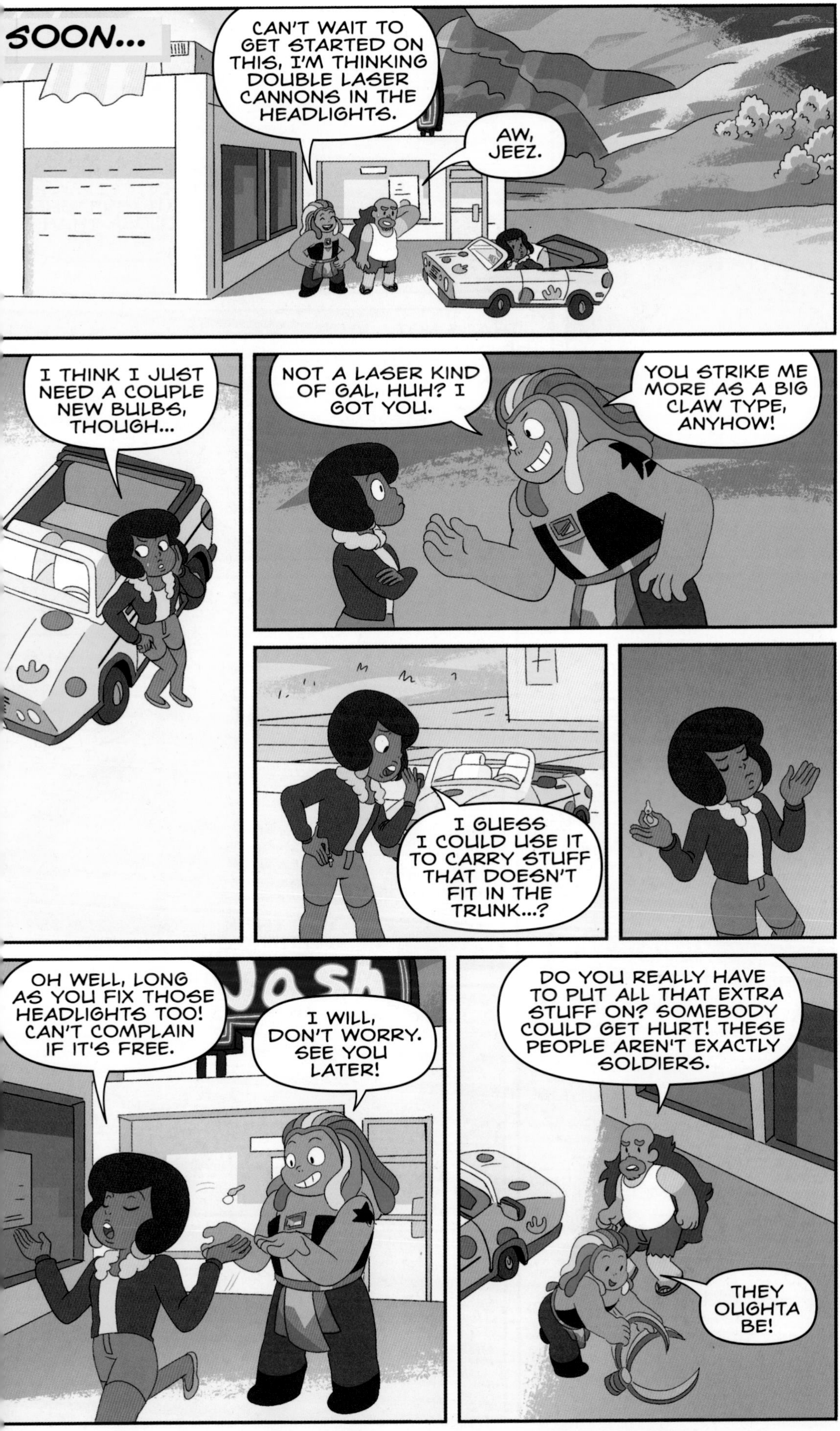
SOON...
CAN'T WAIT TO GET STARTED ON THIS, I'M THINKING DOUBLE LASER CANNONS IN THE HEADLIGHTS.
AW, JEEZ.
I THINK I JUST NEED A COUPLE NEW BULBS, THOUGH...
NOT A LASER KIND OF GAL, HUH? I GOT YOU.
YOU STRIKE ME MORE AS A BIG CLAW TYPE, ANYHOW!
I GUESS I COULD USE IT TO CARRY STUFF THAT DOESN'T FIT IN THE TRUNK...?
OH WELL, LONG AS YOU FIX THOSE HEADLIGHTS TOO! CAN'T COMPLAIN IF IT'S FREE.
I WILL, DON'T WORRY. SEE YOU LATER!
DO YOU REALLY HAVE TO PUT ALL THAT EXTRA STUFF ON? SOMEBODY COULD GET HURT! THESE PEOPLE AREN'T EXACTLY SOLDIERS.
THEY OUGHTA BE!

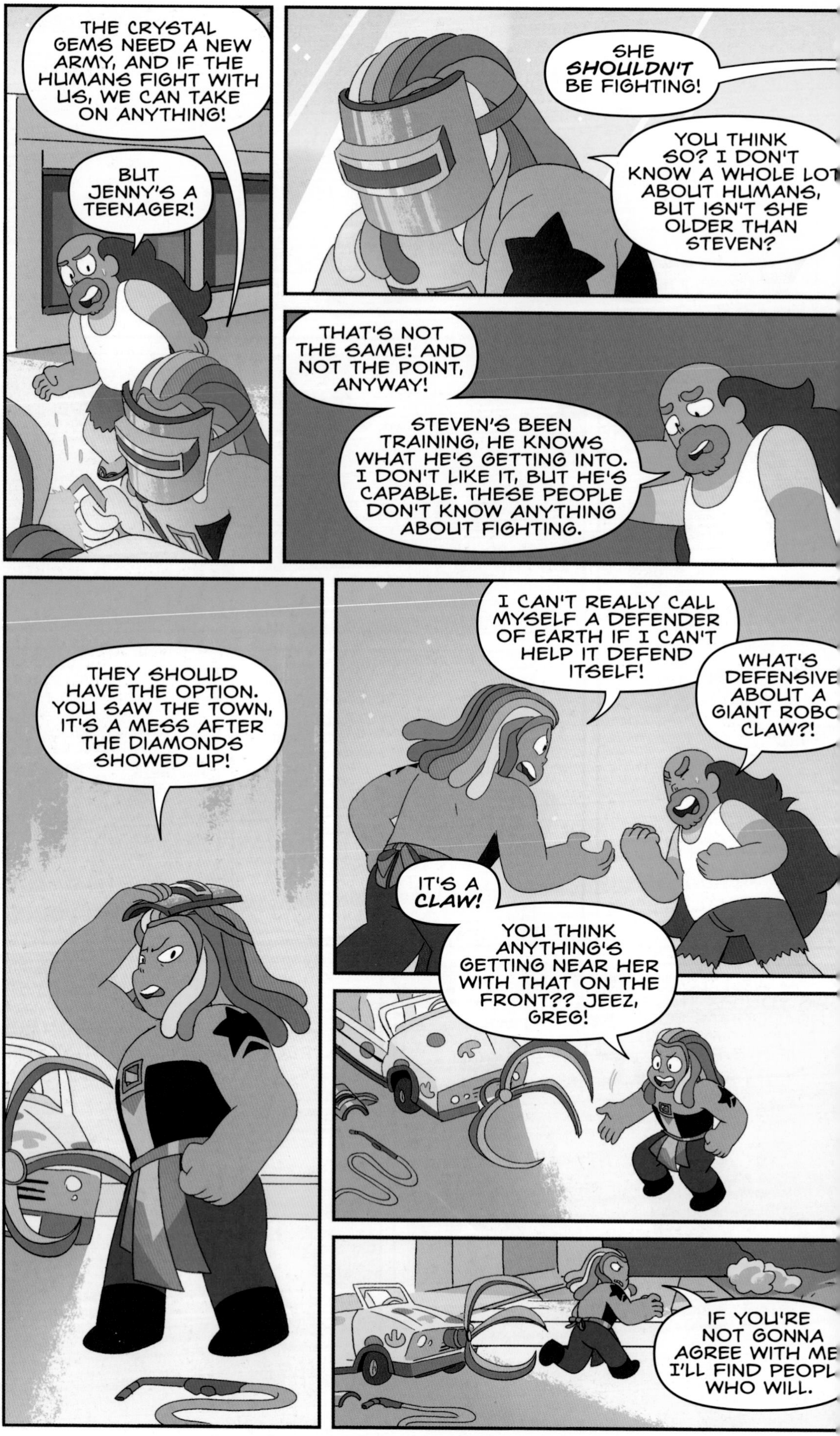
THE CRYSTAL GEMS NEED A NEW ARMY, AND IF THE HUMANS FIGHT WITH US, WE CAN TAKE ON ANYTHING!
BUT JENNY'S A TEENAGER!
SHE *SHOULDN'T* BE FIGHTING!
YOU THINK SO? I DON'T KNOW A WHOLE LOT ABOUT HUMANS, BUT ISN'T SHE OLDER THAN STEVEN?
THAT'S NOT THE SAME! AND NOT THE POINT, ANYWAY!
STEVEN'S BEEN TRAINING, HE KNOWS WHAT HE'S GETTING INTO. I DON'T LIKE IT, BUT HE'S CAPABLE. THESE PEOPLE DON'T KNOW ANYTHING ABOUT FIGHTING.
THEY SHOULD HAVE THE OPTION. YOU SAW THE TOWN, IT'S A MESS AFTER THE DIAMONDS SHOWED UP!
I CAN'T REALLY CALL MYSELF A DEFENDER OF EARTH IF I CAN'T HELP IT DEFEND ITSELF!
WHAT'S DEFENSIVE ABOUT A GIANT ROBO CLAW?!
IT'S A *CLAW!*
YOU THINK ANYTHING'S GETTING NEAR HER WITH THAT ON THE FRONT?? JEEZ, GREG!
IF YOU'RE NOT GONNA AGREE WITH ME I'LL FIND PEOPL WHO WILL.

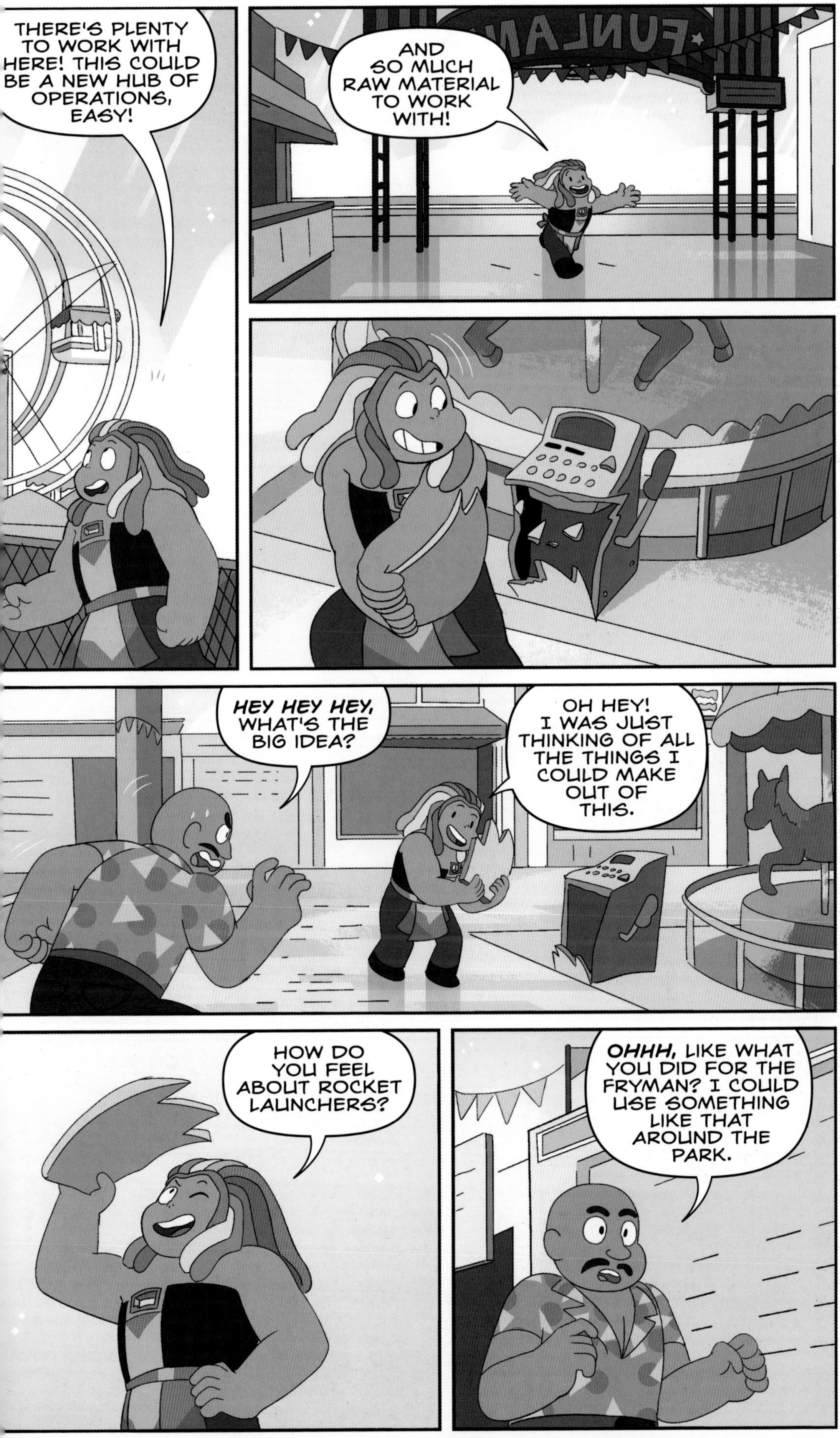
THERE'S PLENTY TO WORK WITH HERE! THIS COULD BE A NEW HUB OF OPERATIONS, EASY!
AND SO MUCH RAW MATERIAL TO WORK WITH!
FUNLAND
HEY HEY HEY, WHAT'S THE BIG IDEA?
OH HEY! I WAS JUST THINKING OF ALL THE THINGS I COULD MAKE OUT OF THIS.
HOW DO YOU FEEL ABOUT ROCKET LAUNCHERS?
OHHH, LIKE WHAT YOU DID FOR THE FRYMAN? I COULD USE SOMETHING LIKE THAT AROUND THE PARK.

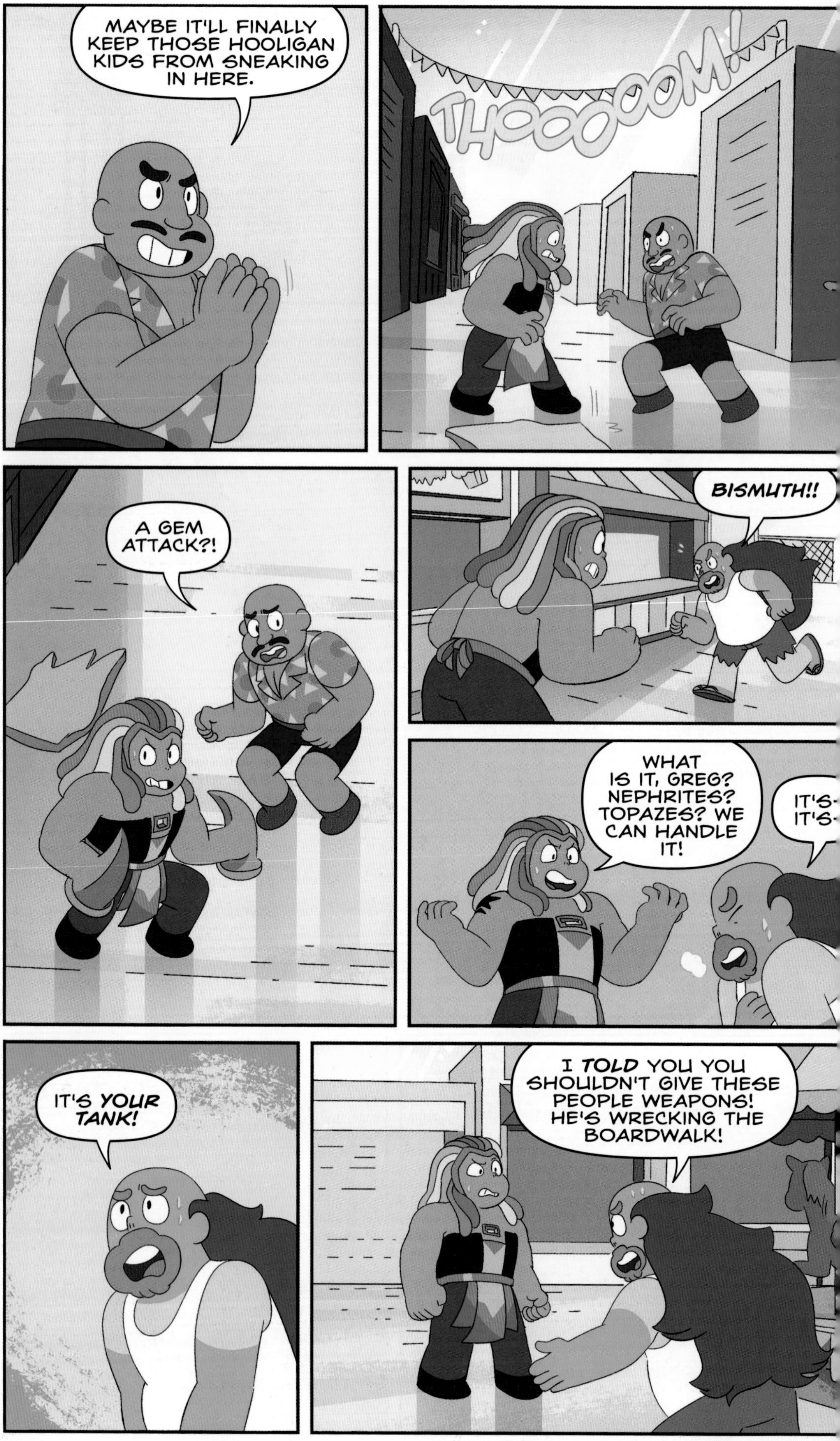
MAYBE IT'LL FINALLY KEEP THOSE HOOLIGAN KIDS FROM SNEAKING IN HERE.
THOOOOOM!!
A GEM ATTACK?!
BISMUTH!!
WHAT IS IT, GREG? NEPHRITES? TOPAZES? WE CAN HANDLE IT!
IT'S- IT'S-
IT'S YOUR TANK!
I TOLD YOU YOU SHOULDN'T GIVE THESE PEOPLE WEAPONS! HE'S WRECKING THE BOARDWALK!

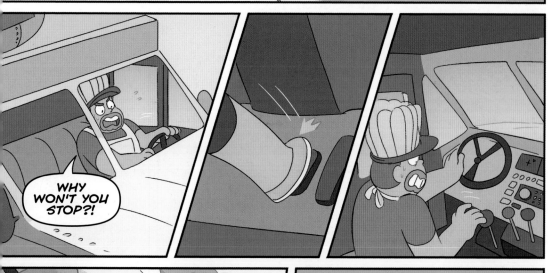

WHY WON'T YOU STOP?!

SORRY!!!

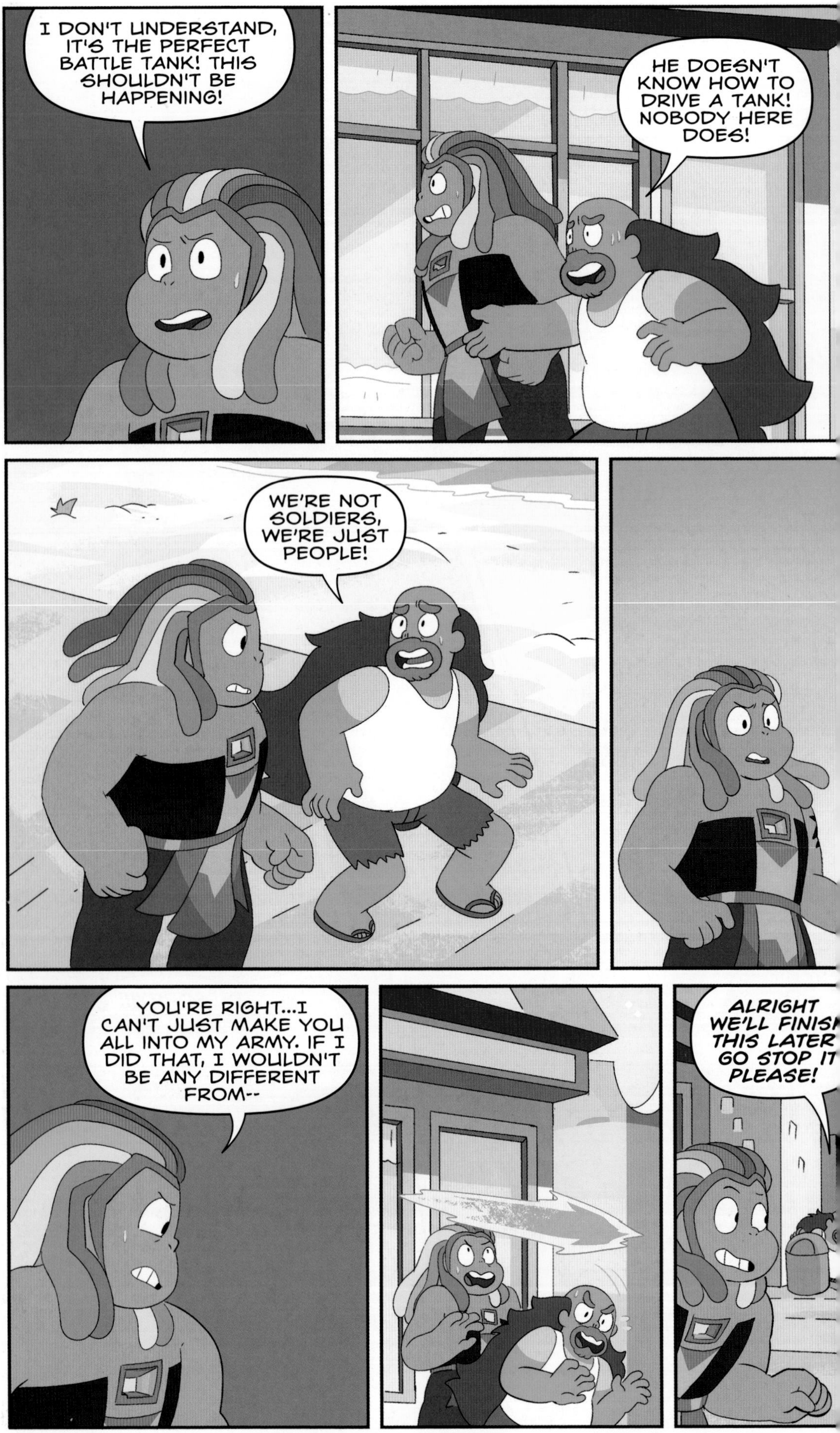
I DON'T UNDERSTAND, IT'S THE PERFECT BATTLE TANK! THIS SHOULDN'T BE HAPPENING!
HE DOESN'T KNOW HOW TO DRIVE A TANK! NOBODY HERE DOES!
WE'RE NOT SOLDIERS, WE'RE JUST PEOPLE!
YOU'RE RIGHT...I CAN'T JUST MAKE YOU ALL INTO MY ARMY. IF I DID THAT, I WOULDN'T BE ANY DIFFERENT FROM--
ALRIGHT WE'LL FINIS THIS LATER GO STOP IT PLEASE!

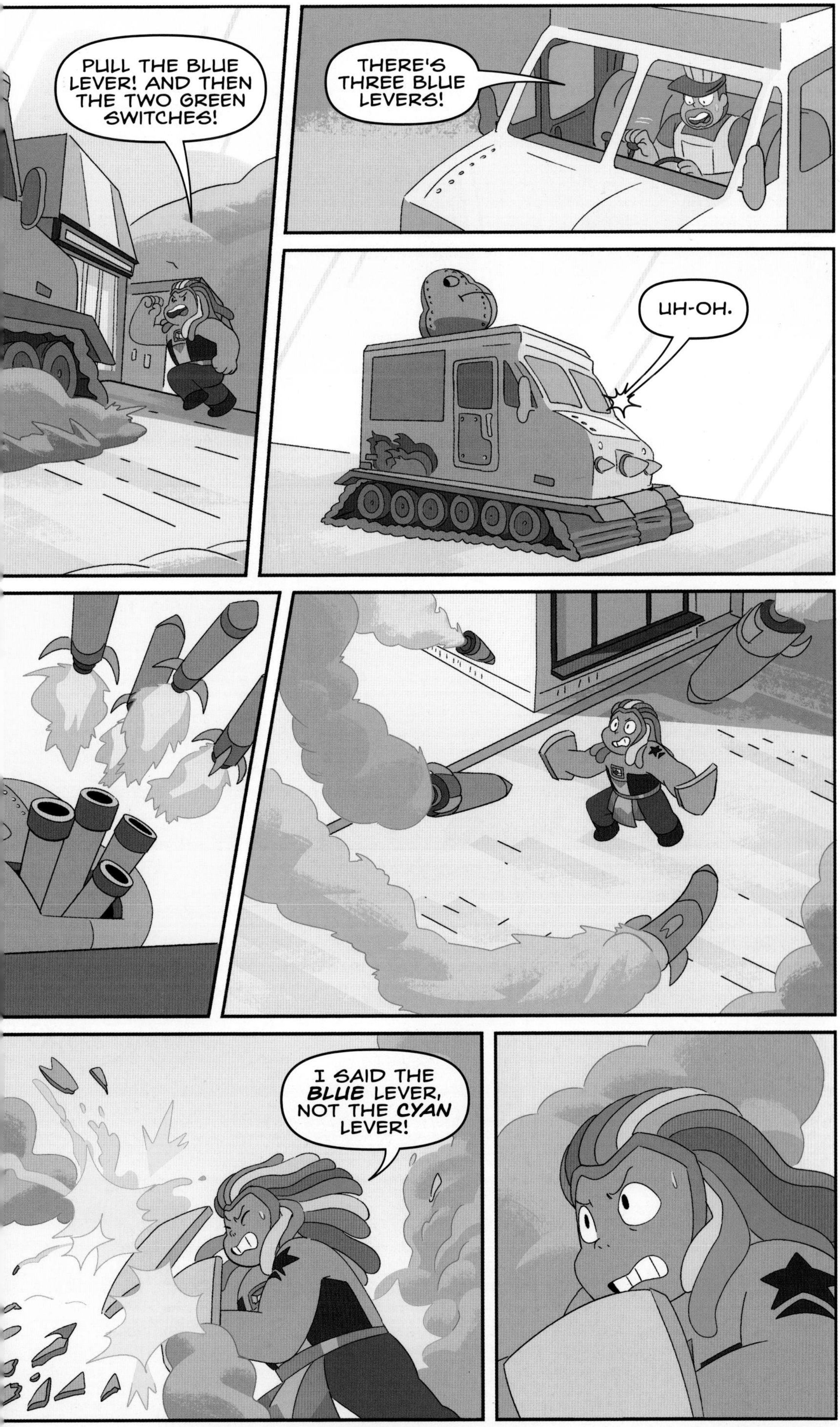
PULL THE BLUE LEVER! AND THEN THE TWO GREEN SWITCHES!
THERE'S THREE BLUE LEVERS!
UH-OH.
I SAID THE **BLUE** LEVER, NOT THE **CYAN** LEVER!

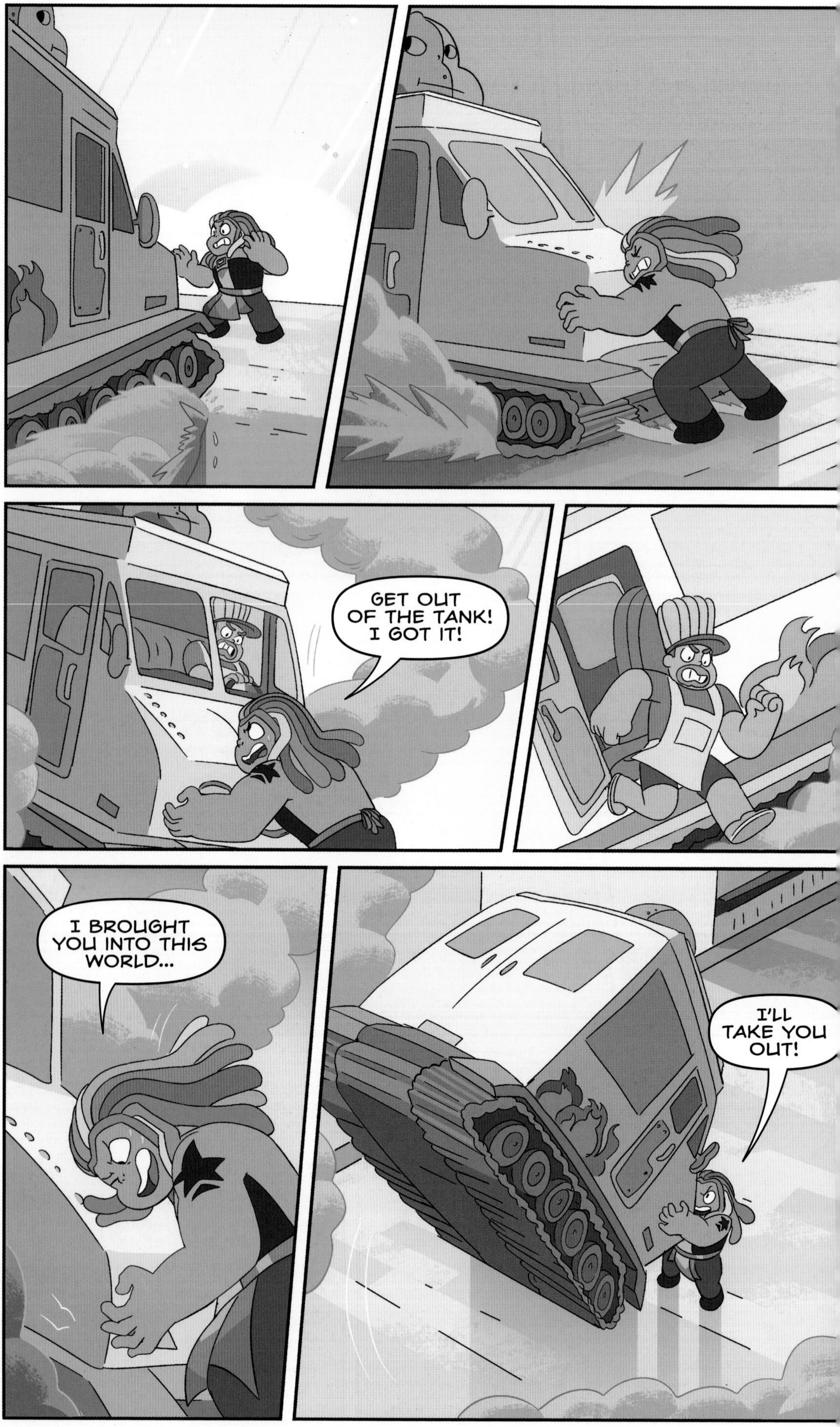
GET OUT
OF THE TANK!
I GOT IT!
I BROUGHT
YOU INTO THIS
WORLD...
I'LL
TAKE YOU
OUT!

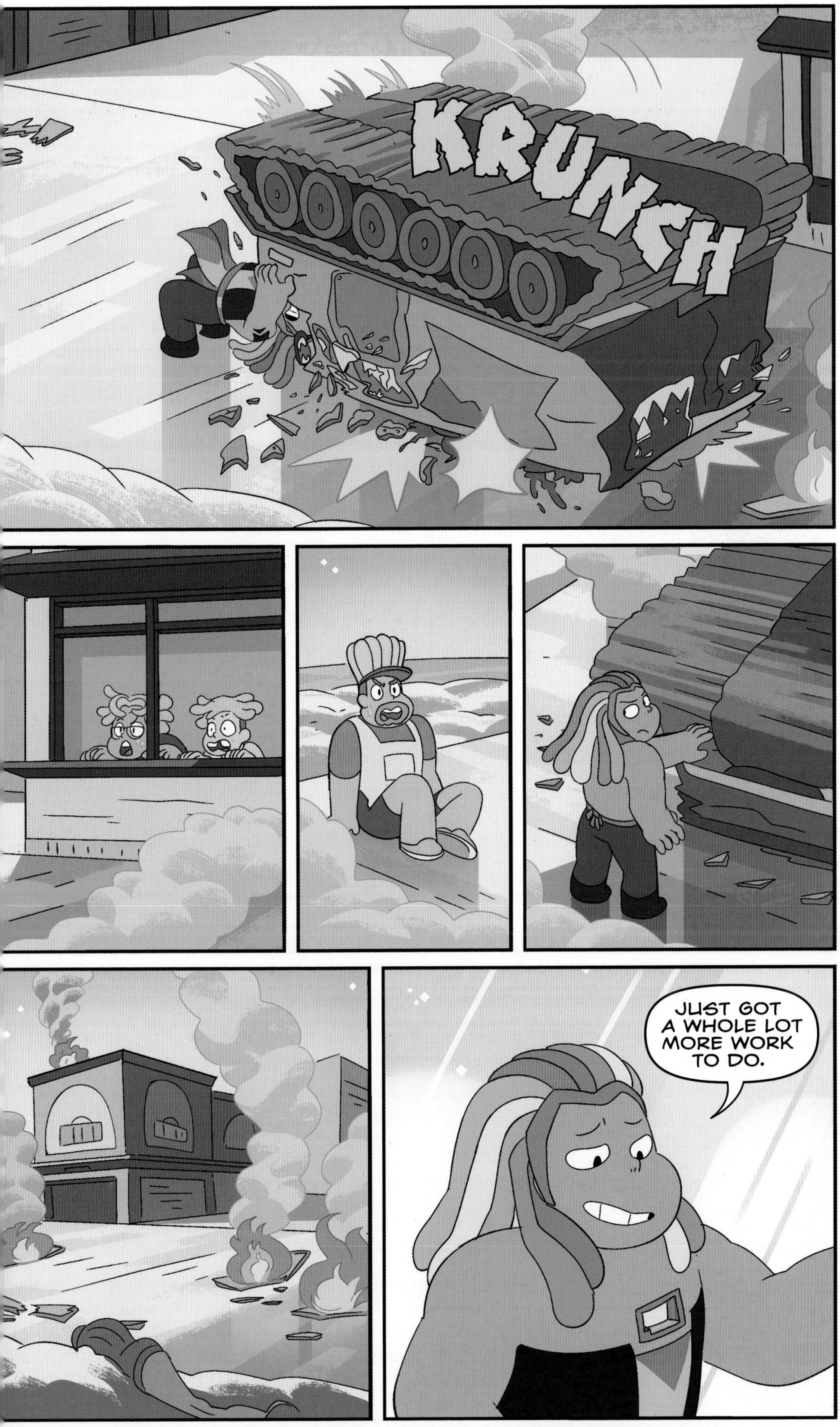
KRUNCH
JUST GOT A WHOLE LOT MORE WORK TO DO.

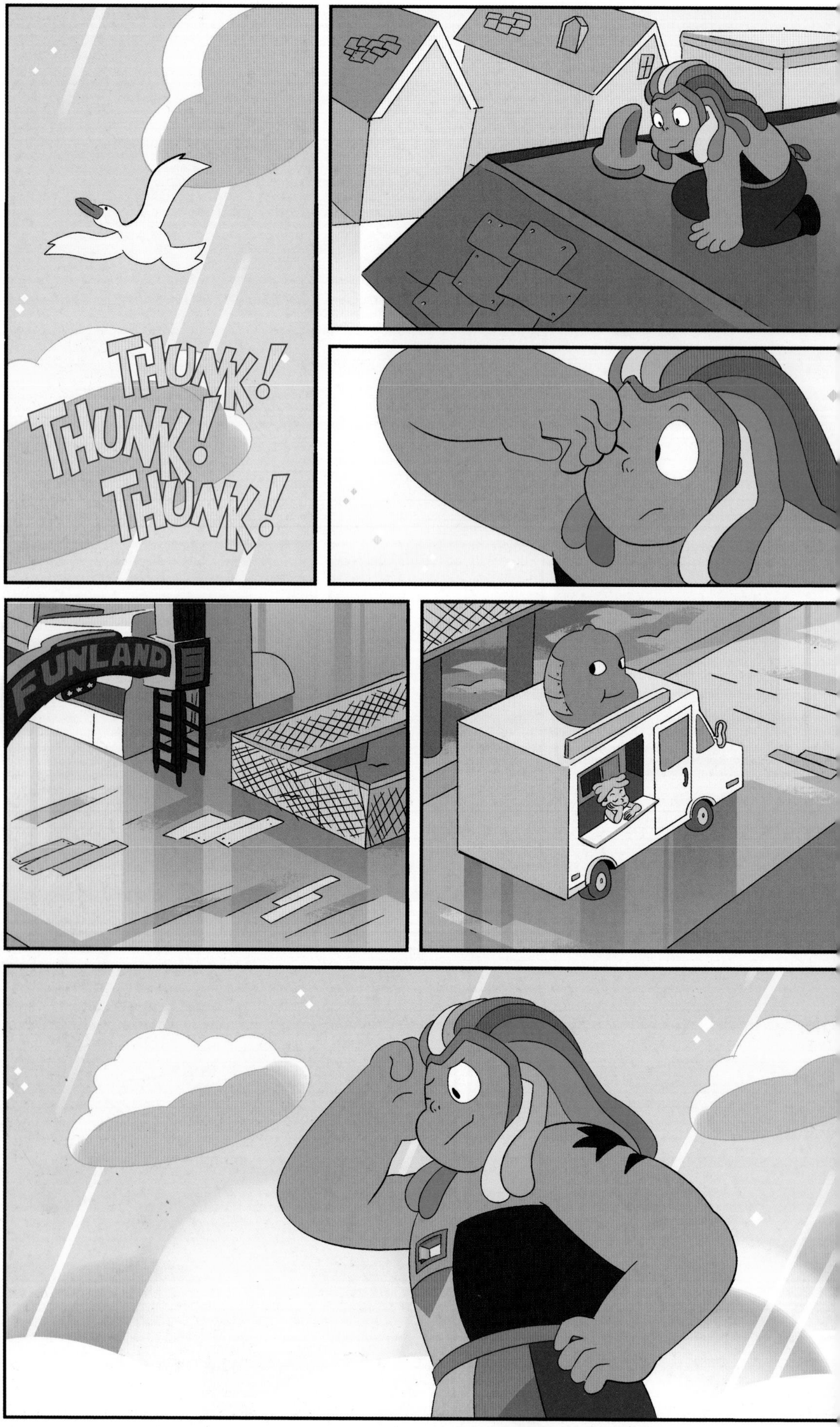
THUNK!
THUNK!
THUNK!
FUNLAND

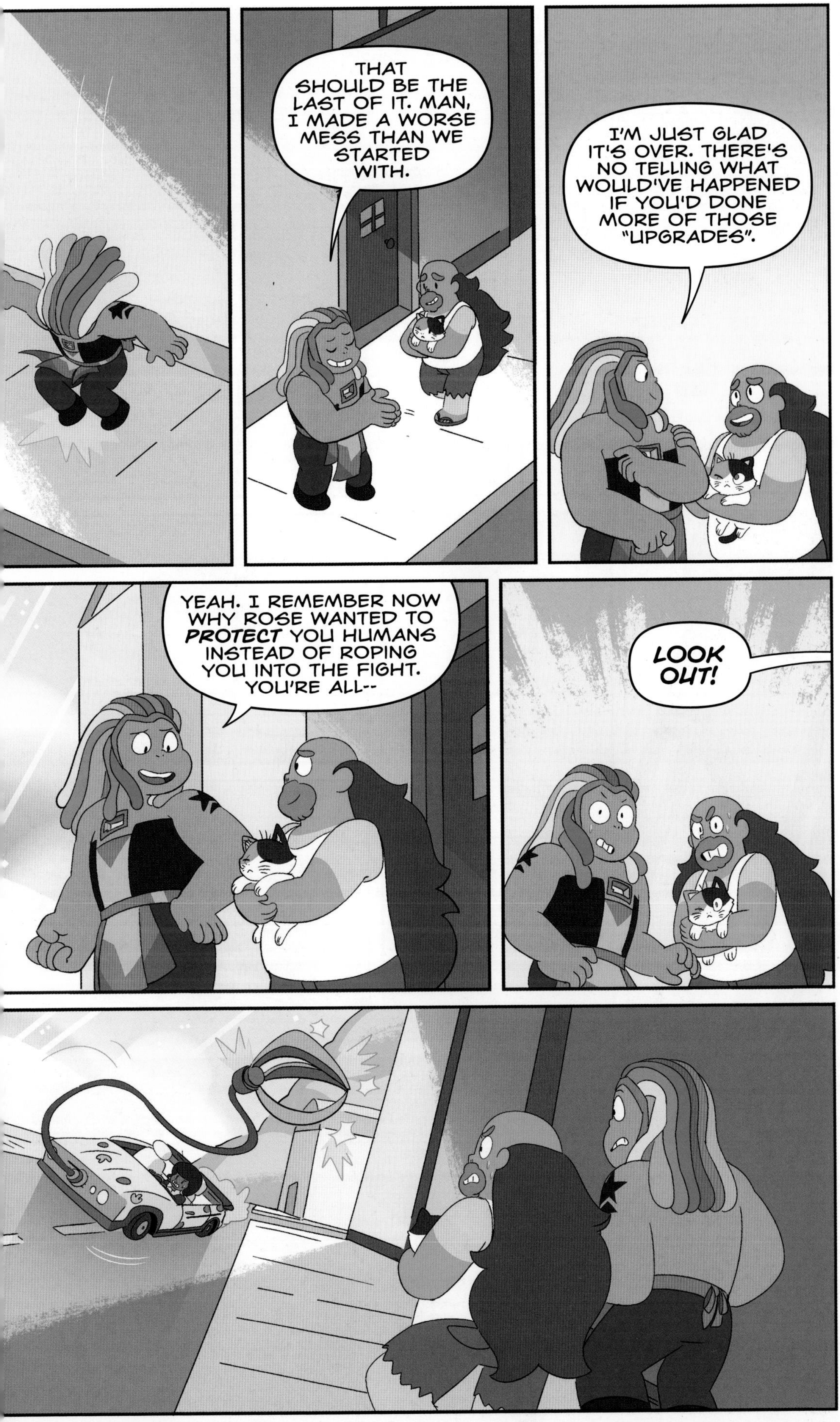
THAT SHOULD BE THE LAST OF IT. MAN, I MADE A WORSE MESS THAN WE STARTED WITH.
I'M JUST GLAD IT'S OVER. THERE'S NO TELLING WHAT WOULD'VE HAPPENED IF YOU'D DONE MORE OF THOSE "UPGRADES".
YEAH. I REMEMBER NOW WHY ROSE WANTED TO *PROTECT* YOU HUMANS INSTEAD OF ROPING YOU INTO THE FIGHT. YOU'RE ALL--
LOOK OUT!

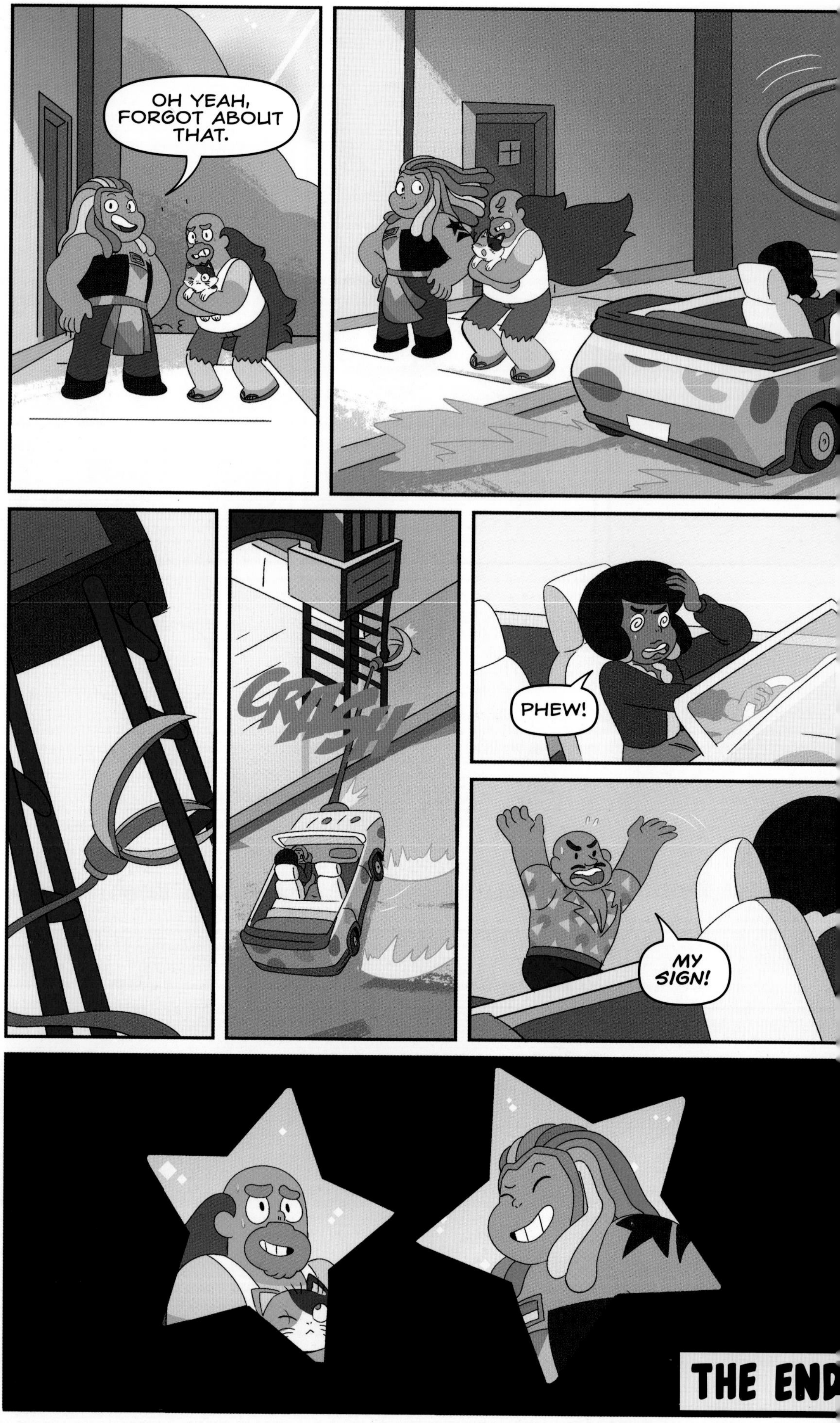
OH YEAH, FORGOT ABOUT THAT.
CRASH
PHEW!
MY SIGN!
THE END

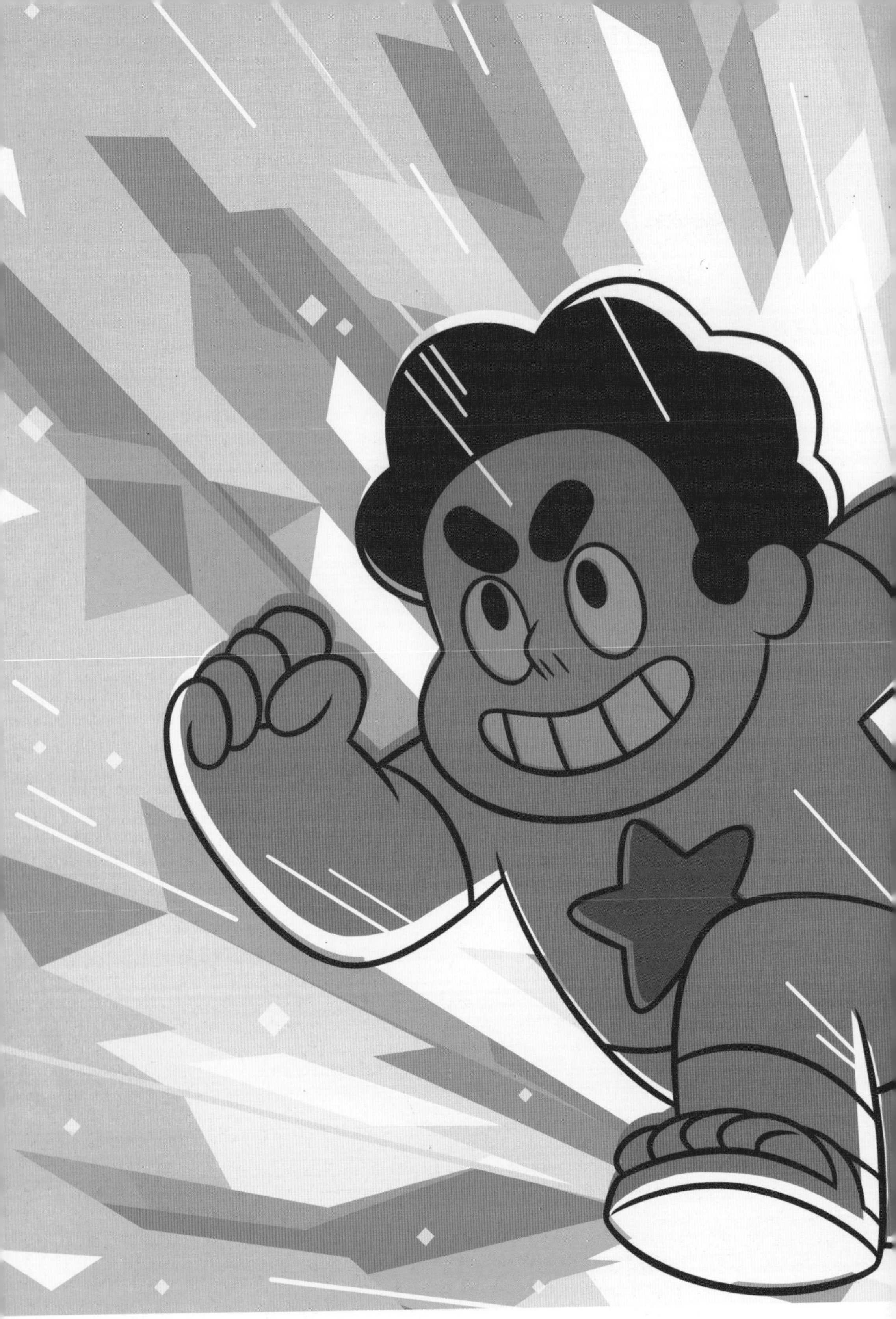

CHAPTER THIRTY-SIX

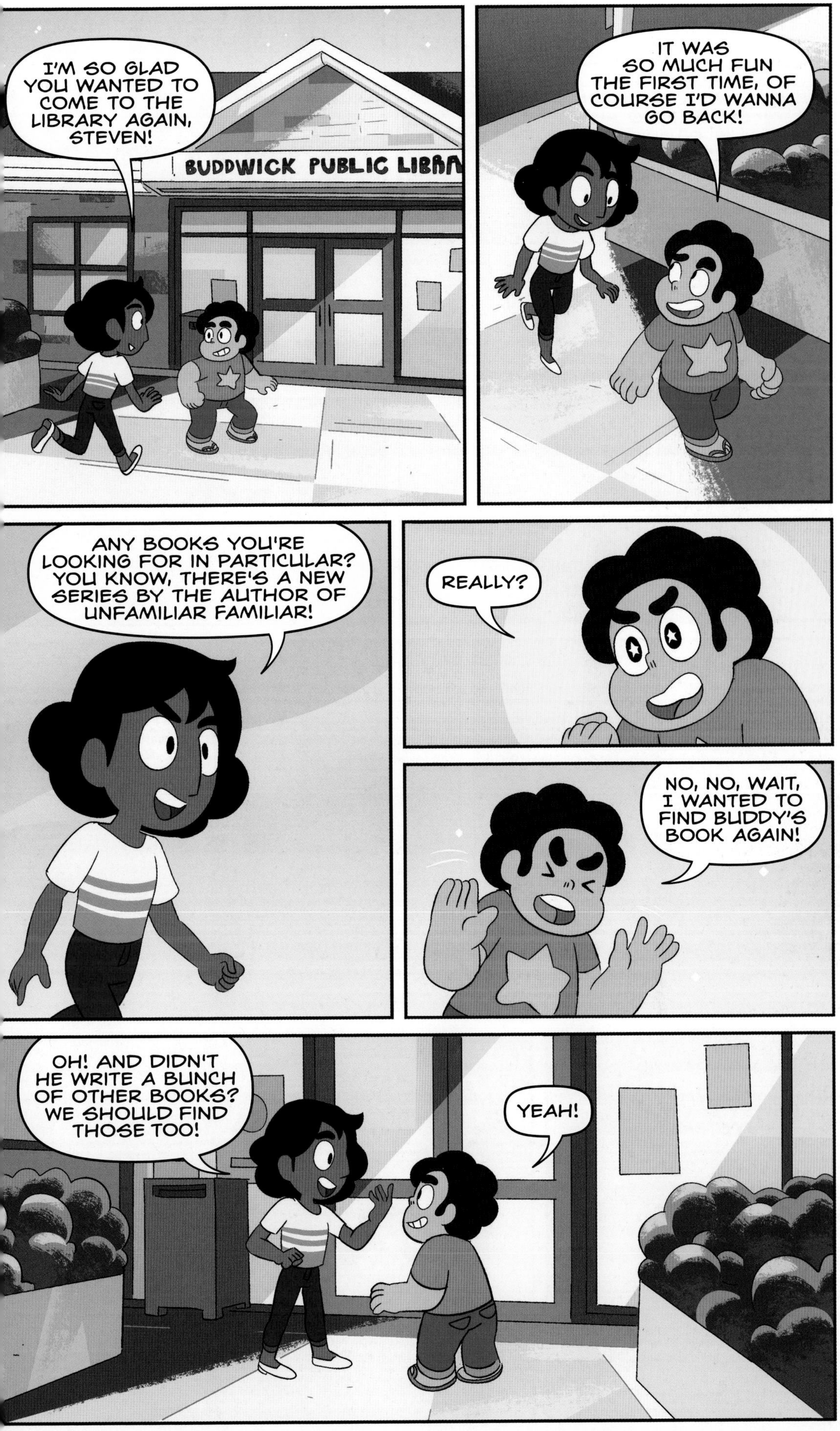
I'M SO GLAD YOU WANTED TO COME TO THE LIBRARY AGAIN, STEVEN!
BUDDWICK PUBLIC LIBRA
IT WAS SO MUCH FUN THE FIRST TIME, OF COURSE I'D WANNA GO BACK!
ANY BOOKS YOU'RE LOOKING FOR IN PARTICULAR? YOU KNOW, THERE'S A NEW SERIES BY THE AUTHOR OF UNFAMILIAR FAMILIAR!
REALLY?
NO, NO, WAIT, I WANTED TO FIND BUDDY'S BOOK AGAIN!
OH! AND DIDN'T HE WRITE A BUNCH OF OTHER BOOKS? WE SHOULD FIND THOSE TOO!
YEAH!

MAYBE WE CAN LEARN SOMETHING ABOUT ALL THE STUFF THE GEMS LEFT BEHIND!

GREAT IDEA!

SHHHHHH

THIS PLACE IS BIGGER THAN I REMEMBER IT. HOW DOES ANYONE FIND ANYTHING?

WITH THE DEWEY DECIMAL SYSTEM!

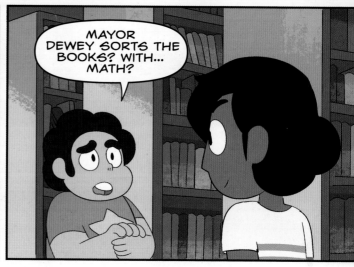

MAYOR DEWEY SORTS THE BOOKS? WITH... MATH?

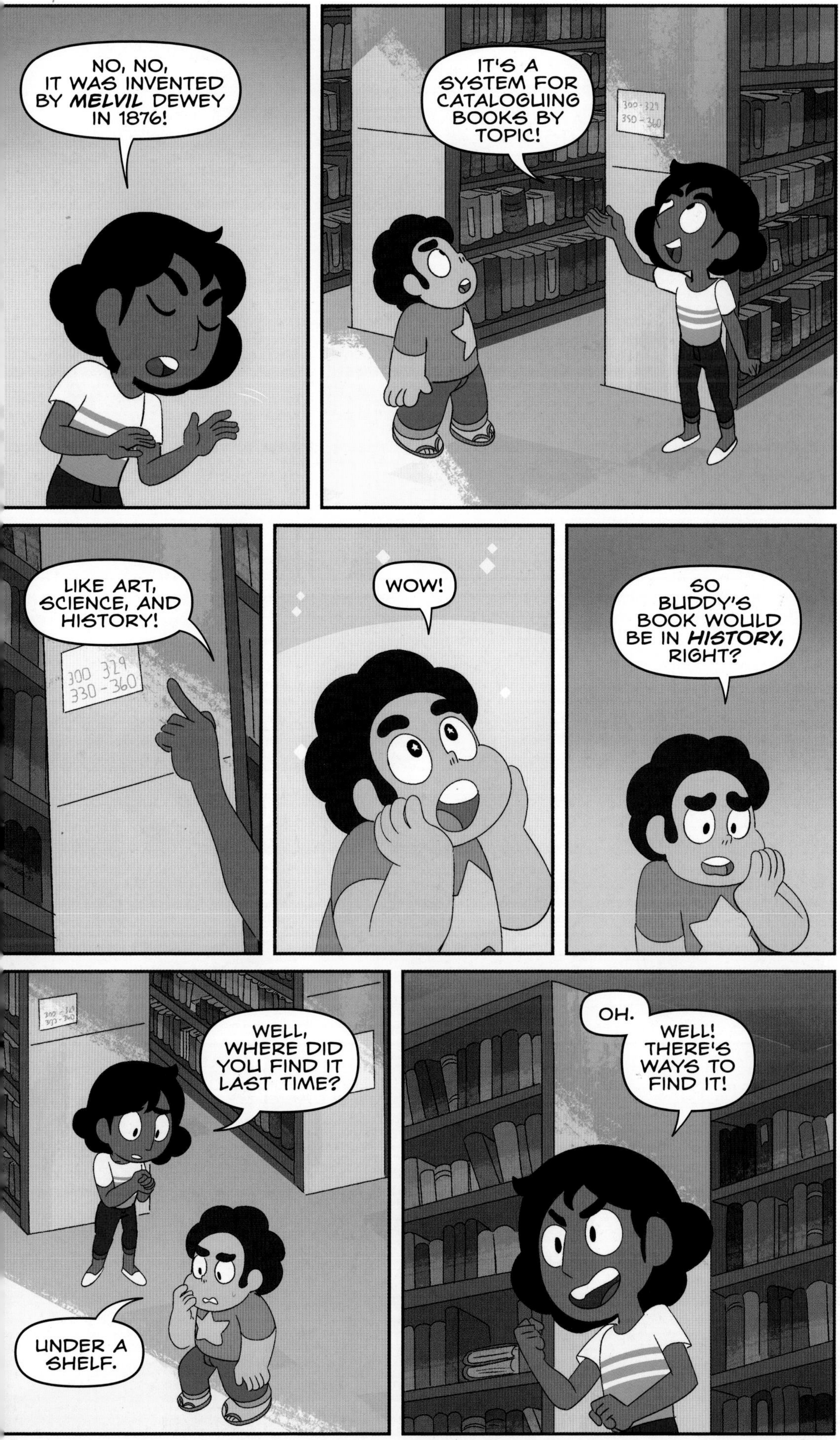
NO, NO, IT WAS INVENTED BY MELVIL DEWEY IN 1876!
IT'S A SYSTEM FOR CATALOGUING BOOKS BY TOPIC!
300-329
350-360
LIKE ART, SCIENCE, AND HISTORY!
300 329
330-360
WOW!
SO BUDDY'S BOOK WOULD BE IN HISTORY, RIGHT?
WELL, WHERE DID YOU FIND IT LAST TIME?
UNDER A SHELF.
OH.
WELL! THERE'S WAYS TO FIND IT!

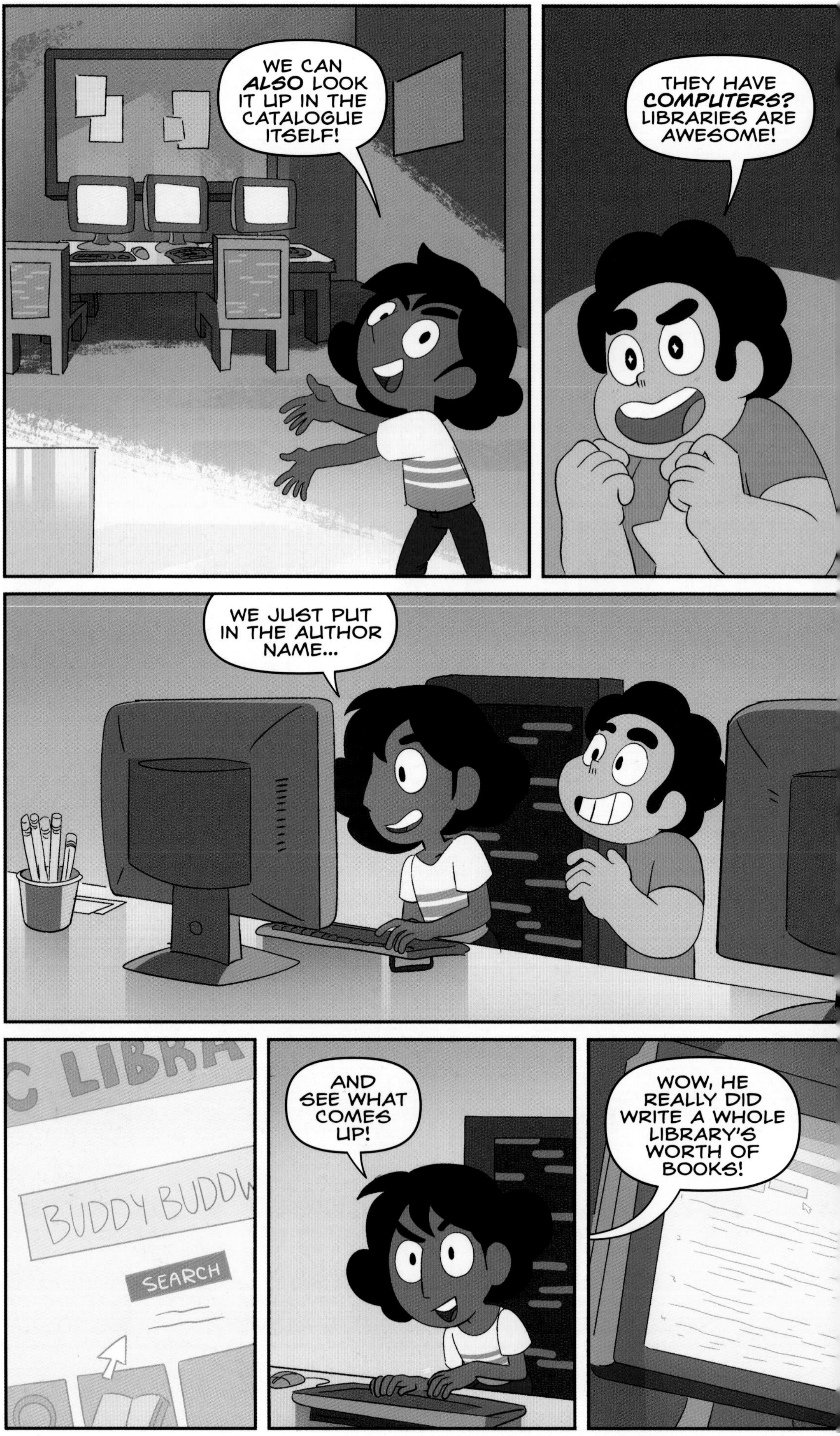
WE CAN ALSO LOOK IT UP IN THE CATALOGUE ITSELF!
THEY HAVE COMPUTERS? LIBRARIES ARE AWESOME!
WE JUST PUT IN THE AUTHOR NAME...
C LIBRA
BUDDY BUDDW
SEARCH
AND SEE WHAT COMES UP!
WOW, HE REALLY DID WRITE A WHOLE LIBRARY'S WORTH OF BOOKS!

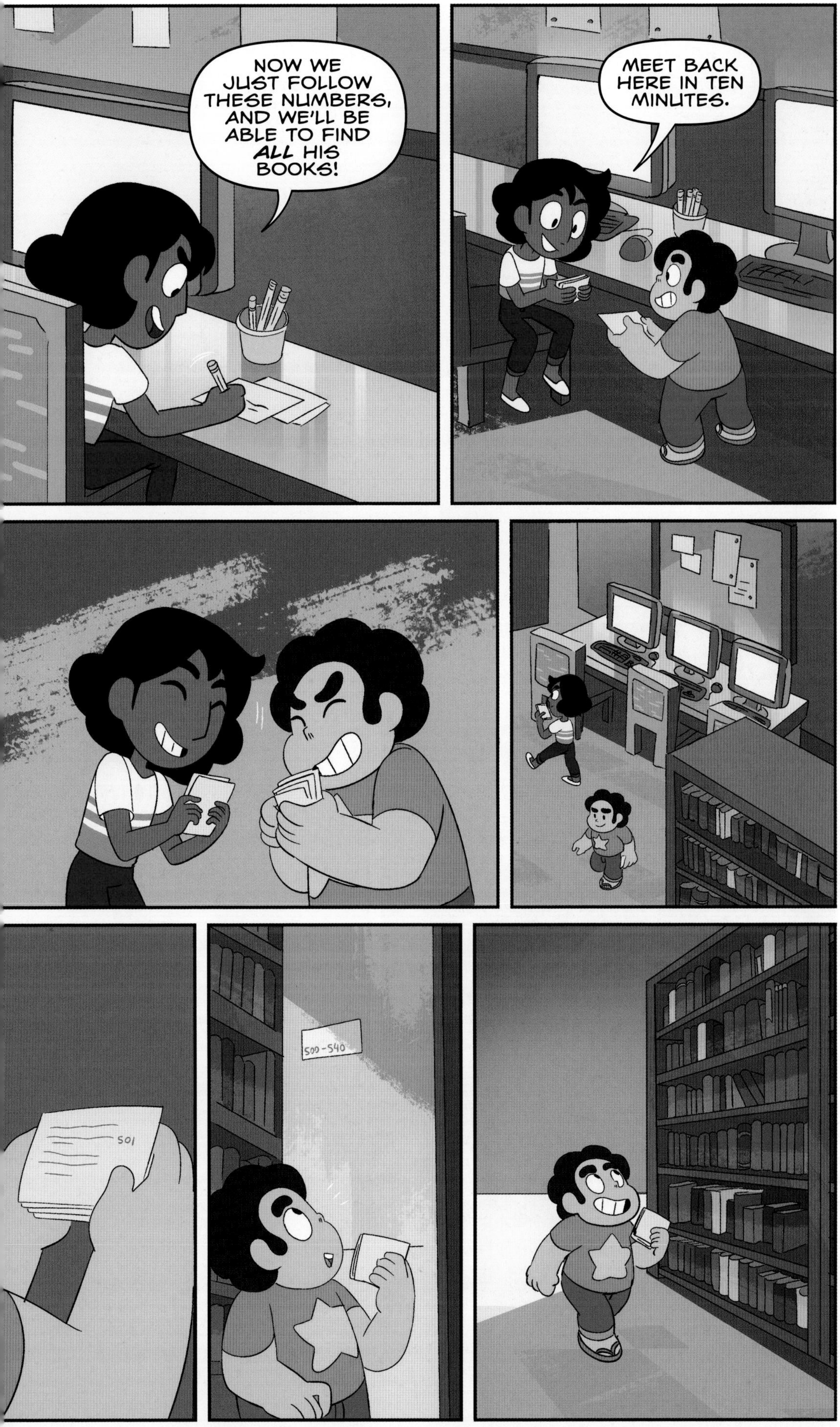
NOW WE JUST FOLLOW THESE NUMBERS, AND WE'LL BE ABLE TO FIND ALL HIS BOOKS!
MEET BACK HERE IN TEN MINUTES.
500-540
501

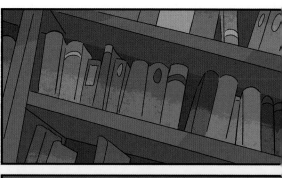

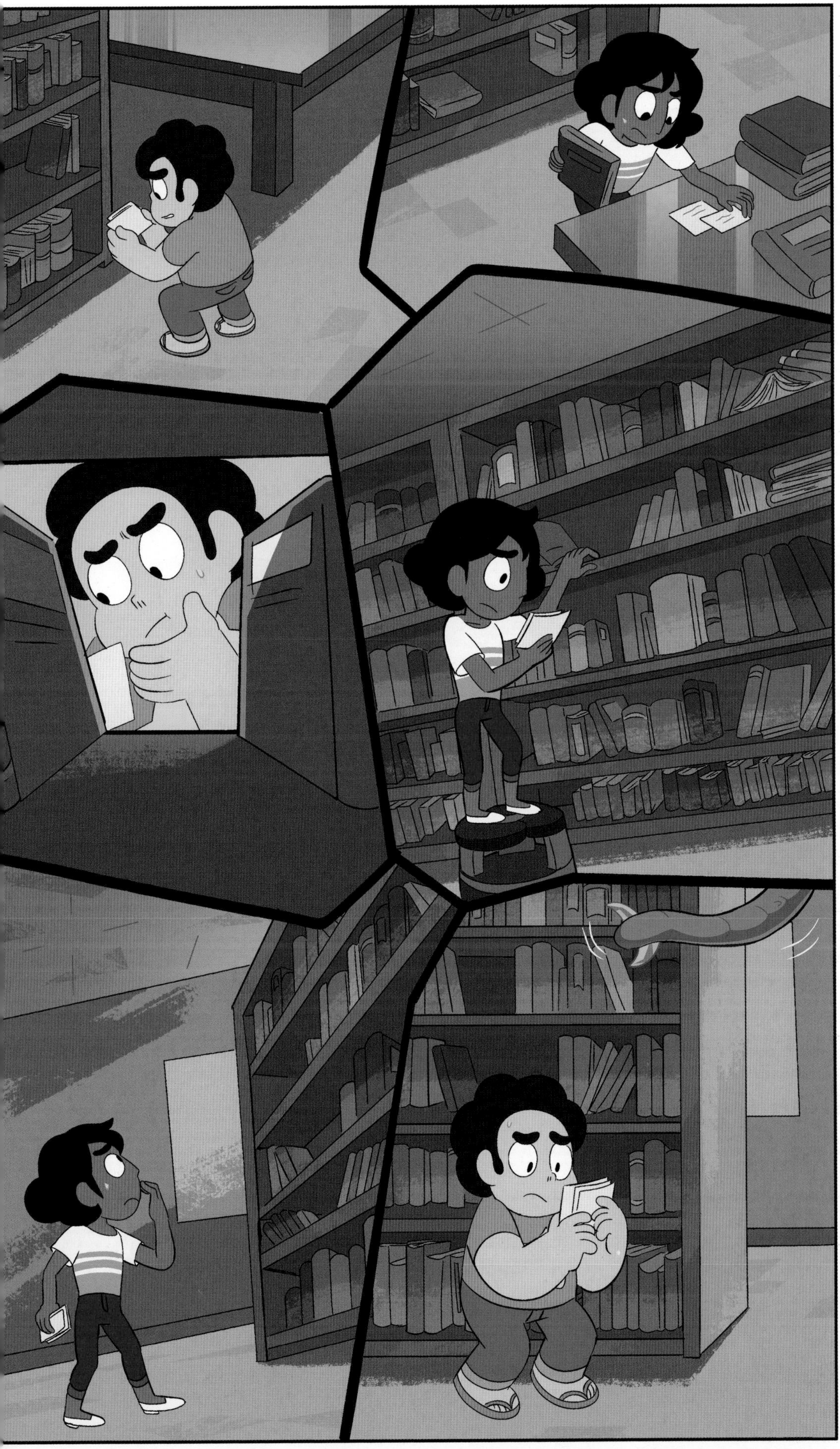

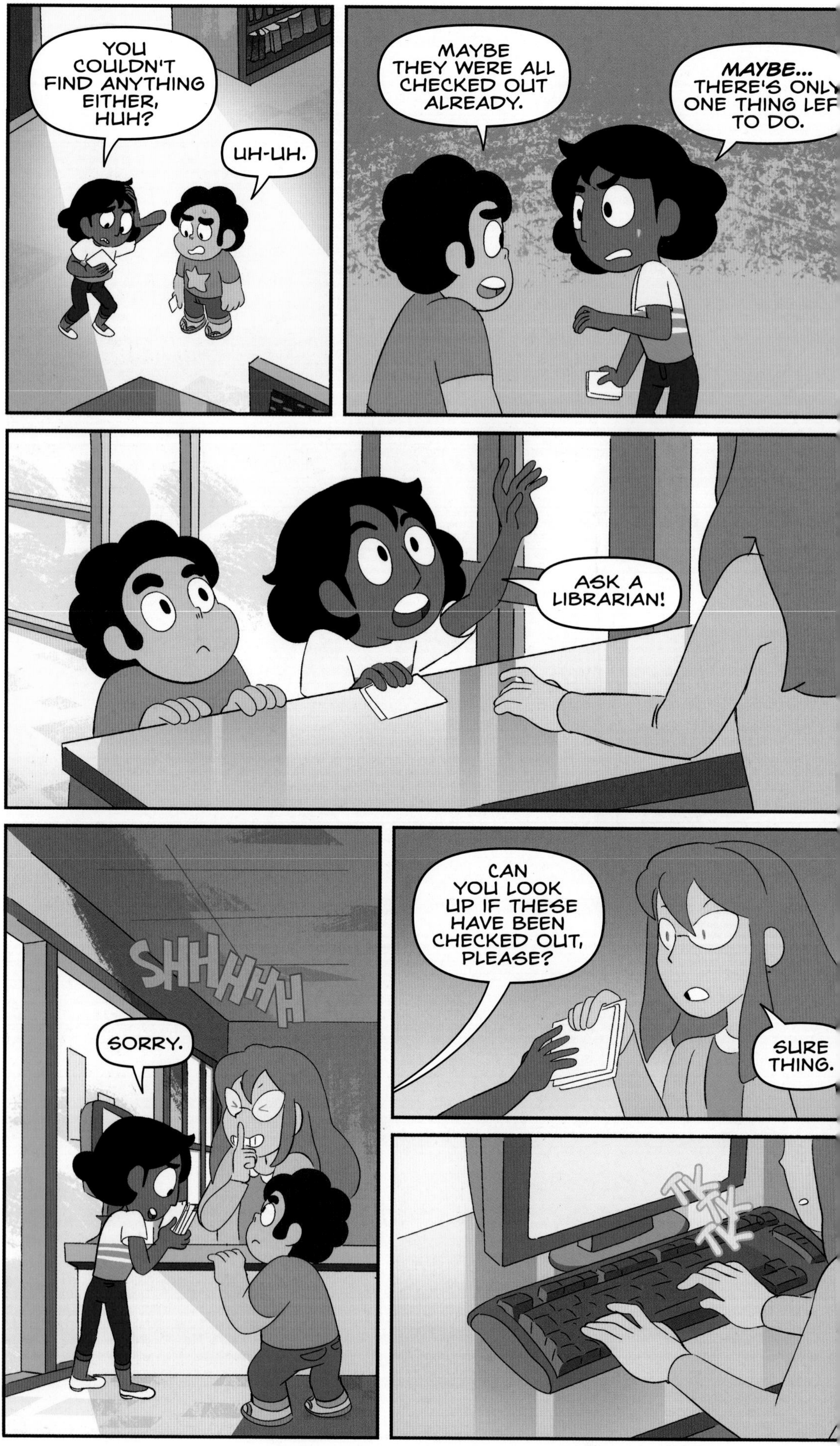

YOU COULDN'T FIND ANYTHING EITHER, HUH?
UH-UH.
MAYBE THEY WERE ALL CHECKED OUT ALREADY.
MAYBE... THERE'S ONLY ONE THING LEFT TO DO.
ASK A LIBRARIAN!
SHHHHH
SORRY.
CAN YOU LOOK UP IF THESE HAVE BEEN CHECKED OUT, PLEASE?
SURE THING.
TK TK TK

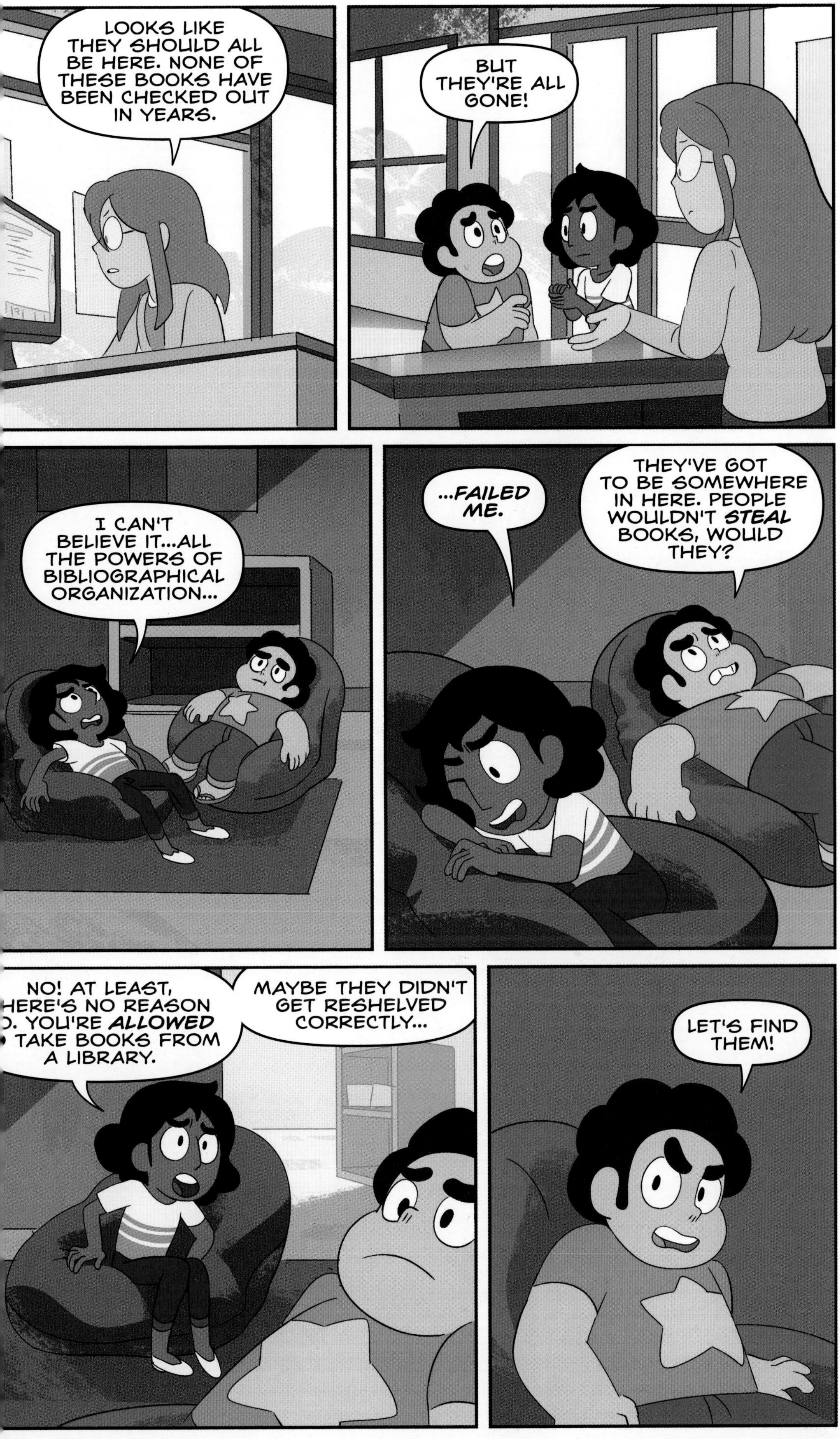
LOOKS LIKE THEY SHOULD ALL BE HERE. NONE OF THESE BOOKS HAVE BEEN CHECKED OUT IN YEARS.
BUT THEY'RE ALL GONE!
I CAN'T BELIEVE IT...ALL THE POWERS OF BIBLIOGRAPHICAL ORGANIZATION...
...FAILED ME.
THEY'VE GOT TO BE SOMEWHERE IN HERE. PEOPLE WOULDN'T STEAL BOOKS, WOULD THEY?
NO! AT LEAST, HERE'S NO REASON O. YOU'RE ALLOWED TAKE BOOKS FROM A LIBRARY.
MAYBE THEY DIDN'T GET RESHELVED CORRECTLY...
LET'S FIND THEM!

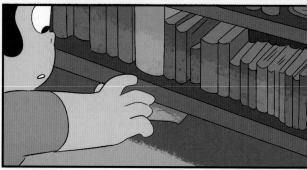

BY
BUDDY
BUDDWICK

HUH?

WAIT!

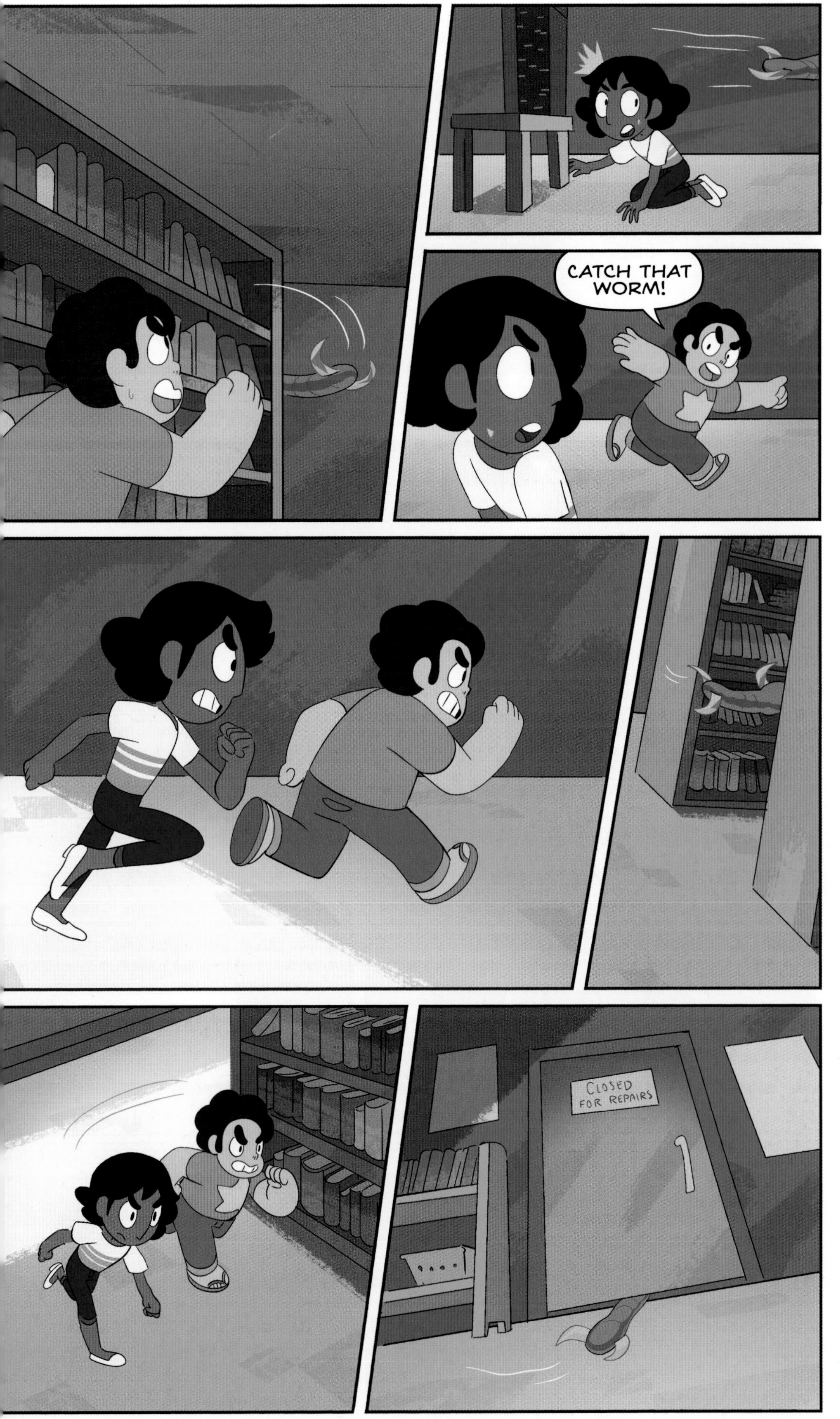
CATCH THAT WORM!
CLOSED FOR REPAIRS

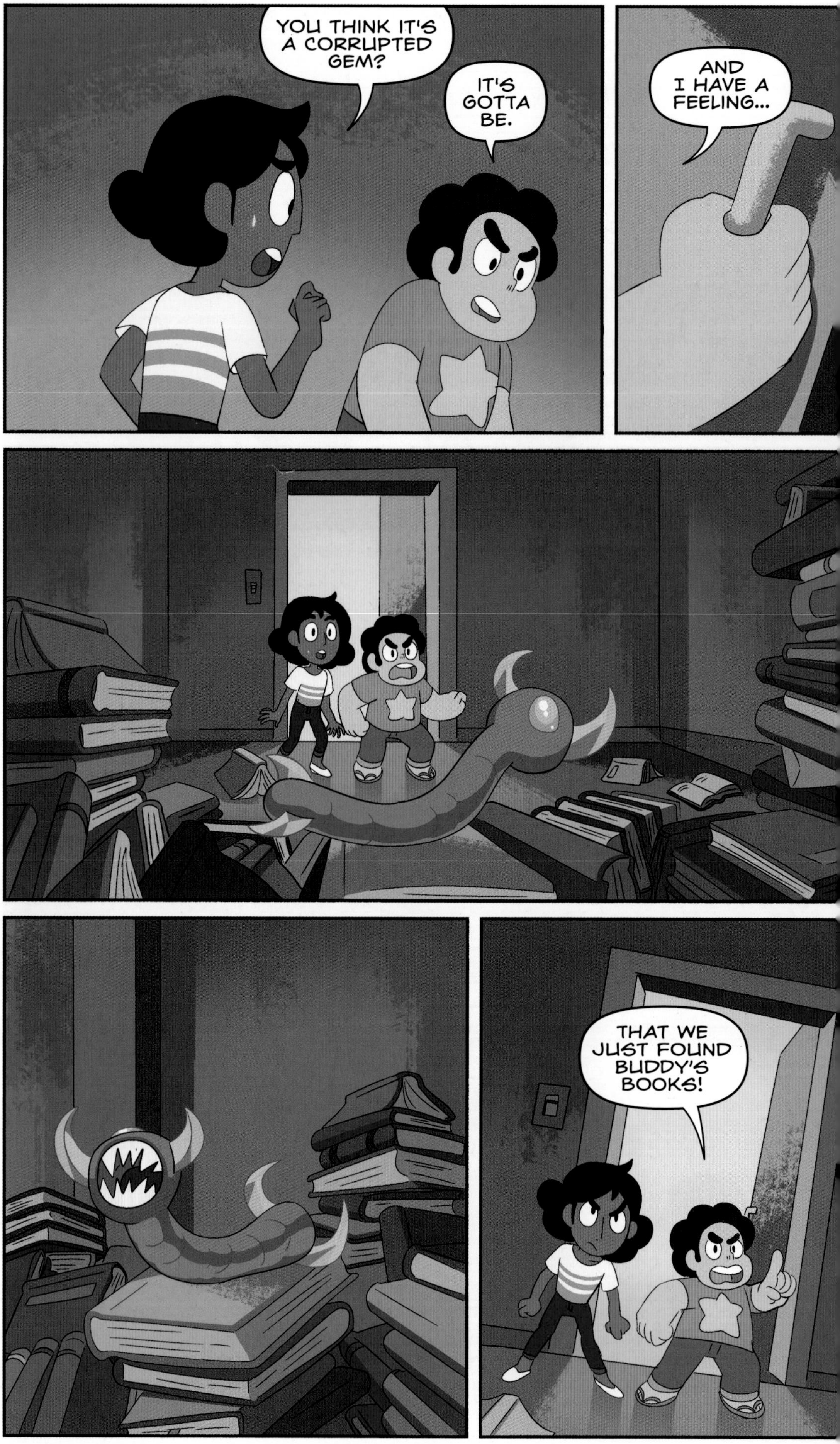
YOU THINK IT'S A CORRUPTED GEM?
IT'S GOTTA BE.
AND I HAVE A FEELING...
THAT WE JUST FOUND BUDDY'S BOOKS!

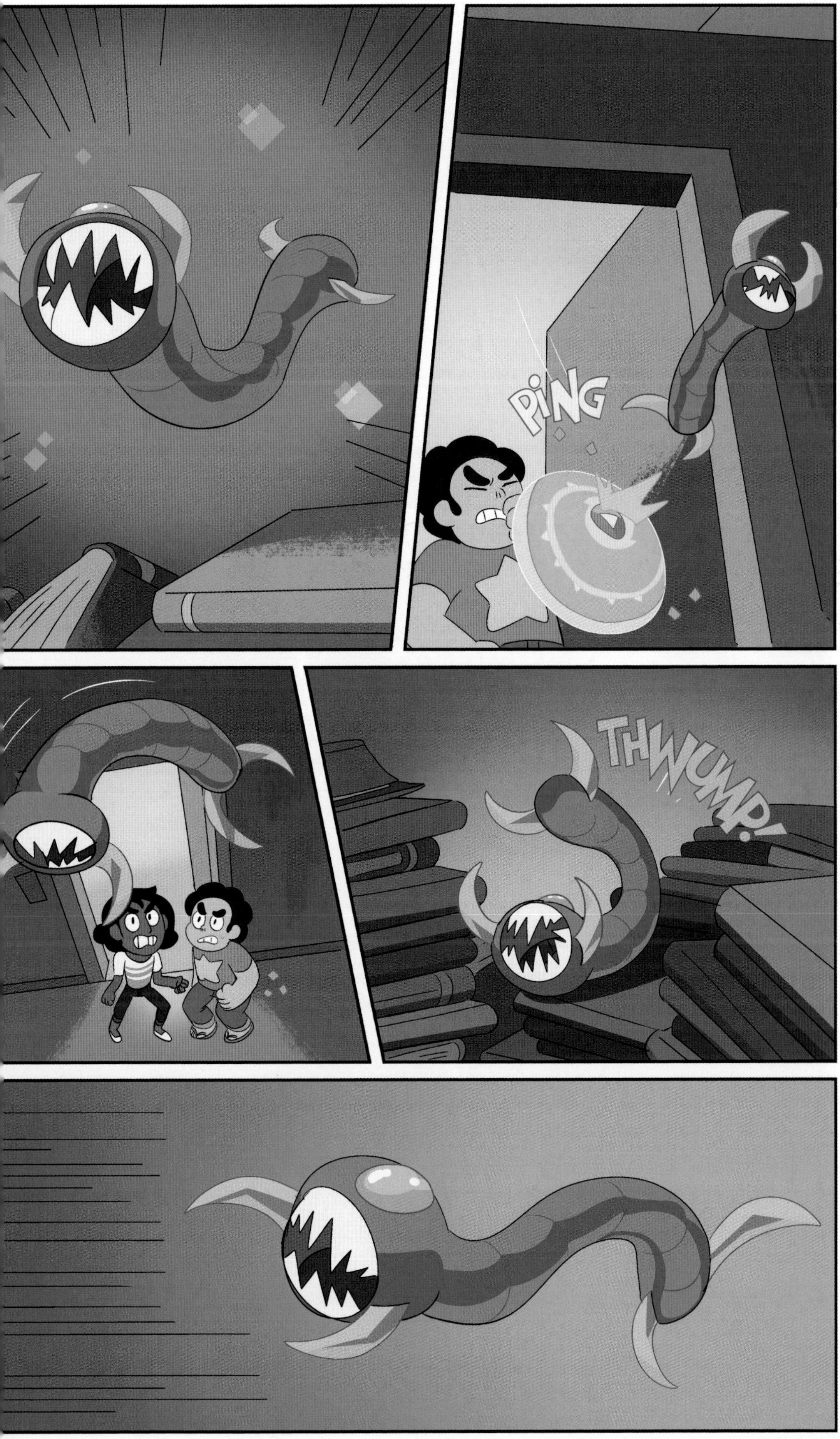
PING
THWUMP!

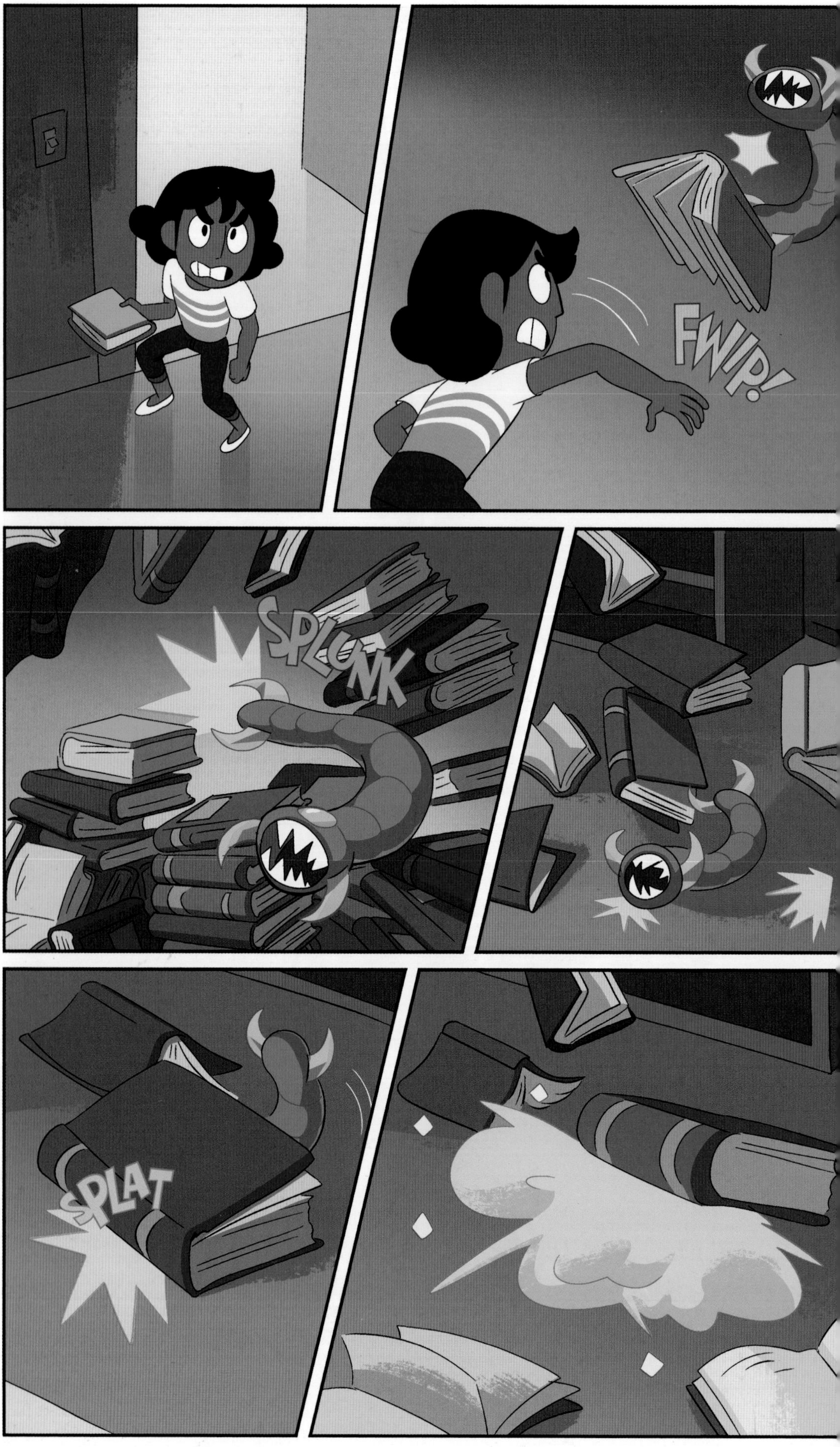
FWIP!
SPLUNK
SPLAT

FOUND THE JOURNAL! BUT LOOK, THIS ONE'S BUDDY'S TOO! ALL OF THEM ARE!

WHAT'S THAT ONE?

IT'S--!

THE DIAMONDS!

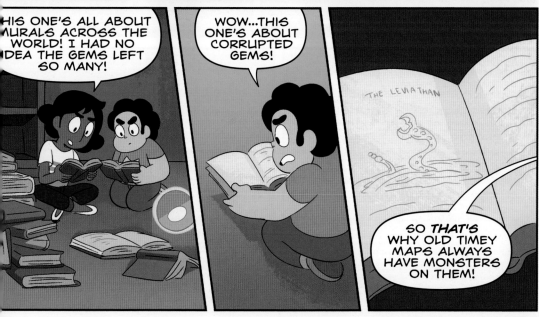

HIS ONE'S ALL ABOUT MURALS ACROSS THE WORLD! I HAD NO IDEA THE GEMS LEFT SO MANY!

WOW...THIS ONE'S ABOUT CORRUPTED GEMS!

THE LEVIATHAN

SO THAT'S WHY OLD TIMEY MAPS ALWAYS HAVE MONSTERS ON THEM!

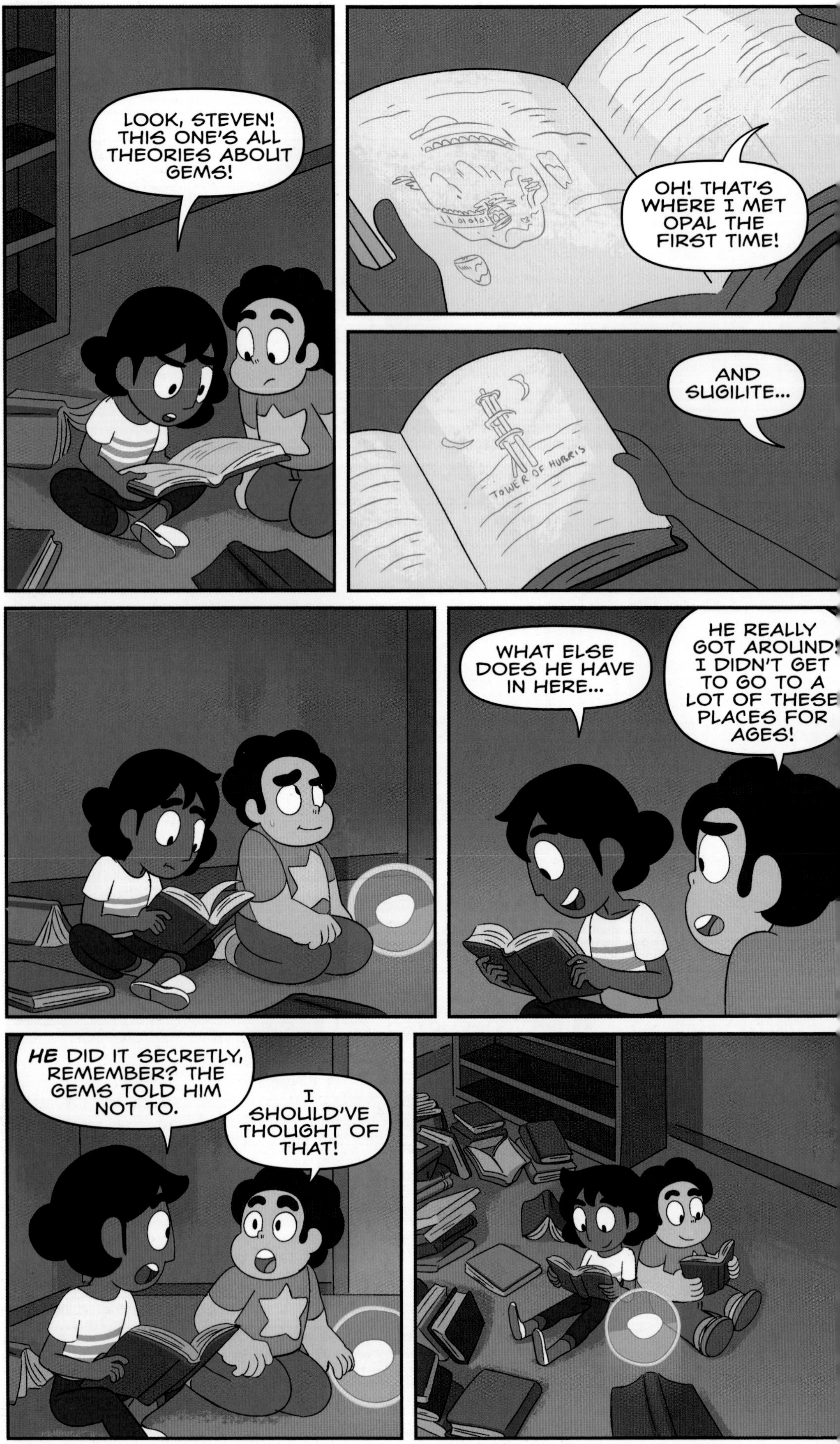
LOOK, STEVEN! THIS ONE'S ALL THEORIES ABOUT GEMS!
OH! THAT'S WHERE I MET OPAL THE FIRST TIME!
AND SUGILITE...
TOWER OF HUBRIS
WHAT ELSE DOES HE HAVE IN HERE...
HE REALLY GOT AROUND! I DIDN'T GET TO GO TO A LOT OF THESE PLACES FOR AGES!
HE DID IT SECRETLY, REMEMBER? THE GEMS TOLD HIM NOT TO.
I SHOULD'VE THOUGHT OF THAT!

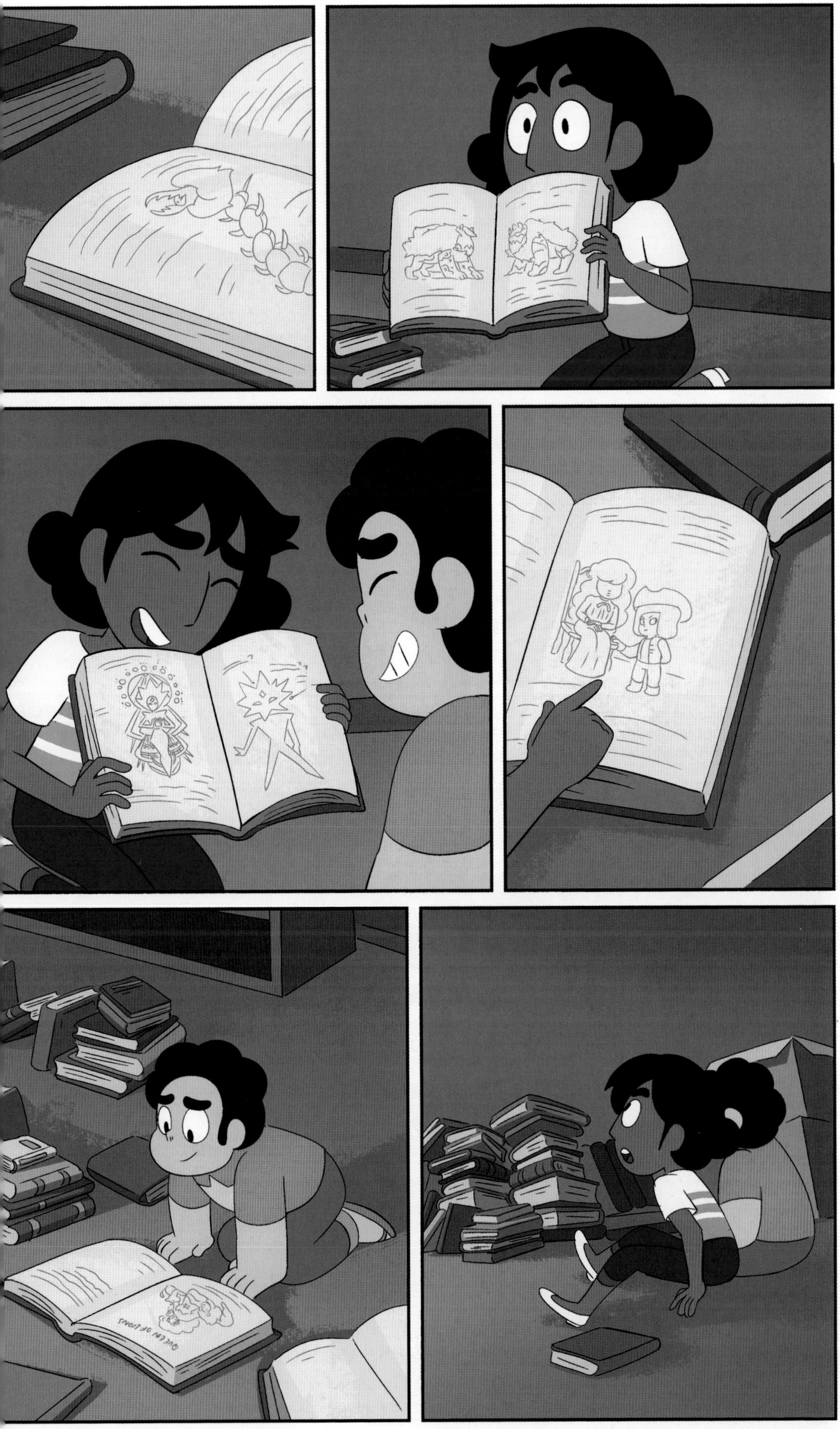
QUEEN OF LIONS

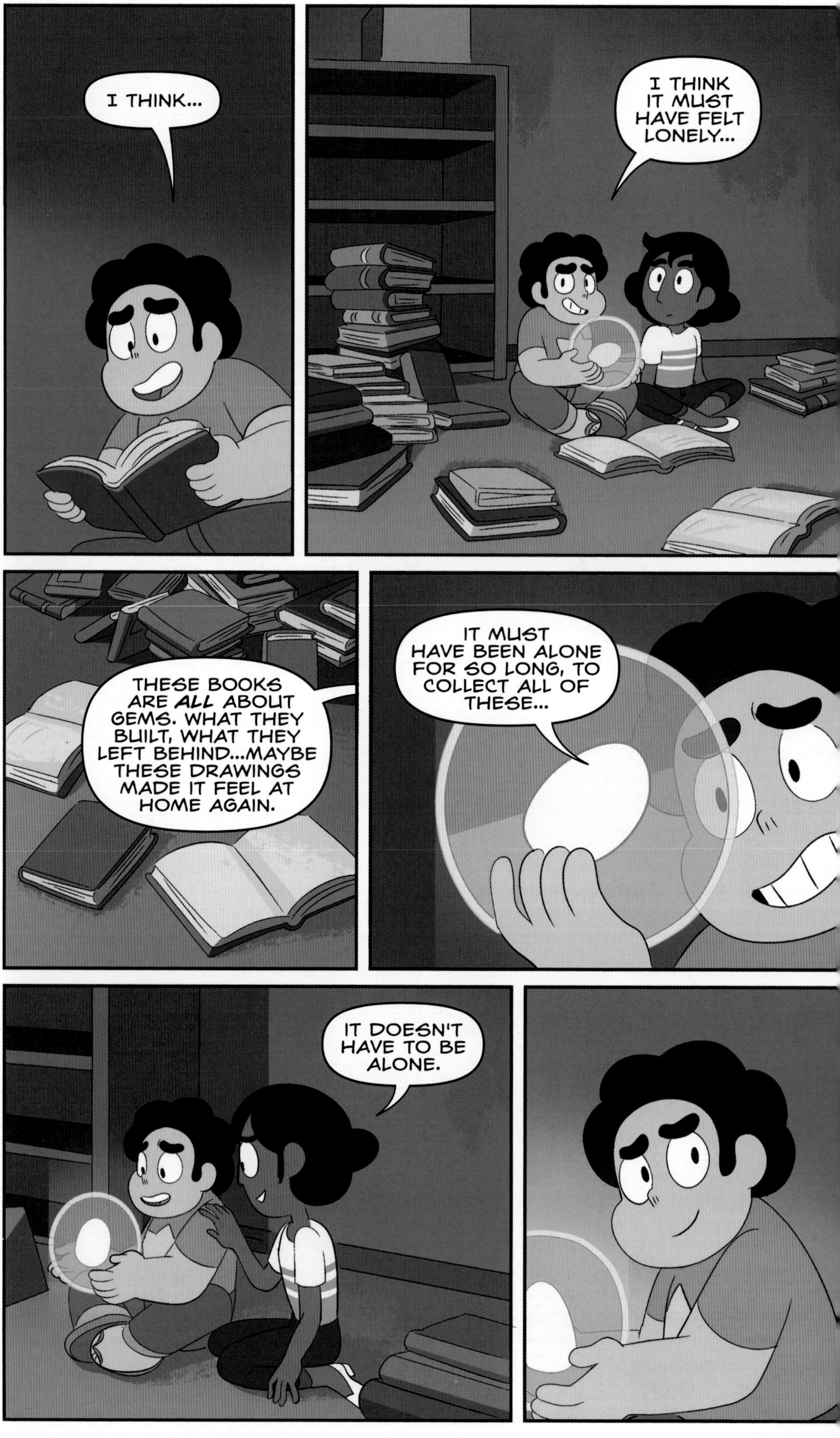
I THINK...
I THINK IT MUST HAVE FELT LONELY...
THESE BOOKS ARE ALL ABOUT GEMS. WHAT THEY BUILT, WHAT THEY LEFT BEHIND...MAYBE THESE DRAWINGS MADE IT FEEL AT HOME AGAIN.
IT MUST HAVE BEEN ALONE FOR SO LONG, TO COLLECT ALL OF THESE...
IT DOESN'T HAVE TO BE ALONE.

YEAH.

WE FOUND EACH OTHER.

NONE OF US HAVE TO BE ALONE ANYMORE.

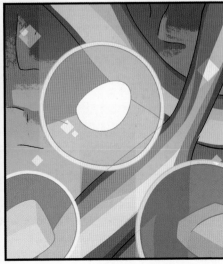

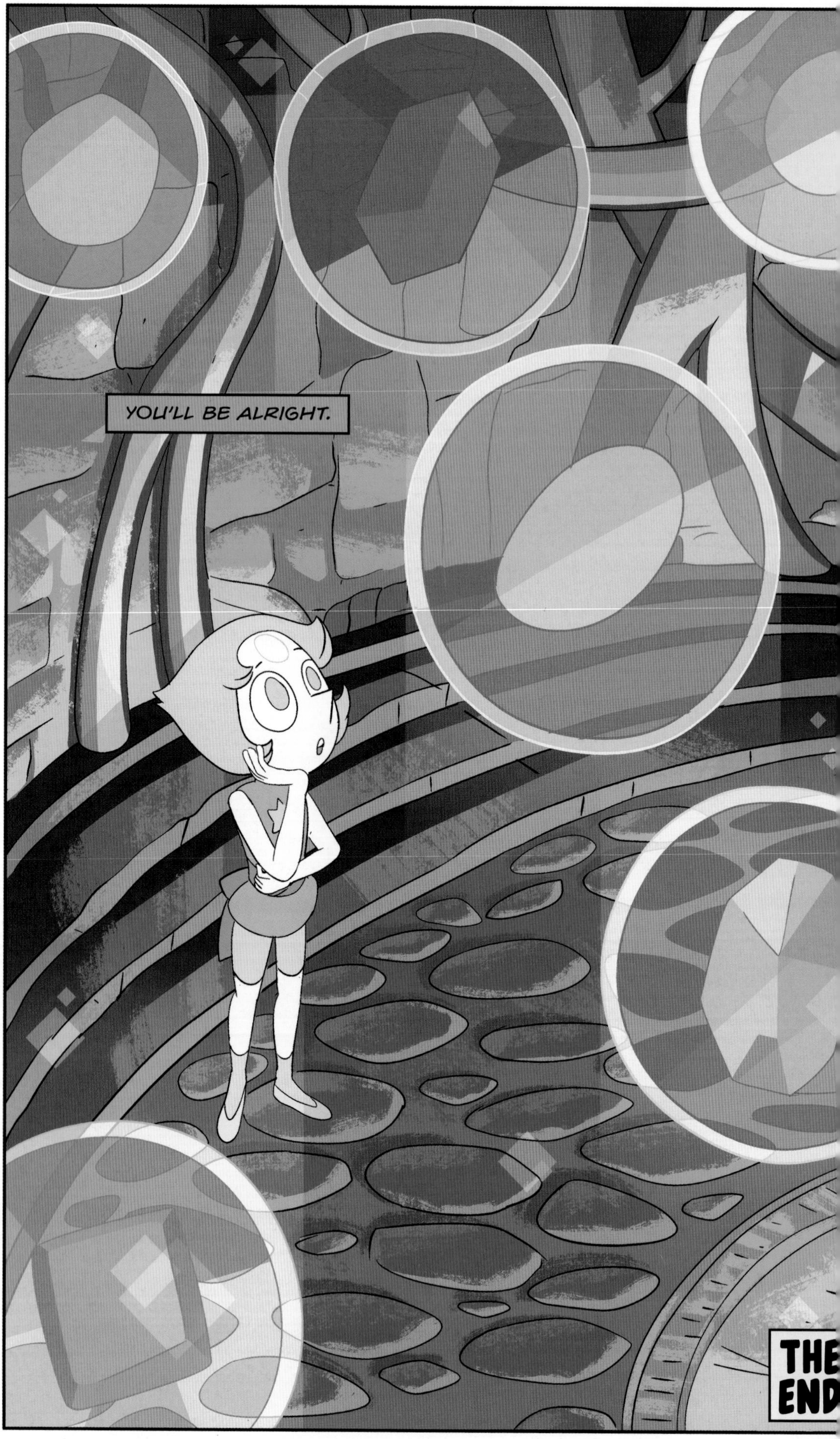
YOU'LL BE ALRIGHT.
THE END

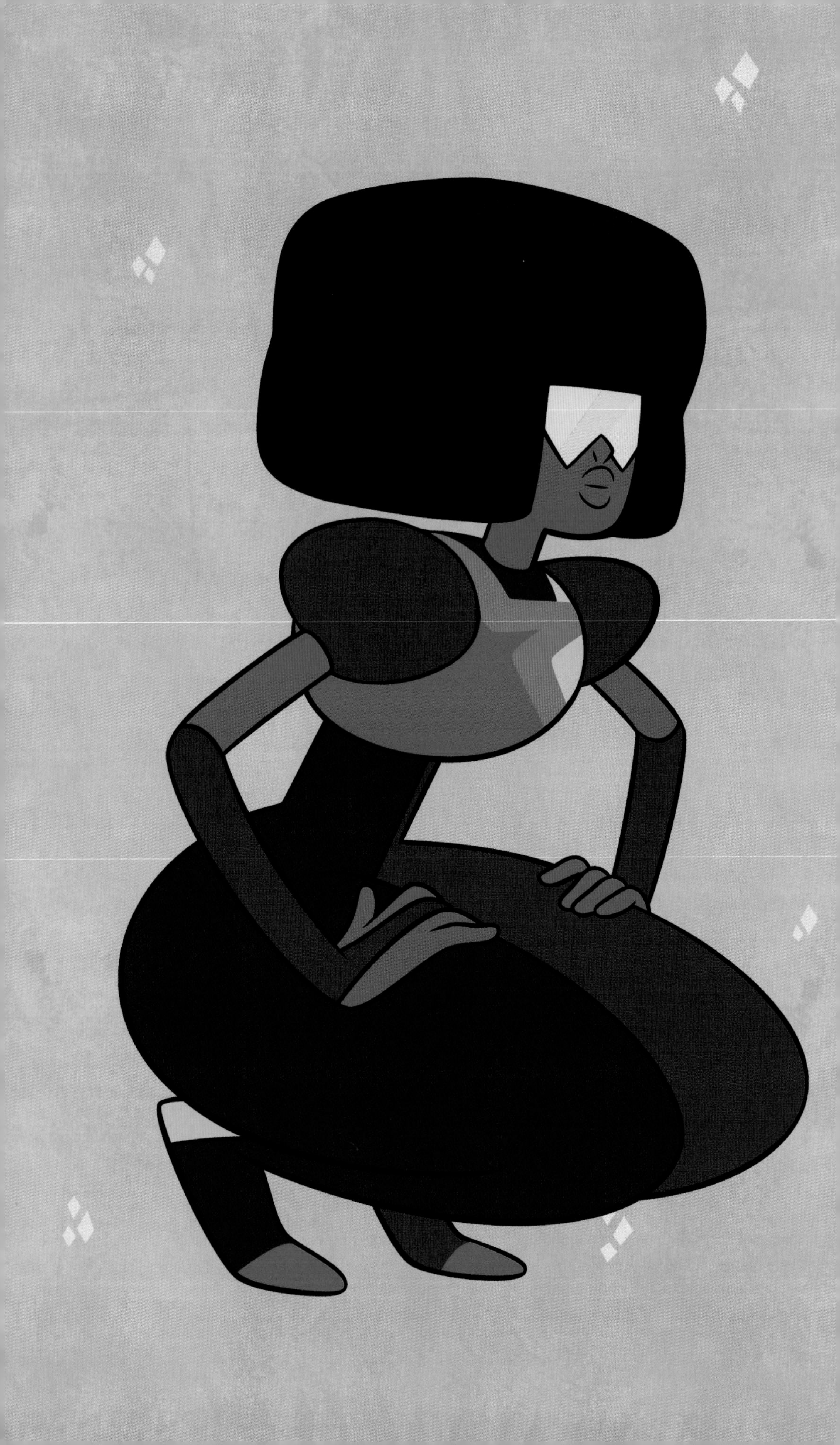

COVER GALLERY

Issue Thirty-Three Main Cover
MISSY PEÑA

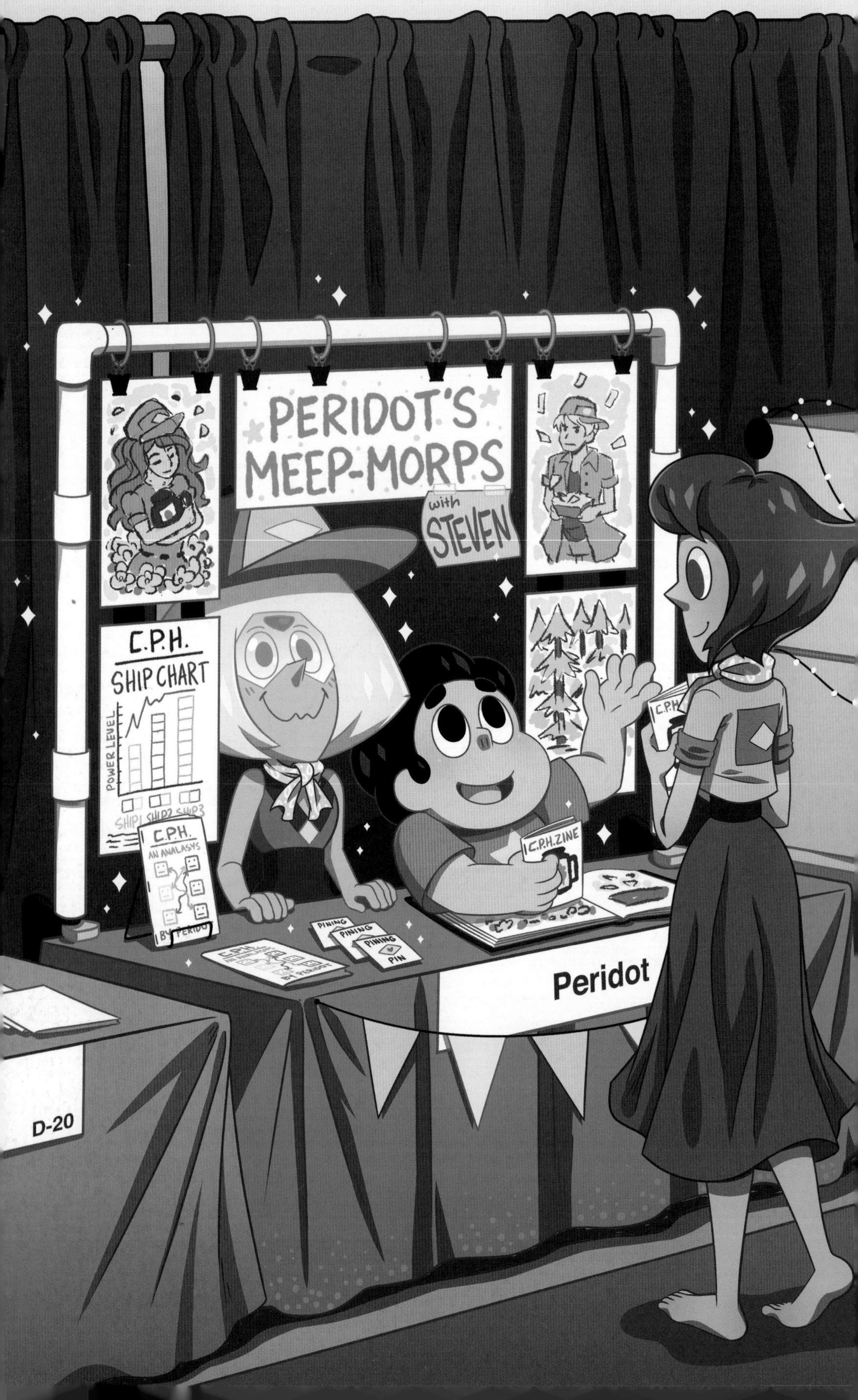
PERIDOT'S MEEP-MORPS
with STEVEN
C.P.H.
SHIP CHART
POWER LEVEL
SHIP1 SHIP2 SHIP3
C.P.H.
AN ANALASYS
BY PERIDOT
C.P.H.ZINE
PINING
PINING
PINING PIN
Peridot
D-20

Issue Thirty-Three Preorder Cover
CY VENDIVIL

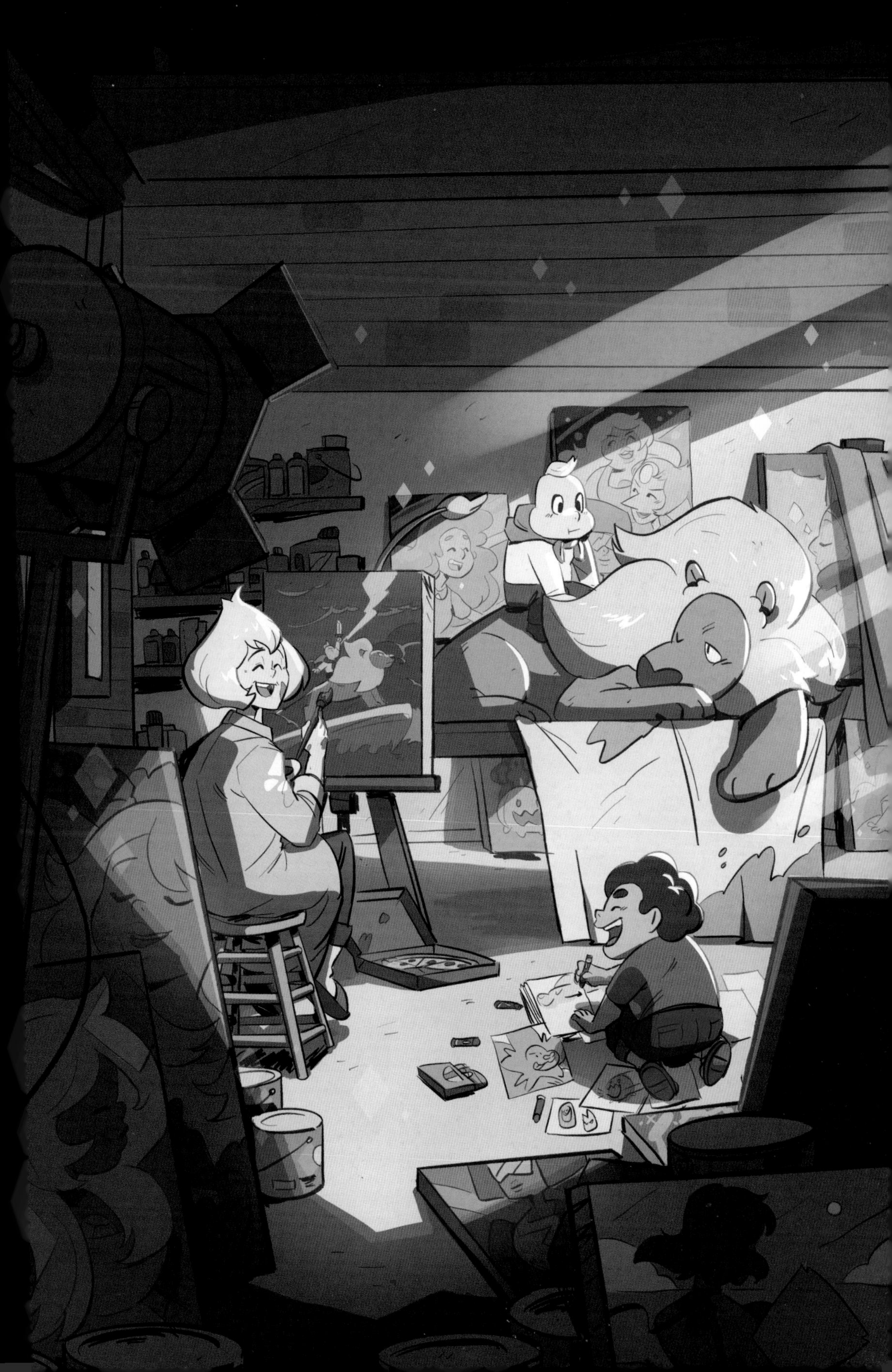

Issue Thirty-Four Main Cover
MISSY PEÑA

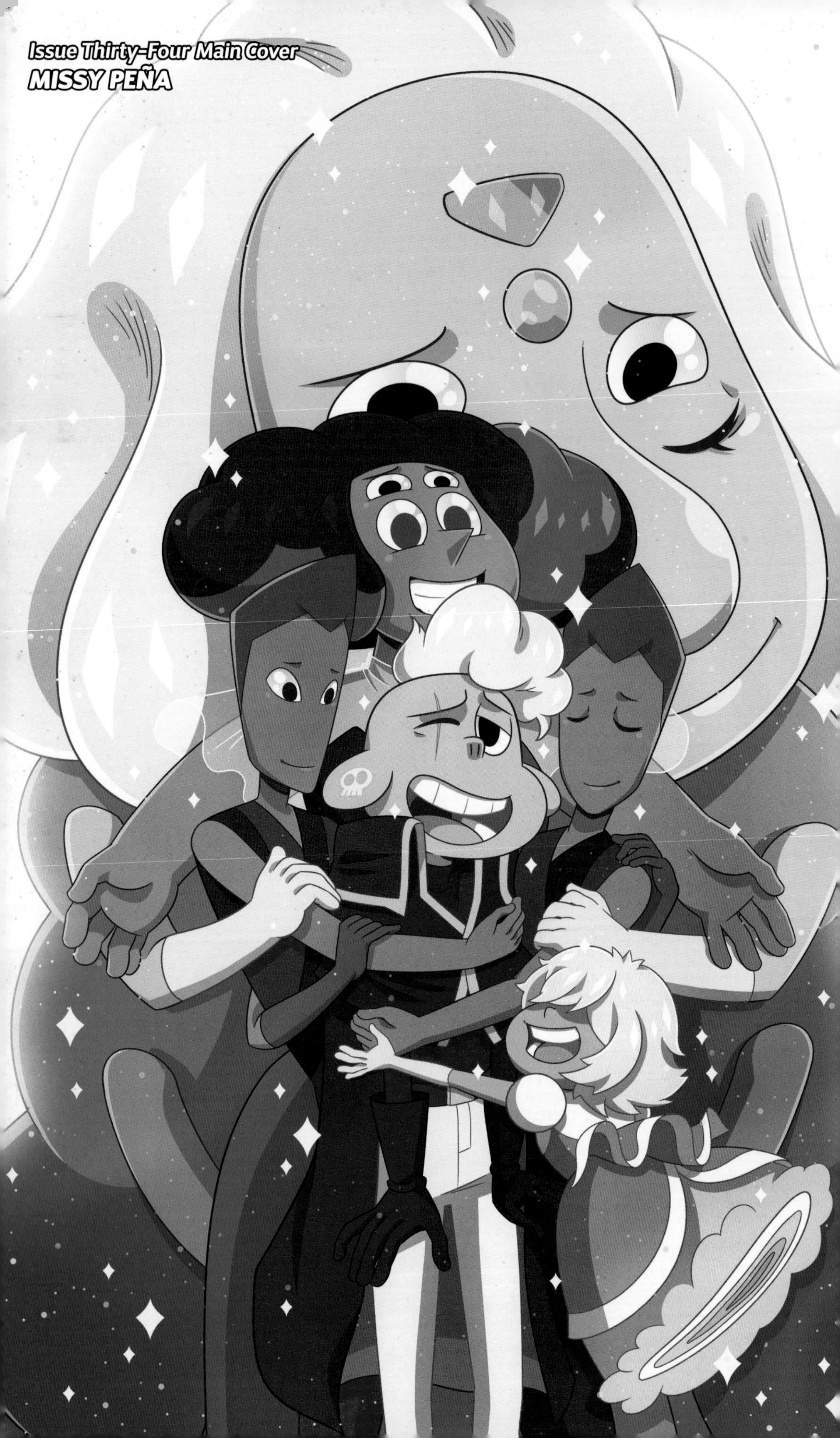

Issue Thirty-Four Preorder Cover
CHAN CHAU

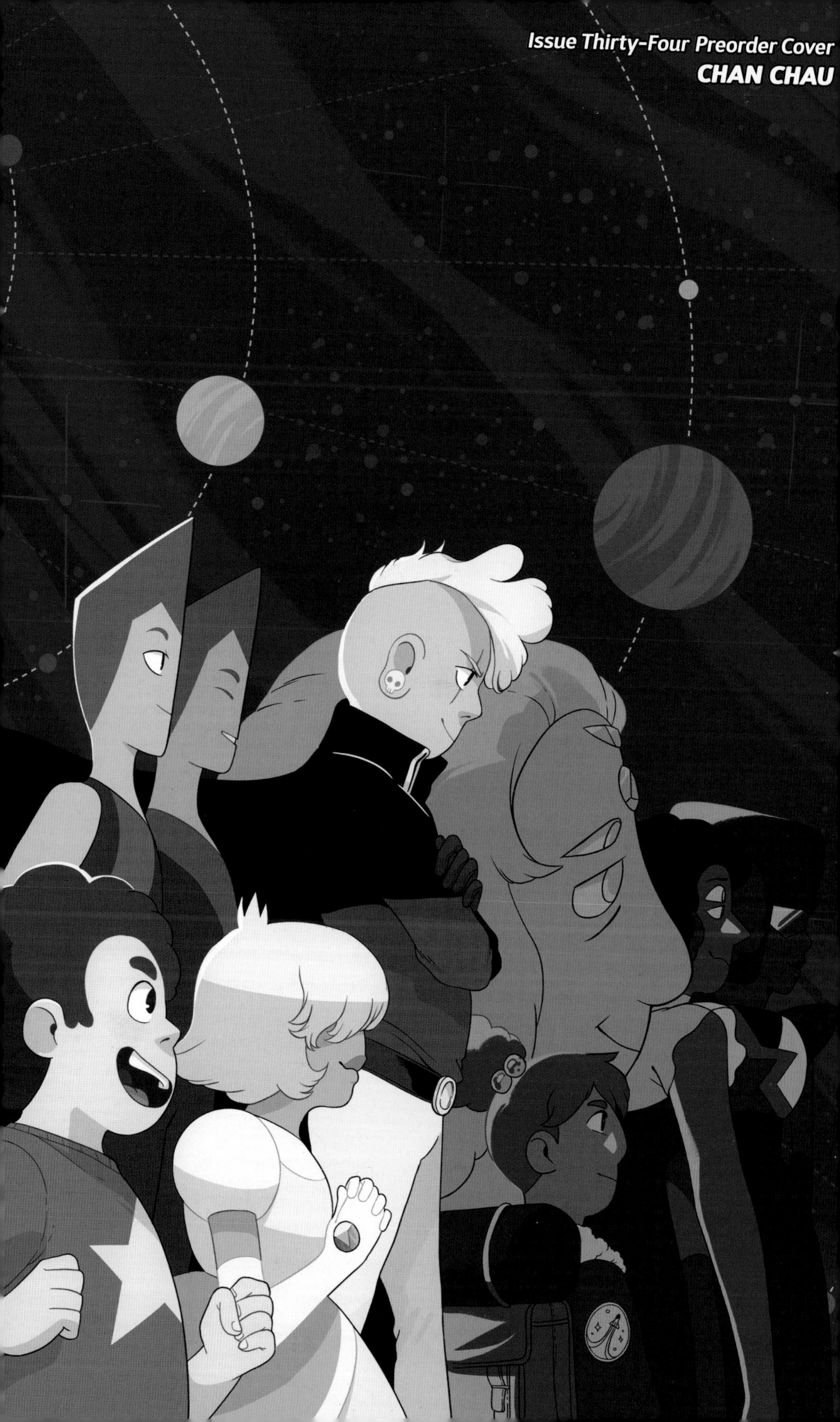

Issue Thirty-Five Main Cover
MISSY PEÑA

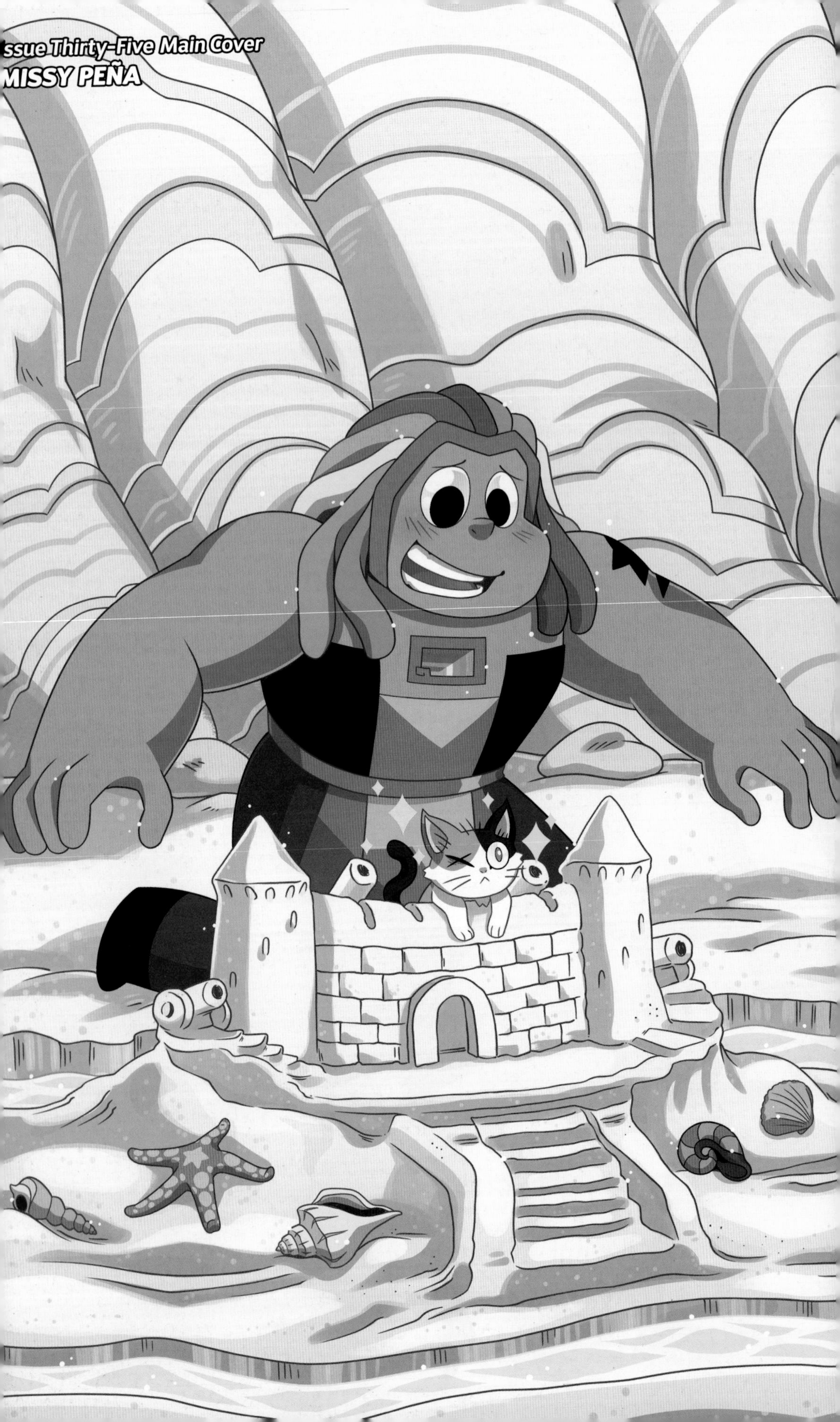

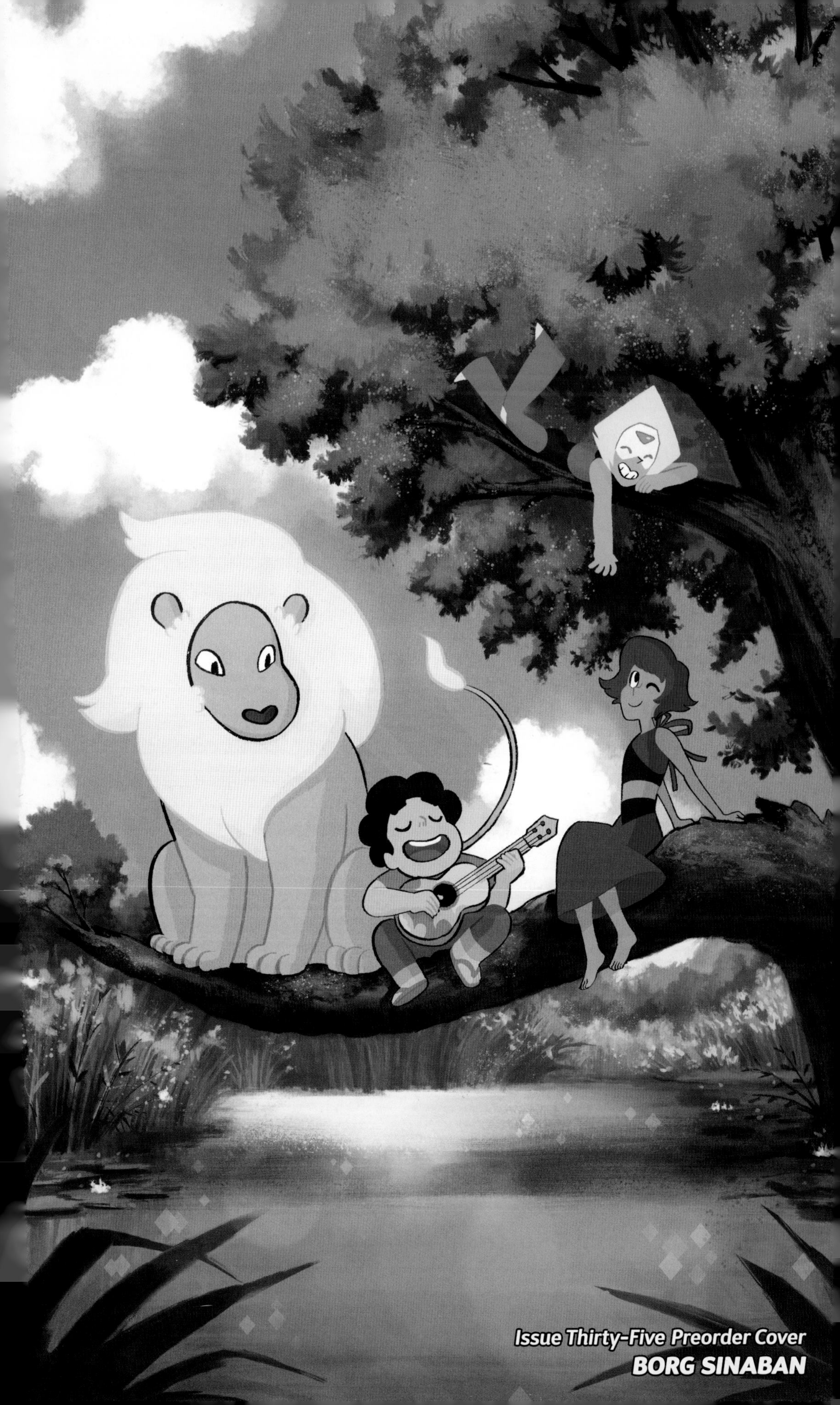

Issue Thirty-Five Preorder Cover
BORG SINABAN

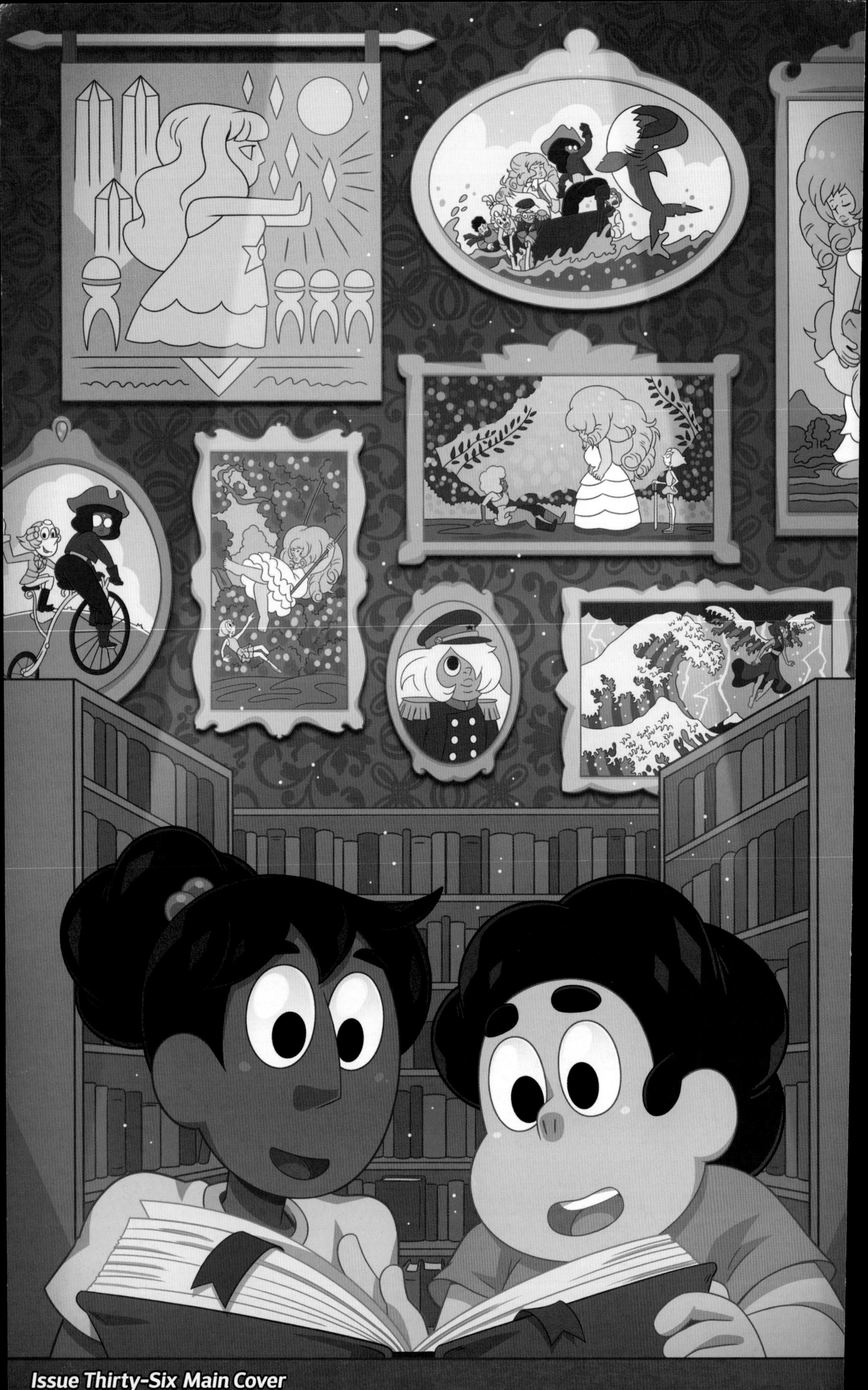

Issue Thirty-Six Main Cover
MISSY PEÑA

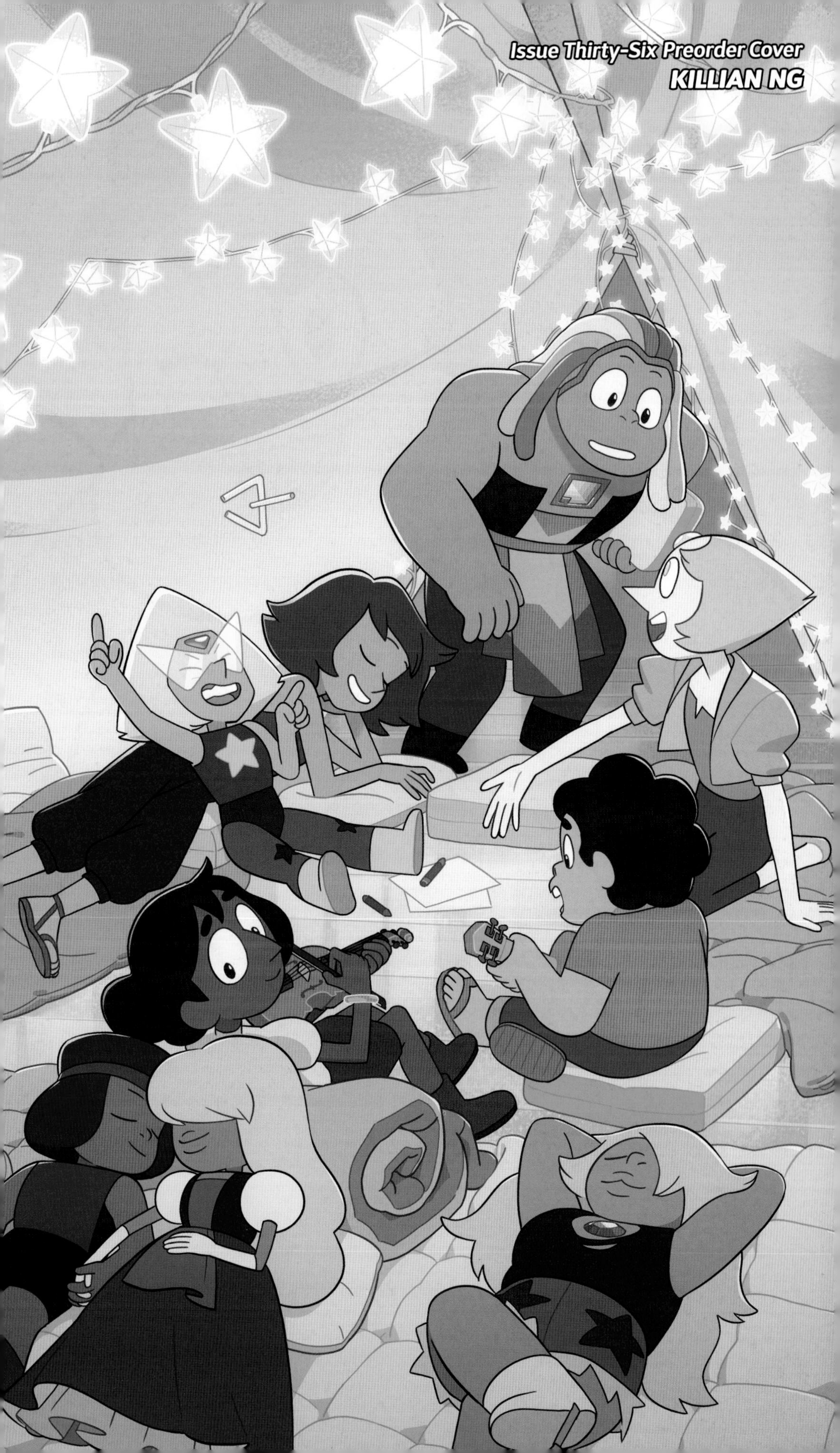
Issue Thirty-Six Preorder Cover
KILLIAN NG

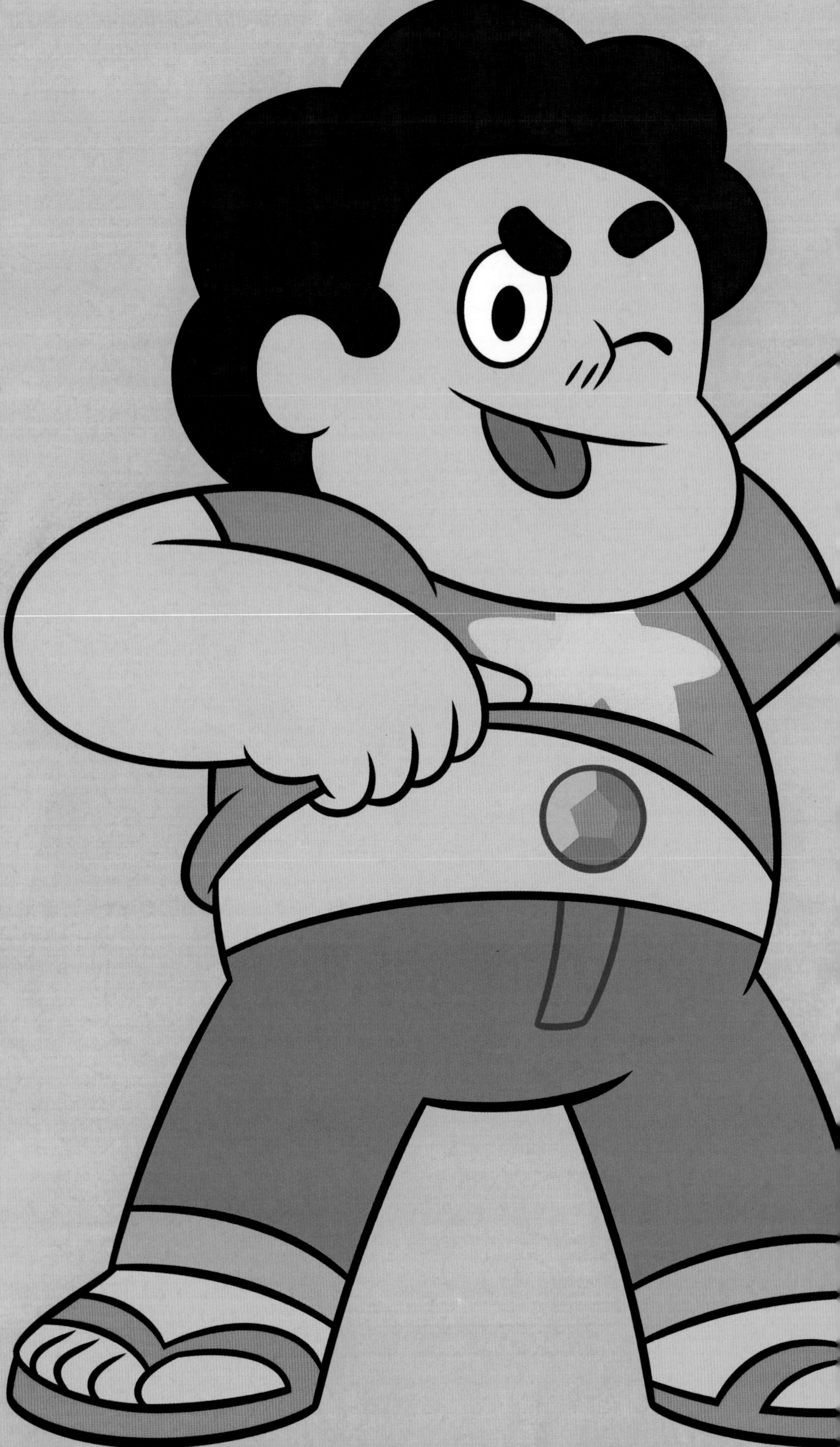

FROM THE PAGES OF CARTOON NETWORK

STEVEN UNIVERSE

WELCOME TO BEACH CITY

SNAP SHOTS

Written by
GRACE KRAFT

Illustrated by
KELLY TURNBUL

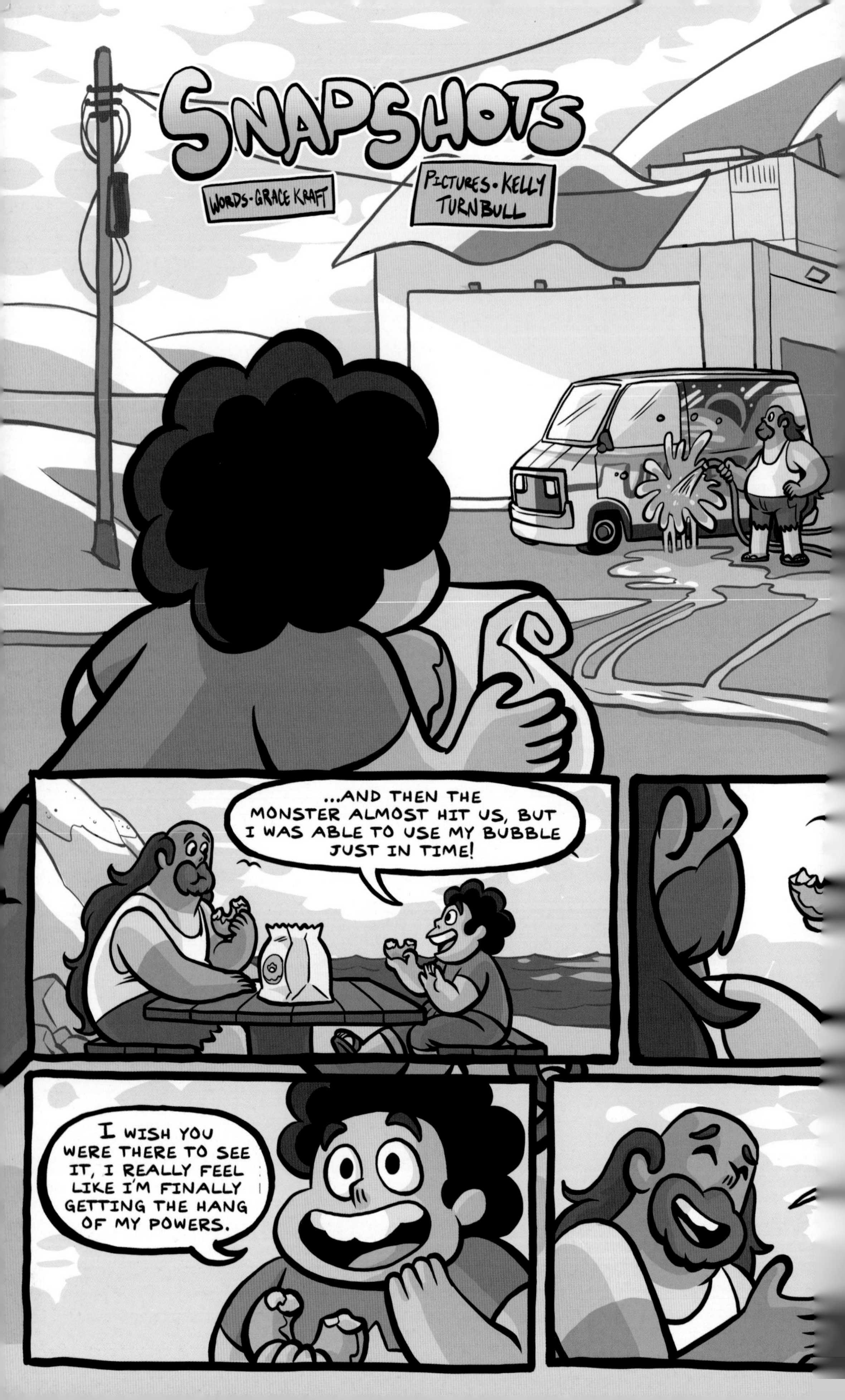
SNAPSHOTS
WORDS-GRACE KRAFT
PICTURES-KELLY TURNBULL
...AND THEN THE MONSTER ALMOST HIT US, BUT I WAS ABLE TO USE MY BUBBLE JUST IN TIME!
I WISH YOU WERE THERE TO SEE IT, I REALLY FEEL LIKE I'M FINALLY GETTING THE HANG OF MY POWERS.

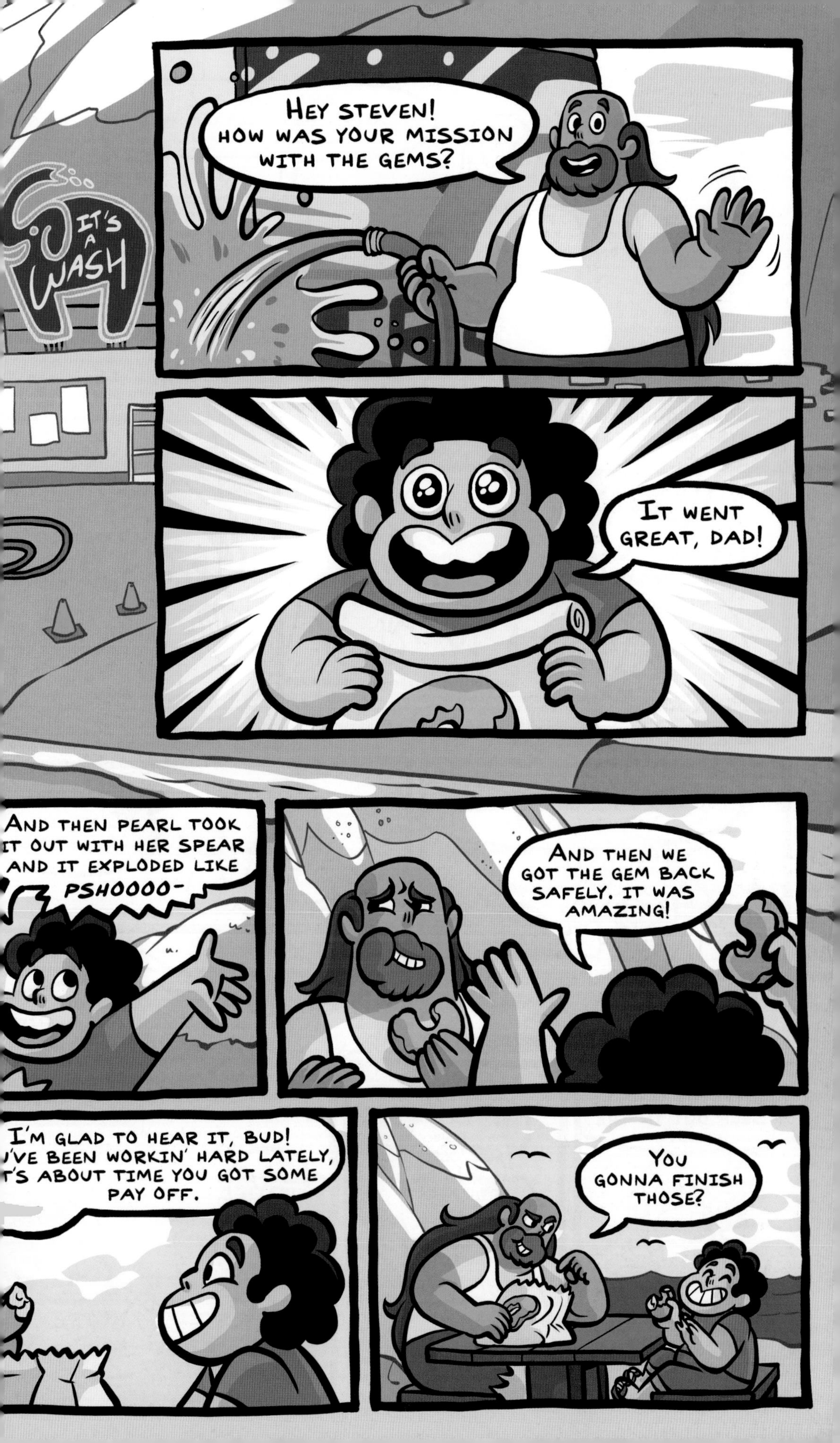
IT'S A WASH
HEY STEVEN! HOW WAS YOUR MISSION WITH THE GEMS?
IT WENT GREAT, DAD!
AND THEN PEARL TOOK IT OUT WITH HER SPEAR AND IT EXPLODED LIKE PSHOOOO-
AND THEN WE GOT THE GEM BACK SAFELY. IT WAS AMAZING!
I'M GLAD TO HEAR IT, BUD! I'VE BEEN WORKIN' HARD LATELY, IT'S ABOUT TIME YOU GOT SOME PAY OFF.
YOU GONNA FINISH THOSE?

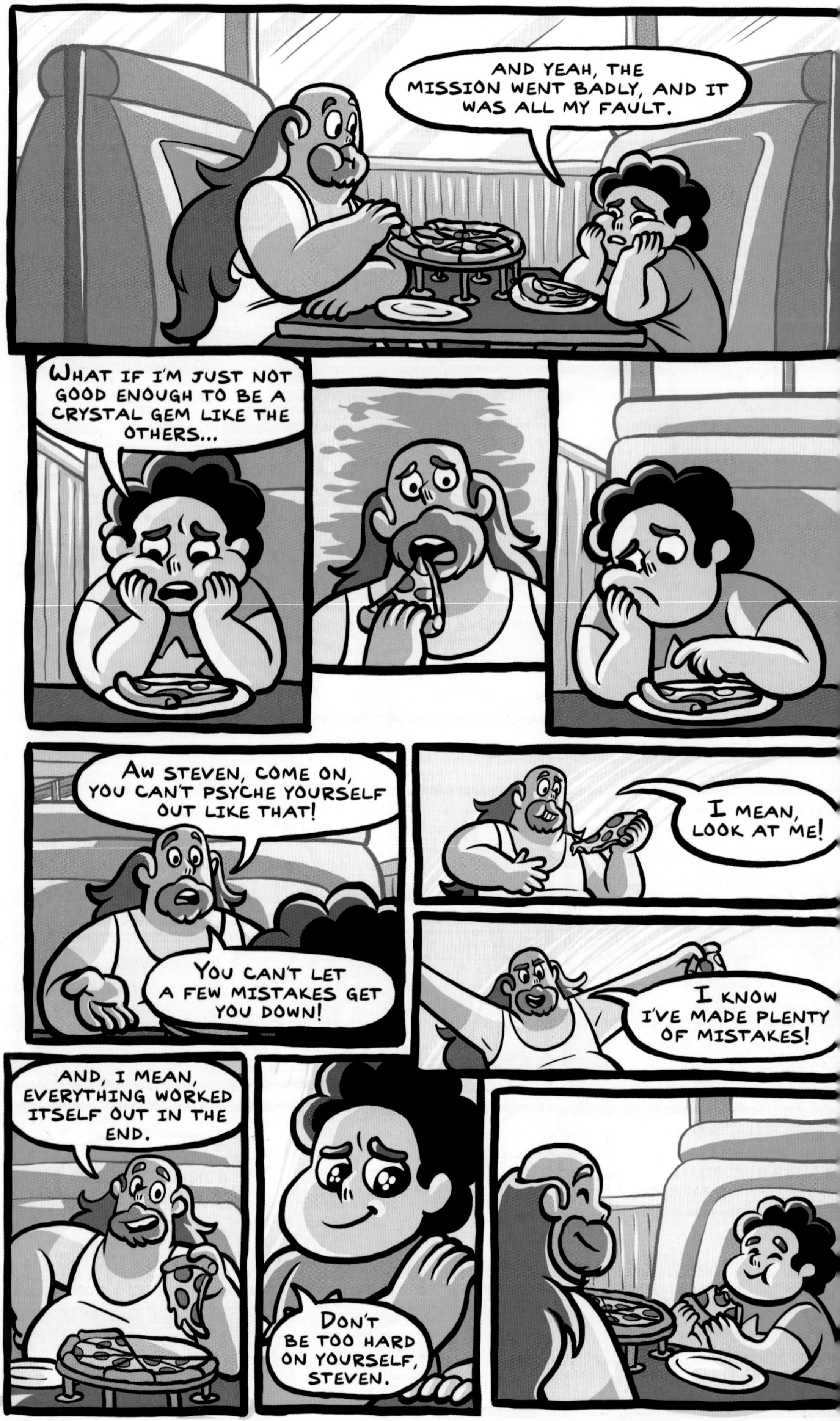
AND YEAH, THE MISSION WENT BADLY, AND IT WAS ALL MY FAULT.
WHAT IF I'M JUST NOT GOOD ENOUGH TO BE A CRYSTAL GEM LIKE THE OTHERS...
AW STEVEN, COME ON, YOU CAN'T PSYCHE YOURSELF OUT LIKE THAT!
YOU CAN'T LET A FEW MISTAKES GET YOU DOWN!
I MEAN, LOOK AT ME!
I KNOW I'VE MADE PLENTY OF MISTAKES!
AND, I MEAN, EVERYTHING WORKED ITSELF OUT IN THE END.
DON'T BE TOO HARD ON YOURSELF, STEVEN.

WHY CAN'T I GET MY OTHER POWERS TO WORK!?

I FEEL LIKE I'VE TRIED EVERYTHING...

WELL... IF IT'S NOT WORKING THEN MAYBE... YOU SHOULD JUST STEP BACK FOR A WHILE...

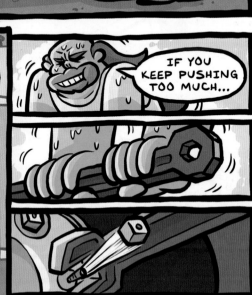

IF YOU KEEP PUSHING TOO MUCH...

SEE WHAT I MEAN?

HAHA, YEAH, MAYBE YOU'RE RIGHT. IF I TRY TO FORCE MY POWERS THEY MIGHT JUST EXPLODE IN MY FACE.

YEAH, AND WE WOULDN'T WANT THAT.

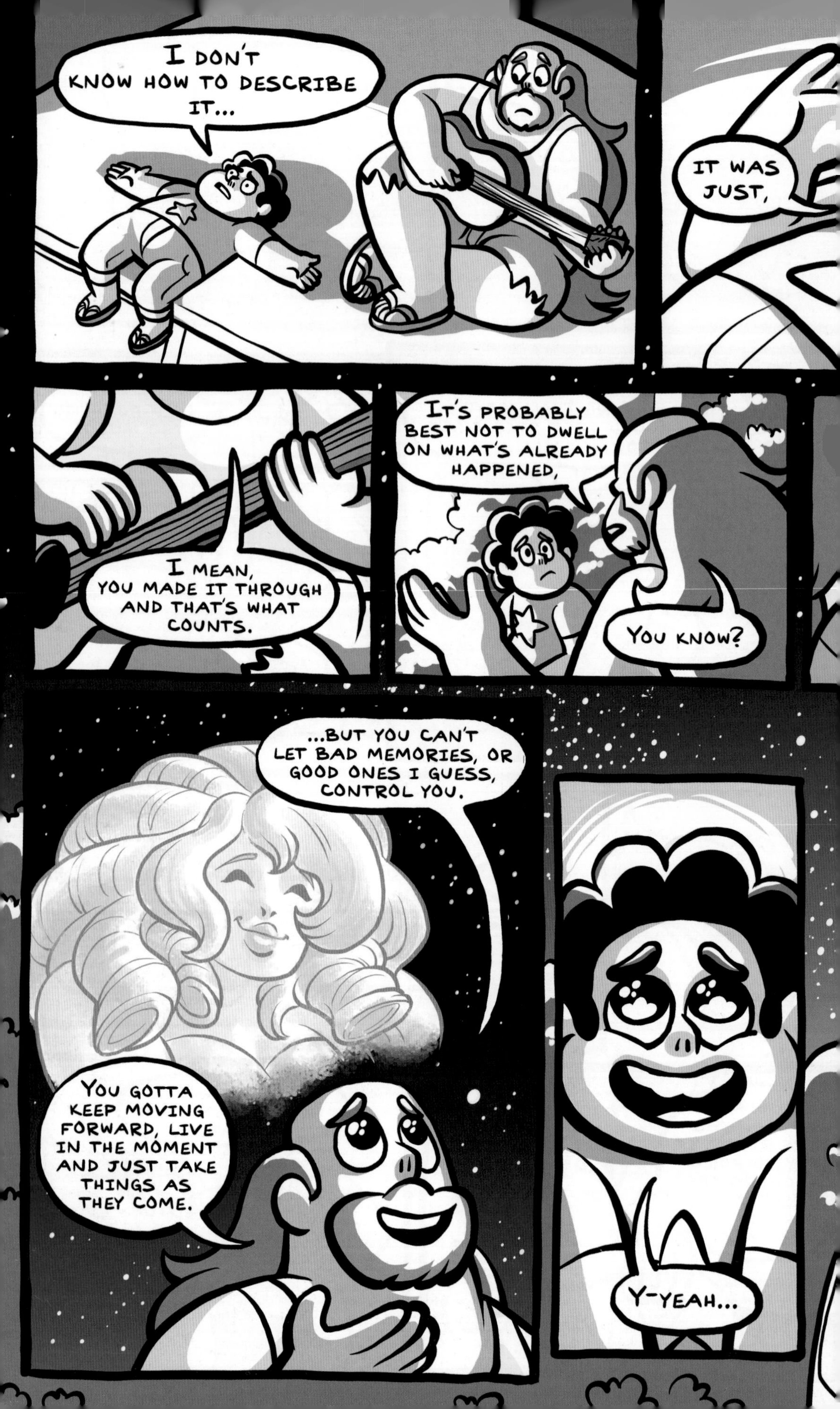
I DON'T KNOW HOW TO DESCRIBE IT...
IT WAS JUST,
I MEAN, YOU MADE IT THROUGH AND THAT'S WHAT COUNTS.
IT'S PROBABLY BEST NOT TO DWELL ON WHAT'S ALREADY HAPPENED,
YOU KNOW?
...BUT YOU CAN'T LET BAD MEMORIES, OR GOOD ONES I GUESS, CONTROL YOU.
YOU GOTTA KEEP MOVING FORWARD, LIVE IN THE MOMENT AND JUST TAKE THINGS AS THEY COME.
Y-YEAH...

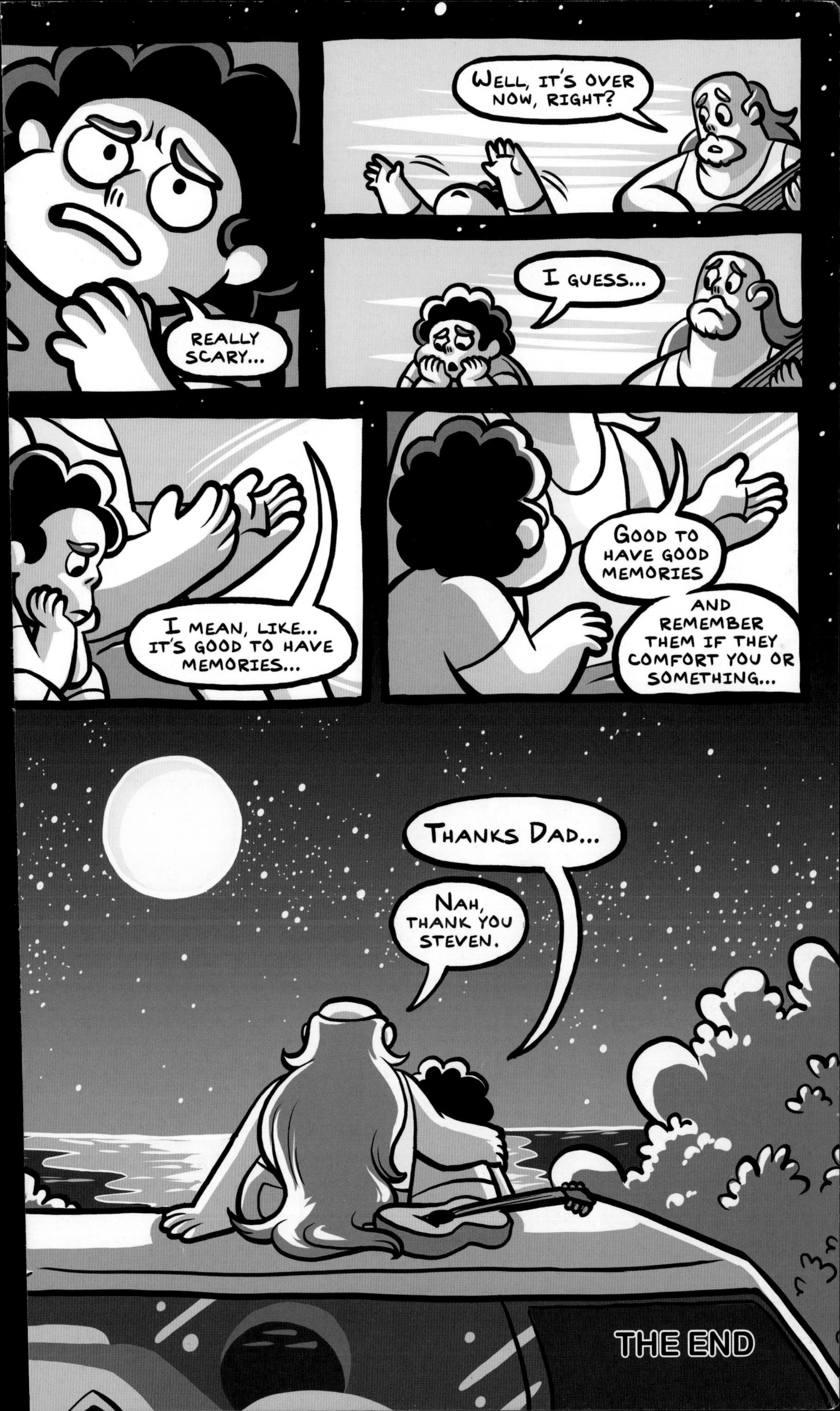
REALLY SCARY...
WELL, IT'S OVER NOW, RIGHT?
I GUESS...
I MEAN, LIKE... IT'S GOOD TO HAVE MEMORIES...
GOOD TO HAVE GOOD MEMORIES
AND REMEMBER THEM IF THEY COMFORT YOU OR SOMETHING...
THANKS DAD...
NAH, THANK YOU STEVEN.
THE END

DISCOVER
EXPLOSIVE NEW WORLDS

ADVENTURE TIME

Sam Sykes · Selina Espiritu · Sarah Stern
Brave Chef Brianna

KELLY THOMPSON BRIANNE DROUHARD M. VICTORIA ROBADO
MEGA PRINCESS

THE NOT-SO SECRET SOCIETY
DALEY · CRAFTS · CLARK · BRUNI

OVER THE GARDEN WALL

STEVEN UNIVERSE
VOLUME ONE

kaboom!™

AVAILABLE AT YOUR LOCAL COMICS SHOP AND BOOKSTORE

To find a comics shop in your area, visit www.comicshoplocator.com

WWW.**BOOM-STUDIOS**.COM

Adventure Time
Pendleton Ward and Others
Volume 1
ISBN: 978-1-60886-280-1 | $14.99 US
Volume 2
ISBN: 978-1-60886-323-5 | $14.99 US
Adventure Time: Islands
ISBN: 978-1-60886-972-5 | $9.99 US

The Amazing World of Gumball
Ben Bocquelet and Others
Volume 1
ISBN: 978-1-60886-488-1 | $14.99 US
Volume 2
ISBN: 978-1-60886-793-6 | $14.99 US

Brave Chef Brianna
Sam Sykes, Selina Espiritu
ISBN: 978-1-68415-050-2 | $14.99 US

Mega Princess
Kelly Thompson, Brianne Drouhard
ISBN: 978-1-68415-007-6 | $14.99 US

The Not-So Secret Society
Matthew Daley, Arlene Daley, Wook Jin Clark
ISBN: 978-1-60886-997-8 | $9.99 US

Over the Garden Wall
Patrick McHale, Jim Campbell and Others
Volume 1
ISBN: 978-1-60886-940-4 | $14.99 US
Volume 2
ISBN: 978-1-68415-006-9 | $14.99 US

Steven Universe
Rebecca Sugar and Others
Volume 1
ISBN: 978-1-60886-706-6 | $14.99 US
Volume 2
ISBN: 978-1-60886-796-7 | $14.99 US

Steven Universe & The Crystal Gems
ISBN: 978-1-60886-921-3 | $14.99 US

Steven Universe: Too Cool for School
ISBN: 978-1-60886-771-4 | $14.99 US